Leaving Gary

www.mascotbooks.com

Leaving Gary

For more information, please contact:
Mascot Books, an imprint of Amplify Publishing Group
620 Herndon Parkway, Suite 320
Herndon, VA 20170
info@mascotbooks.com

Library of Congress Control Number: 2022912229

CPSIA Code: PRV1222A
ISBN-13: 978-1-63755-272-8

Printed in the United States

Other Books by John V. Amodeo

Voices of Hell's Kitchen

Believe: Journey from Jacksonville

Blessed or Cursed

The Captain's Coin

Revolutionary War Series: Francis Lewis

The Sharecropper's Son

Not Yet

To the people of Gary.

LEAVING GARY

A NOVEL

JOHN V. AMODEO

CHAPTER ONE

Nineteen seventy-four was not a good year for Rust Belt cities like Gary, Indiana. It wasn't any better for Gary resident Kevin Bolton. The twenty-one-year-old, just released from state prison, faced a two-month parole period, which was not usually a problem. Two months wasn't a big deal. Yet, for Kevin, it was a major problem. He was alone. Without any nearby family, Kevin faced an uncertain future. Worse, he had nowhere to stay. And, of course, he had no job. Now on the outside, he wandered the cold, lonely, dangerous streets of Gary. The crestfallen young man felt like a stranger in his own hometown. The reclusive, moody, introverted young man set foot in a town he had called home his whole life. Now, it was not the same town. It had changed in such a short span.

Gary, "The Steel City," once a thriving, industrial powerhouse east of Chicago, had undergone a transformation. Symptomatic of many medium-sized Midwest cities, its decline was replicated throughout the vast stretch of the Upper Midwest in city after city. The Steel City, a magnet for European immigrants and Black people leaving the South at the beginning of the twentieth century, had indeed fallen on hard times.

Kevin found himself misplaced, a stranger in his hometown. Like many paroled inmates, his future was forever stigmatized with a record. His future indeed seemed bleak like the city of his birth. Like Gary, he needed help.

Kevin's return to his native city, normally an occasion for joy for both family and friends, went unnoticed. There were no reunions. *Got no one here for me anymore. The city looks as if it was hit by a tornado—at least, my old neighborhood does.* Navigating his way by foot to his former street, he thought back to that fateful day two years earlier.

Kevin, then a nineteen-year-old kid from a dysfunctional single-parent household, had just lost his mother to cancer. He was angry. Angry at God, angry at himself, and angry at his mom for dying so young at forty-four. He had no one to turn to. "I just didn't know what to do. And no one was there. I wasn't easy to be around. I was irresponsible, irritable, and regular pain in the ass that people avoided."

His temper got in the way. It controlled him, making him unpredictable. Confrontational, bellicose, and challenging anyone he felt was a threat or in his way, he was a person no one wanted to confront. He needed help. Yet, he had no one to turn to. Proud, defiant, and feeling empty, he thought he could handle the grief. He couldn't.

His mom's death sealed the deal. No one wanted to be near him. "I had [an] attitude, big time. If people looked at me the wrong way, I was ready to challenge them." Kevin's anger and hostility soon got him in trouble. When he was fired from his part-time, entry-level job as a UPS packer, his funds—meager as they were—ran out. With limited skills, that rage inside boiled over. "That crazy me was different two and half years ago. I was a stupid kid hell-bent on listening to nobody. People like my boxing trainer tried to help. It didn't do any good. I listened to nobody. I was thrown out of the gym twice. Don't understand why they let me back. I was a loser. I guess someone felt I had some future."

Back in Gary, he needed to redirect himself. Yet, the arrest still hung over him. Kevin kept going over the circumstances that led to his arrest. Like a bad dream, he tried to dismiss the circumstance that led to his confinement in state prison. But it still hurt. "It shouldn't have happened. I let a stupid infraction turn nothing into something."

An entrapment arrest. "Bought a little weed from a young, rookie, punk undercover cop with an attitude like mine. Didn't help that I had a worse attitude, too. Should have known better and walked away, but I let my emotions get the best of me. Yelled at him, and he got backup. Thought I was threatening him. Wanted to charge me with assault. Thanks to the judge, that was dropped due to lack of evidence or any weapon. But, I probably would have hit him, and then I'd really have a problem. I'm a little more clear headed now. Should have known I couldn't win with the cop version of the story over mine."

Able for some introspection, Kevin wished he could turn back the clock to that fateful day. Shaking his head as if to brush off the past, he sighed. He knew he reacted badly that dark day outside the gym. As he approached his old street, the dilapidated, abandoned buildings and old, abandoned, rusty cars were more numerous than before he was sent away. Eerily silent, the once vibrant street now resembled a wasteland. Looking around, he saw few people and was overcome with a sense of loss. This was his city. Not the model citizen, he nevertheless had time to reflect on his own situation as he moved about his former neighborhood. What he witnessed made him depressed.

He had had a few minor incidents prior to the arrest outside the gym—all misdemeanors for disorderly conduct and fighting in a local bar. Yet, he never let his guard down until the incident with the rookie cop. He could have avoided jail time but didn't. His anger boiling over, he wanted to do things his way, refusing to listen to his court-appointed lawyer. "Young, stupid, angry, and refusing to listen to reason. What an idiot I was."

A high school dropout, Kevin Bolton had little prospect of getting ahead. Today, with a prison record and no place to call home, his arrival in his hometown of Gary was as gloomy as the cold, cloudy weather that had greeted him getting off the Greyhound bus, which was just a ten-minute walk from his former address.

He zipped up the plain, black jacket given to him by the prison to fight off the brisk, October wind. It was quiet, with few people nearby. Picking up his pace, he set out to the one place he used to call home. He knew no one would be at his address. Who cared? What was he to do? He just wanted to bond.

Kevin had completed two years of the two-and-a-half-year- to three-year sentence. His stay at Indiana State Prison normally would go unnoticed. He was just another inmate assigned to a number. Kevin's was 8L3024. Like most incoming prisoners, he was subjected to scrutiny not only from the correctional officers but also the curious and often hostile prison population. Nothing was expected from the young man from Gary. But, as fate would have it, Kevin's prison term would have lasting effects on him and others. It would prove to be a seminal moment in the young man's life.

When he arrived at the high-walled, concrete prison, something happened. Events have a way of changing our lives. They impact us and transform us. With lasting effects, changes occur. For Kevin, this change came as a surprise.

He came into the prison like others and went through the process. Raw, scared, but not wanting to show any fear, he kept his guard up. He was assigned a single cell in the minimum-security area. Indiana State, Indiana's second oldest prison, was founded in 1859. It also housed maximum prisoners—lifers. In fact, John Dillinger was perhaps its most famous prisoner. It was here that the notorious Dillinger served time from 1924 to 1932. By the time of his parole in 1933, he set out doing what he had done before—robbing banks and getting the FBI on his track. The FBI had him on its famous Most Wanted list. Dillinger would have a bad exit—coming out of the nearby Chicago Biograph Theater, he was gunned down in 1934 after a showing of *Manhattan Melodrama* starring Clark Gable. Kevin often wondered what cell Dillinger had occupied. "If these walls could talk, I'm sure it would make for a great movie."

The maximum-security section was separate and certainly one to avoid. It was the place that witnessed the executions of murderers, rapists, and kidnappers. Up to 1913, convicted murderers were hanged. Starting in 1913, it used the electric chair and in 1994 resorted to lethal injection. Kevin, having committed a nonviolent crime, was secured in a minimum quad area away from those who committed the most heinous acts. Yet, unlike the notorious gangster who ended up dead in front of a Chicago theater, Kevin would experience an entire metamorphosis in jail.

Kevin became a ward of the state of Indiana just like the others in his quad. Nothing else. Most would forget about him. He was one fewer problem on the streets of Gary. It was time for him to dwell on his past, repent, maybe reassess his priorities, and hopefully come out a better individual. It sometimes didn't work that way for many inmates. Many would come back. For Kevin, prison—however dismal and foreboding—transformed him. His was a total transformation. Most people who had met Kevin knew his level of his anger and detachment. They felt he was a loser—even his teachers at Theodore Roosevelt High School in Gary. He was the underachiever who was too busy looking at girls and trying to impress them with his good looks and alluring physique. That is, until they got to know him.

He was someone no one wanted to be near. He was a loser in the eyes of most people. His term at the prison, many felt, would be just the start of a long life of incarceration due to his attitude. He would be just another ward of the state. The conservative populace of the state of Indiana didn't care about such subnormals. But something did happen. A change was about to occur.

Unexpectedly, it came in the form of a dream. Yes, a dream one night changed his outlook. It happened just a week after he arrived at Indiana State. It would have a major impact on his life. A dream completely changed his outlook on life and set him on a new course. He would never be the same. It was, indeed, an epiphany. It was a breakthrough that left Kevin a completely changed man.

"Had a dream soon after being locked up. My mom came to me. It was surreal. As if she were in front of me. I swear she was there. Couldn't believe it. My mom told me to make something of myself. Said she had faith in me and that I needed to get myself together. It was weird. Like I said, it was as if she was right there. It scared me. I woke up in a cold sweat. I remember I looked at the naked light bulbs outside my cell in the cold and dark corridor and just stared at those lonely light bulbs. Like them, I had nothing to hide. Alone and isolated, I realized my mom sent me a message. I started crying. Big time. This was the first time since Mom died that I cried. I don't know why. I got up, pacing my cell. Thank God, we had private cells. Others would have thought I was a pussy. I paced for what seemed a long time.

"Wondering. Wondering. What did Mom want? It just was so weird. It's just a dream. It's nothing. Go back to bed, idiot! I went back to my bunk. My pillow was wet, even though it was March and cold and damp. I put my hands up to my head and ran my fingers through my hair, looking down at the barren, concrete floor. What did this mean? Change? Yeah, I was ready—more than ready. Where do I begin? I didn't get back to sleep that night and actually said a Hail Mary or two. I hadn't been to a church since Mom's funeral. I didn't go to Mass and stayed away from any church. But the message kept haunting me. I kept going over what my mom said: *Change. Do something positive*."

That dream did, indeed, become a seminal moment in Kevin's life. He was haunted by the words relayed by his late mother pleading for to him to make something of his life. Getting up from a sleepless, fitful night, he looked at himself in the small mirror above the steel wash basin. He didn't like what he saw—an angry, hostile man with an attitude. Over and over, his mom's pleas kept haunting him. "Do something with your life." As he stared back in the mirror, he nodded at himself and then, at that moment, decided he had to make changes.

Kevin followed her advice. He decided he had to act. Remembering the message, he knew it was time for him to change. No one else would be there for him. It was solely up to him to make any changes. His mind was made up. The message conveyed: "It's time to act."

He sat down. In his cell, he had a yellow-lined paper pad. He started something that would resonate with him from that day onward—writing a list of daily things he wanted to accomplish before his release date. "Perhaps a word for the day or week." He would live by these words. He was scheduled to get out in two years with good behavior. That list, Mom's Book, became his Bible. He kept it under his pillow, knowing full well that if there was any inspection of his cell, it would be found. He didn't care. "Nothing earth shattering except for me. If anything, the guards probably would like that I was doing something positive." He decided he'd have to enter a word of the day. It was something to adhere and try to be faithful to.

"I did change. Yeah, I guess I became the model prisoner—reading a lot and working out, reading and working out. Staying out of trouble. Not responding to lurid and racist remarks. Guys that had attitude, guys trying to egg me on, or worse, wanting to be too friendly. Straight or gay, I was afraid of no one, but I would look at anyone who I thought was threatening and eyeball them. It was like being in the boxing ring before a bout. It worked. I didn't want to get into fights. Guys are always in your face, testing you. Hell, it's a jail, not a country club. I knew how to handle them. My size and physique intimidated many, and those who were trying to test me soon found out not to mess with me. My advantage was my height, body, and attitude. Thank God, it worked. I made it a priority in the Mom's Book—don't get into fights, respect others, and stay the hell out of trouble. I just would look at the other dudes straight up and down and walk away, sometimes with a smirk on my face. Yeah, it worked. I soon got respect, getting attention from both the correctional officers and fellow cellies.

"Some knew I was an amateur boxer back in Gary. A boxer with an attitude, as my trainer Joe Montalvo often remarked. But, that dream did something. It did so much. Prison changed my life forever. It made me grow up.

"Inmates locked up from Gary knew me—some of them didn't like me, while others were still intimidated by me." Kevin's reputation preceded him. "Three of the inmates from Gary remembered me. I wasn't easy to be around. They soon became okay with me once I let them know that I was there just to do time and not get into any fights. I was grateful that others looked up to me, this White kid—messed up and in need. I still got the respect from others locked up and eventually even the correctional officers. Maybe the time spent behind bars made me a man and got me to take responsibility seriously. I kept remembering that dream. That dream! It changed me.

"Didn't like being locked up, but no one bothered me. The brothers, Black and White in the joint—especially those from Gary—especially respected me, too. Some of them had seen me in the boxing gym. I had won all three bouts I fought. Was focused then; before all the BS started with me. I liked boxing. I was thinking of the fight in Chicago. It was my moment of glory. It made me feel like somebody. In a packed, smoky arena in downtown Chicago, not far from the Miracle Mile. Didn't pay any attention to the crowd—just focused on my job. I guess that's why I got respect in jail. Decided to grow up and act right. Just pissed that I should have listened to people who tried to help me from the start, like my trainer Joe Montalvo and that lawyer assigned to me after I got busted. Now, here, locked up, I decided to help some of the guys in the joint. Guys saw my intensity and came up to me.

"Soon, I focused my energy and started helping them. What else was there to do? Training some of the other inmates in the yard with weights, yeah, that was a good release of my tension and gave me the respect I needed. I showed them a lot—shadowboxing, proper foot moves, sparring, and the right cardio workout. Too bad we didn't have a boxing program. I would've done okay. But, I stayed focused. I'm glad that I actually enrolled in a GED. I think Mom would be proud."

Kevin's positive efforts didn't go unnoticed by both correctional officers and inmates. In the yard, he attracted a following. The correctional officers remarked how steady and intense he was in training others. Methodical and concentrating on details, he led by example. Showing the right moves, he gained the respect of the most jaded and suspicious convicts in the yard. Kevin's resolve—his pledge to his deceased mom—became a catalyst for change. And it soon touched others.

He checked his Mom's Book every day, adding or deleting but always making sure he accomplished an item from it. "Today, it's legs; tomorrow, upper jabs." He added a word of the day to his list—one day, *respect*; next, *responsibility*; the next, *kindness,* etc. Kevin's dedication to this quest was part of the dream from his mom. It motivated him. That list became a game changer and guidepost. And it worked. Results followed.

Taking charge indeed got attention and respect from others. His dedication soon made him popular. Soon, word got out to the administration that Kevin—the amateur, undefeated, kid boxer who was on his way as a pro before events got in his way—had a following. And it showed. The prison officials noticed a change in tone. Tension seemed lower. Fights were less frequent in the yard. Things quieted down in the yard as more inmates asked Kevin to display his skills. It got the attention of the education program director, Ana Matos, as well.

Asked if he would like to enroll in the GED program, Kevin, never a serious student in high school, hesitated. Encouraged by several of the inmates in the yard and a few officers, he had a change of mind when the director of the GED program asked him to report to her office. A tense Kevin walked into the spartan office that was located at the end of the classrooms reserved for special programs like the GED, rap sessions, and social events. Escorted by Captain Otis Brown, he tapped on the door and was greeted with a smile by the administrator, Ana Matos.

"Mr. Bolton"—Ana Matos's greeting brought a smile to his face—"please have a seat." Greeting him with an extended hand and smile, she at once relaxed the nervous young man. Kevin stared at the wall and noticed her credentials: a BS from Indiana State University and a MSW from Notre Dame. Pictures of John F. Kennedy and Martin Luther King were above the green file cabinets. On her desk was a picture of a young female. Kevin guessed the child in the picture was about four years old. "Probably her kid." He glanced at Matos—a smile on her face sent the right message. Matos was middle aged, five foot ten inches, and wore a black dress with a cross around her neck. Her presence and her calm demeanor did the trick. What happened next was yet another moment in Kevin's troubled life. It was something that would give his Mom's Book a special entry.

She pulled up a similarly sized chair adjacent to Kevin. Holding a manila folder, she sat next to him with Captain Brown just outside the door. With eye-to-eye contact, her manner eased whatever tension Kevin showed. "Don't want him to feel uncomfortable with me behind my desk." This slight, albeit nice, gesture was important—Kevin relaxed. A slight smile at Matos enabled her to get to the point.

Ana Matos, a no-holds-barred administrator, had seen many come and go in her education program. In addition to the popular

GED, the prison education program offered classes in literature, writing, US history, and psychology. She wanted to get funding from the state of Indiana to establish a college program. Dragging its feet, the conservative state legislature did not want to reward people who were wards of the state. Yet, each year, she proposed a program and wouldn't give up.

Proud of her eight-member staff, she was a fair, albeit tough, person who demanded much from her teaching staff. Her proudest moments were the commencement exercises of those who successfully completed the GED. The ceremony also gave her the chance to meet families of inmates who excelled and were ready to go back into society. Her staff of six teachers and two teacher's-aides liked working with her. During her three-year tenure, she implemented sessions that alleviated tensions, allowing inmates to express their frustrations, be it with the rules, their families, or emotional issues. The result was an easing of tensions and fewer incidents of violence at Indiana State Prison.

Her intentions for sitting alongside Kevin were twofold—make him feel at ease and have direct contact that at once sent a message that signaled she was there to listen, as well. The tall, black-haired Matos, with her penetrating, dark eyes focusing on Kevin, began, "I'm glad to finally meet up with you."

Looking up at her for the first time with a nervous smile on his face, his voice low and hesitant, Kevin added, "Nice to meet you, too." Kevin liked her approach and the message she sent. He nervously added, "Thanks for this. I hope I'll be okay."

Embarrassed and not knowing what else to say, Matos, aware of his situation, added, "If you put the same effort in your studies as you do in the yard, you should have no problem. I've seen the impact you've had on others, and I'm not alone." This response worked. Kevin took a deep breath as Matos sized him up correctly: He was a lonely, withdrawn young man who was starting to come of age when given some responsibility.

Matos had asked to see Kevin as the result of observing him leading several inmates in weight training. She liked what she saw. What she noticed was a dedication to the art of weight lifting and boxing. And she saw something else. Noticing that he got respect from both Black and White inmates sent a clear signal. "This kid knows how to reach out to others. He needs an extra push," she remarked to Captain Brown, the officer in charge of recreation. The yard, as it was called, had seen some bad incidents sparked by the wrong look, a misinterpreted comment, or racial slurs and hostility. Captain Brown, initially skeptical of Kevin's assertiveness, realized that Kevin indeed had a way with people that got him respect. Captain Brown came on board, telling Matos that Kevin's positive attitude transcended to others.

Kevin was an anomaly at Indiana State, a blond White guy of Irish, Polish, and German ancestry who got along with others. This was in part due to his upbringing in a largely Black neighborhood of Gary. Also, his family, like many in the city, had financial troubles. They had struggled with alcoholism with his dad. It became a constant ordeal for his mother. "She was the bedrock of the family." Her desire to keep the family intact became an ongoing task.

Like many from a troubled family, Kevin's young life was rife with troubles, living with a drunk, verbally and physically abusive dad who was quick with his fists when his only son answered back at him and who shouted obscenities at his wife. He abruptly left his wife and three kids in the dead of night when Kevin was just twelve. "I was actually relieved that he left. I heard he headed out West somewhere. My aunt Maggie, his sister, said she thought he was in Montana. I don't care where the hell he landed his ass. He never had the decency to contact Mom. She went through hell. To this day, I don't care to find out what happened to him. When she died, I was glad we weren't able to contact him. My aunt made so many calls, but not one came through. I probably would have decked him if he showed up at the funeral Mass."

The family, now headed by a single mom, needed help. His mom received food stamps. She couldn't work due to her debilitating and declining health. She ended up moving into public housing—a three-story unit in one of the most crime-ridden sections of Gary. Kevin hated the area. Alone most of the time, he started hanging out outside. Kevin wanted to leave the house often, hanging out and eventually gravitating toward the boxing gym, where a friend, Gerard Jenkins, noticed his quick jabs after a brief encounter with a bully who was bothering some younger kids on the street. "Kev's the real deal. He wasn't afraid to pounce on those street punks trying to steal a kid's lunch money." What resulted was a purpose and interest in boxing.

With Kevin's arrival at Indiana State Prison, his presence quickly got the attention of several Gary inmates. They knew of his time spent in the ring and his deft, sharp jabs, which made him a formidable boxer. He soon got respect. "Maybe Mom wanted me to help others. I don't know. But that dream did something to me." The end result displayed a confident Kevin helping others in the art of boxing.

Captain Brown had asked Matos to come to the yard and see for herself. She agreed. What she saw impressed her. Captain Brown's assessment helped, adding, "He was not a bad boxer from Gary. He's not a problem. My cousin worked with young kids and remembered him from Gary. Said that he could have gone pro if he straightened himself out. Had a bad temper. Lost his mother, and everything seemed to change. I liked the way he took his time to explain the art of shadowboxing and how he moved on his feet in the ring. Too bad we don't have the gloves or ring!"

Having seen Kevin and having gotten a good endorsement from Captain Brown—a tough veteran of fourteen years who had seen fights, near riots, and racial tensions—Matos knew it was time to act. "He's a leader whether he realizes it or not." The resulting meeting in her office not only gave her a chance to size up Kevin but also enhance his self-esteem by offering him a chance to excel. She knew that the yard could be a cauldron for violence and fights. Kevin had impressed her greatly with his command of the ad hoc workout group he organized in the yard. She knew he was someone whom others would listen to, follow, and benefit from his boxing skills. Now was her opportunity to act. It was worth a try. That meeting in her office would be the start of a big change for Kevin. It had the effect of a calming after a storm—the yard did not have to be a confrontational, one-on-one show of bravado. Kevin managed to give some of the inmates a purpose. The tone in the jail seemed to calm down almost overnight. Kevin's intense interest in the sport of boxing that he loved so much was clearly evident. He gave it his all, resulting in a renewed interest in the sport. More importantly, it served as a catalyst for others to get involved and display good team spirit. Matos, clearly satisfied at the meeting in her office, knew she had someone who would make a difference.

CHAPTER TWO

The yard. The place where inmates could get some air, walk, jog the periphery of the oval track, lift weights outdoors, and exchange some small talk. The back-and-forth discussions ranged from sports, queries as to release date, parole board appearances, and quality of life in the single-cell dorms. Captain Otis Brown had seen the best and worst in the yard. His job was to maintain order. It wasn't an easy task. Each day could bring about a volatile confrontation over a misinterpreted glance, an inane comment taken much too seriously, or a casual bump, intentional or not. Yes, Brown had seen it all. Today, he was in a buoyant mood as the yard was buzzing over Kevin's recent meeting with Matos. One veteran inmate remarked, "If that young White dude can get us some new equipment and allow us a bit of more time out here, I'm all for it."

When Kevin began his program, Brown noticed the change. Brown and several other correctional officers observed a calmer yard once Kevin initiated his impromptu training. It was spontaneous—the result of fellow inmate Sean Givens, also from Gary, who knew Kevin from the boxing gym. In fact, Givens had sparred with Kevin on several occasions. "He floored me in the second round of the three allowed in the gym for sparring."

Before long, Kevin and Givens decided to act, attracting other inmates in the yard. Kevin got permission from the captain to lead in not only additional cardio and weight training but also shadow boxing, footwork used in the ring, and finally, a bit of sparring sans gloves. It took on a life of its own. Not only did younger inmates come up, but also some of the more seasoned ones helped. What started as an attempt to pass the time became a communal effort, uniting Black and White, young and old. Advice, whether wanted or not, was quick. But Kevin listened. He respected the older inmates. He didn't forget the dream he had and continued to live by his word of the day.

When Matos inquired about Kevin, Captain Brown, impressed by the changes he saw, gave a solid evaluation of the former young pugilist from Gary. The meeting in Matos's office had quickly followed.

"Officer Otis Brown liked the intense workout I did. He also liked the fact that I was helping some of the others in the yard by pushing them to work out and showing them boxing techniques, like shadowboxing. Sean also was great. We were not good friends in Gary, but I respected him. Sorry he ended up here, too. Told me he got into a spat with a girlfriend, and she pressed charges of assault with a deadly weapon. Since he had several misdemeanors, he plea bargained, getting a mandatory three-year sentence. Never asked him details, as it's not good to do that. As for Captain Brown, he finally got the warden, Jack Molton, to give us three pairs of boxing gloves. Took two months. The warden, I'm sure, saw what we were up to. Thanks to Captain Brown, I could now really show them some moves. So, I set up a little boxing ring without the ropes, of course, but it caught the attention of people."

Matos knew he was ready to act. After the meeting in her office with Kevin, she listed a few items that a second meeting would address. Matos invited Kevin to take courses to complete his high school diploma. Her purpose was to use the popular inmate as a showcase to further the educational component at Indiana State. She was impressed by the intensity which she observed in Kevin with a few of the inmates. Observing him in the yard, she felt she could be of additional help. On one visit to the yard, she saw Kevin explaining the art of shadowboxing with quick jabs in the air. He followed this with an exercise that incorporated sparring and the right leg moves used in the ring.

He was calm, focused, and in control. Matos recognized leadership and saw it in young Kevin Bolton.

Matos knew she had to call Kevin back to her office. She reached out to the young man. The second meeting was exactly what he needed—attention and a modicum of respect from a higher-up prison official. That was apparent, given Matos's methodical way of observing Kevin. The reclusive and usually hesitant young man, when surrounded by authority figures, at last had people in his life who cared. The second meeting was much more relaxed and uplifting. At least, he hoped so. "Matos seems like she really wants me to get into her program with the GED."

Matos, aware of the impact Kevin had on others, quickly added, "I'll make sure that your classes won't interfere with the time in the yard with the others."

Pleased by this gesture, Kevin thanked her, adding, "I hope I can do it. I wasn't much of a student."

"That's in the past. You're now ready. I hope you take up the challenge, right? If you put as much time and attention in your studies as you do in the yard, I'm certain you'll even surprise yourself." Matos's comment did wonders for Kevin's ego. The smile on Kevin's face was enough for Matos to know she had reached him.

Nodding, Kevin responded, "Yeah, you're right. I hope so."

Kevin was correct. Matos had checked his record. Knowing he was a first-time offender, she reached out to Kevin after checking his high school record, which showed he left Theodore Roosevelt High School in his junior year. She wanted to make a difference. It was now her turn to act.

"I saw in Kevin Bolton a diamond in the rough. He just needed a little attention and tough love, and I knew I could reach him. I saw in his report that his mom had recently passed and that he had issues that weren't addressed. I knew if I could just reach out, we could do a positive." It worked.

Matos had seen the best and worst while working in such a tense and intimidating environment. To her, each individual who was locked up was a challenge. "I want to make a difference in their lives. Most of them, regardless of their age, race, and religious background are reaching out." Tough and straightforward, she would confront the most angry, seasoned, and menacing inmate who enrolled in her class, often reaching them with a good dose of that tough love. That's what many of the guys locked up lacked—someone who cared and showed it. This was evident in the manner in which she and her staff conducted themselves. "We're here to make a difference, and I want to see results." Her staff of teachers and aides respected her, and it showed. The teachers performed well, often getting the most reclusive, angry, and jaded inmate to open up. Such was the case with Kevin.

She was looking for a leader or someone who just needed a good dose of self-esteem. Kevin fit the profile. Sizing him up by observing his leadership in both weights and boxing exercises, she knew he would be a great candidate to shine. Her objective, as with all of her pupils, was to make them feel human and a person who could contribute. And the results of her dogged determination manifested in an overall rate of 78 percent passing the GED. Proud of this accomplishment, when asked what her secret to overall success was, she summed it up perfectly by saying, "I did what I'm supposed to do—get the job done and show some degree of compassion to even the most hardened inmate." So, it was no accident that she approached Kevin.

When Kevin was first asked by Matos to consider taking classes, his reluctance showed itself. "Didn't want to go into the class and make a fool of myself. I hated math and knew that I probably would fail the damn test." Yet, Matos wouldn't give up. After his initial skepticism, she called him back to her office. Matos got right to the point. She pressed on, adding, "You're not a quitter." She looked directly at him, touched his shoulder, and again reaffirmed, "Use your energy and zest for life that you display in the yard in the classroom. Your teachers and I will be there for you. Look, I know this is a change, but think of it as a challenge. A challenge that you succeeded in before—I know about your success in Gary with some boxing venues."

"That's it. She's right. I can apply myself." He kept his Mom's Book, and he knew what word to enter for the day—*determination*. Kevin calmed down. He knew he owed it to her to make something of himself.

Matos knew from experience that he could be reached. And work, it did. Matos's approach, gentle yet with a firm resolve, finally convinced the apprehensive young man, bringing a smile to Kevin's face. Matos's direct approach did the trick. It worked. Matos's endorsement of Kevin, after a bit of introspection, got him board. He decided to take the plunge.

While Kevin had never been one to take responsibility too seriously except for boxing and football in high school, this was a game changer for him. He felt his mom's presence. His Mom's Book, his own private Bible, kept him going. He decided he would get on board and take the classes. It was a decision that witnessed an internal change, giving the jaded young man confidence that he could get the job done. Like the intensity displayed in the yard, Kevin, with the backing of others, soon plunged headlong into his new venture. A challenge that heretofore he would have avoided, it became the perfect setting for a change in his outlook on life. His entry of determination into his Mom's Book soon became a reality.

The classroom. "How strange to be back in a school setting," the thought bringing a smile to his face. The six classrooms were close to the prison library. They were in a separate unit, two on each side, and at the far end was the prison library. The library had many books donated from charitable organizations and had some of the current bestsellers on the *New York Times* list. A first-time visitor, he noticed the bright yellow concrete walls in one classroom and blue in another, while the other four had an appealing off-white color.

In each classroom was a blackboard. The teacher's desk—small and wooden with a chair—was unlike the one Kevin saw in his high school, which had a big desk in front and a large, often straight-back wooden chair for the teacher. Here, the desk looked like it belonged in the bedroom of a young student. Small and unassuming, the desk was complemented by a chair for the teacher that was the same as the students'. That setting sent the right message. The teacher was there to facilitate their journey. The warmth of the classroom of 1972 was highlighted with walls decorated with pictures of notable people: Washington, Lincoln, Harriet Tubman, Frederick Douglass, as well as sports stars from all venues.

Kevin liked the history room that had pictures of Muhammad Ali, JFK, MLK, Lincoln, and Willie Mays. There were posters added to the mix that had positive statements from people in the arts and sports worlds.

Matos achieved her goal of making the classroom an unintimidating place. "They see enough going on in this place; I want the classrooms to be our minischool." Making each room a warm place in which to feel at ease, Matos included bookshelves displaying works of classic literature from *The Canterbury Tales*, the complete works of Shakespeare, and contemporary literary giants such as Ernest Hemingway, Eugene O'Neill, F. Scott Fitzgerald, Alex Haley, Zora Neale Hurston, and James Baldwin.

Several of the inmates had protested when the state wouldn't allow *The Autobiography of Malcolm X*. It took a special effort to finally get a copy, thanks to letters to the governor and local state officials. Matos and her librarian, Mary Alice Hurley, started a writing project that had involved over 300 inmates signing a petition for the controversial Malcolm X autobiography to be part of the library collection. Matos fought hard for the inmates and was a catalyst in bringing reforms such as halal meals for Muslims and more free time in the yard. It was not a surprise when, as an advocate for change, she convinced Warden Molton that Kevin's success should be recognized by adding a boxing program in the prison yard. She saw something special in Kevin and, as in most cases, her intuition proved correct.

True to form, Kevin became a model student. He studied hard. The message in the dream from his mom still haunted him. "I know she wants this from me, and I'm not going to disappoint her." It soon paid off. He started helping others with their lessons. Two of his friends from the yard also enrolled. They bonded not only in the yard but also in the prison library. Even the math he hated so much wasn't as difficult. He was not afraid to ask questions. He became more humble, and with it, his attitude changed. That went a long way.

Kevin also got assistance when he needed initial help with mathematics. And the teachers made a difference. His math teacher, Heather McCarthy, a late middle-aged brunette, took a liking to Kevin, making sure his fear of algebraic equations was assuaged as they drilled over and over. She related some of the equations to boxing—a square, sides, angles. He found it entertaining and, more important, wasn't afraid of delving into something he once feared. Soon, he began to excel on the pop quizzes that Heather McCarthy started classes with on occasion.

Finally in his niche, Kevin's progress transcended to a more confident self. No longer brooding, introverted, and angry, he found that others actually liked being around him. He matured. To further his self-esteem, he enrolled in a rap session every Friday. The rap sessions enabled him to self-motivate for one hour with the school psychologist, Dr. Aaron Baker. These sessions brought out his inner fears of not succeeding.

Baker, a veteran and graduate of Northwestern University, had written three books on behavior modification. His method was straight to the point: "Listen first, always. Don't draw any inferences until you have a composite of what makes a person react to a certain event." In his sessions, he examined the inner fears, anger, and distrust of authority that so many incarcerated people felt. By incorporating a passion to help others, he reached Kevin. What resulted was a more mature and happier individual. The classes provided the right mix. Soon, Kevin, at Baker's urging, started speaking up, asking questions, and contributing much to the classroom dynamic. In a short period, he became more self-assured and lent much to the content of the rap sessions, even leading one session on how boxing helped him focus.

Kevin surprised himself but not his teachers by passing the GED exam on the first try. He was proud that administrator Ana Matos cited him for his good grades at the commencement ceremony held for staff, inmates, and families. The graduation ceremony was a big deal. Yet, Kevin didn't want to attend. "Nobody's gonna be there for me, anyway." Matos and several of the inmates felt for Kevin, who had no one from his family at the ceremony. Matos and the staff knew of Kevin's family difficulties. When asked by Matos if a family member would be there, Kevin remained silent, just shaking his head and saying nothing but thinking: *Don't think so. It's ok. I got through this program, and I hope when I get back, I can get a job, and maybe they'll let me back at the gym.* He thought of his mom. He looked at his Mom's Book. He had entered his daily vocabulary word for the day: *perseverance*. Not a quitter, he knew he could get through the graduation with or without anyone cheering him on.

He was in for a big surprise.

Matos made a special effort to cite Kevin as the student who excelled on his first try. She knew he was one of the few graduates who wouldn't have family there. She gave him a hug, and a standing ovation from the crowd followed with sustained applause. It confirmed her initial instinct that this was one individual who just needed to be reached. Other fellow inmates in the program introduced him to their wives, mothers, fathers, siblings, and friends. He was treated as a star. Each one who passed the GED had a borrowed a graduation gown provided by a local church. Wearing the gowns, the graduates also had the traditional mortarboard hats, which made their presence stand out.

The reception that followed the ceremony provided the

opportunity for him to bond with others. The large cafeteria, decorated with blue streamers and white and blue balloons, provided the right mix. Jamal White, the resident artist, true to his talent, had a large graffiti art masterpiece with the names and caricatures of the twelve graduates. His artwork became a subject of discussion among some of the faculty, including Dr. Baker, who urged Jamal to send copies of his work to American Greetings and Hallmark. As Dr. Baker explained it, "He found his niche here, and it should be shared. Hopefully, when he's released his talent will be recognized. Today, Jamal's creative art was solely for the graduates and their families." Taking pictures in front of the large canvas that served as a backdrop to his work, pictures of all twelve inmates who passed the program were taken with their proud families. Matos, mindful of Kevin's absent family, took a photo with him. This eased Kevin's unhappiness and made his day.

Yet, it was painful that neither of his sisters attended. "Really miss Mom today. She would have been proud." His sisters, of course, were another story. He had not been in contact with them, and he made no effort to try. "They don't care, anyway. They got their lives, and I have to get on with mine." Deep inside, he felt his mother's absence but managed to smile when the photo in front of Jamal White's tribute with Matos was taken.

Kevin realized his accomplishments both in school and as a leader in the yard was a start. At age twenty-one, he was ready. He was in his own niche. If he felt depressed or lonely at the prospect of having no one to cheer for him at the ceremony, he didn't show it. But Matos knew it. Her special recognition of Kevin's accomplishments was to be recognized, family or not withstanding. It meant so much to him that others witnessed the creative and sensitive side of the formerly troubled young man.

Kevin felt good about the GED; thinking again, *My mom would've been proud.* This achievement, plus his role as mentor in getting an impromptu boxing program, gave Kevin the recognition he craved. At long last, the angry, introverted kid molded into a solid individual. He became a loyal and dedicated student. When word came that he, along with four others in the quad, had passed the GED program, cheers went up.

Even one hardened lifer who normally was avoided by most in the yard—Jesse Keene—came up and told him he was glad to hear the news. Keene, convicted in a drive-by in Fort Wayne, was a tough, often bitter person to approach. Yet, despite their racial difference, he had also seen in Kevin what others did. "If that White boy got Black and White guys sparring and exercising, he's doing more than any damn program here." Keene's assessment was right on target. Less racial tension was noticed. As Keene aptly put it, "Some of these damn crackers want us dead, and frankly, those skinheads can die for all I care." Yet, the tone and atmosphere of the yard and overall prison seemed to be much calmer. It didn't go unnoticed. Even a hardened killer like Keene, now in his late forties, noticed it. He was not alone.

The administration was grateful. Kevin was, too. Soon, his release date would come. Now, it was time to move on. He was set to go back to Gary. But to go to what? Just when he felt that events were moving in the right direction, a reality check set in—he had no place to go once he was out. His release date was approaching. Normally, this meant a great relief and a chance at life's renewal. But for Kevin, his major problem couldn't be solved overnight. He was homeless. But he still remembered the dream. "I'm on a mission. Don't know where I'm going, but my mom's dream will motivate me." It wouldn't take long for him to find out.

CHAPTER THREE

Four months after the gala GED ceremony that made him a star at the prison, Kevin Bolton was a free man. He had made his mark at the institution. Pictures of his now popular impromptu boxing events lined the wall next to the small weight room in the indoor gym. It was the result of an interview with a local ABC affiliate. The local television station knew from the prison staff that something was going on in the prison yard that would generate much-needed good publicity. And they got their story with Kevin.

After being on the nightly news, Kevin became a reluctant celebrity in the prison. Most of the incarcerated brethren were supportive; a few were jealous, and a few more remarked, "Well, what do you expect—he's White." There was some truth, no doubt, but Kevin was making a difference without even intending to. The overall tone improved in such a bleak environment.

The positive TV coverage resulted in more donations coming in for equipment for the boxing program—gloves, mouth and head guards for sparring, and boxing bags used in the makeshift ring. All of these were needed to alleviate any injury. In addition, correctional officers vied for a spot, as their time allowed, for the boxing program, allowing both staff and inmates to bond. Being outside during most of the year, the inmates got fresh air and time to bond through teamwork to alleviate pressures. Without intending to, Kevin had assisted in creating an overall more tranquil environment in the prison. Those who didn't participate in the boxing program also received additional benefits vis-à-vis more weights, gym shorts, and jump ropes, thanks to an anonymous South Bend philanthropist who donated $2,000.

A renewed energy seemed to permeate the bleak, concrete walls of the austere and foreboding prison. Noting the difference, Matos invited the warden to get out of his office more often and witness the activities. He did. What he saw pleased him. Going into the yard, he smiled at Matos, saying, "You mentioned one Gary inmate."

Matos, gently touching the warden's hand, pointed in the direction of a group of three shadowboxing alongside a group of four jump roping. "You see the White kid with the blond hair?"

Laughing aloud, Warden Jack Molton glanced at Matos and touched his forehead, responding, "This young man has got a team of loyal followers."

Matos, knowing that Kevin had inquired about obtaining new protective equipment, quickly interjected, "That's what I wanted you to see. Kevin Bolton is his name."

The warden stepped up to Kevin. Extending his hand, the ebullient warden added, "Ms. Matos told me to see for myself what you've accomplished, young man. I have to tell you that I'm impressed."

Kevin, looking in the direction of Matos while the group momentarily stopped what they were doing, added, "Thanks very much, sir." This was followed by some small talk by the warden asking him about his roots in Gary and his interest in boxing. Kevin, his newfound status evident, quietly suggested, "We could use some boxing gloves, mouth guards, head protection, and ropes. We got some contributions, and I hope we make good use of them." This comment was reinforced by the boxing squad formed by Kevin.

Nodding approval, the warden remarked, "I'll see what I can do for you. You've gotten some good publicity for the guys, and, yes, I'm certainly aware of some donations. In the meantime, keep up the good work."

Matos knew that Kevin would win over the warden. Good publicity helped him with his image, and the interview with the media and subsequent write-ups in the local papers also helped. More donations came in, totaling over $3,400. One was from an elderly woman in Terre Haute, who sent a $10 check and a note that read: "I'm eighty-nine years old. I want you to continue to help these troubled young men and make good of them for society." Comments like that sealed the deal for the warden.

With the donations, additional tasks that were on hold due to severe budget restrictions from the state capital in Indianapolis could now be addressed. The library and classrooms got a new coat of paint, several new color televisions were purchased, and even the cafeteria got a new oven, which pleased Chef Donatello and his staff.

The pictures that appeared in the newspaper as a result of the TV interview were there for all to see. What they highlighted were the workouts, the attention to detail on proper boxing stance, a description of upper and body cuts, and a jumping rope routine followed by leg moments of ducking and moving side to side. Impressed with Kevin's dedication to the sport of boxing, a reporter, Tom Hurley, summed up his encounter with Kevin by adding, "Kevin Bolton is a powerhouse who I'm sure we will soon hear from once his time here at Indiana State is finished."

Through the efforts of Owens, Matos, and others, Kevin accomplished much—including the first boxing exhibition in the prison. Publicity and donations came in as a result of the TV and newspaper coverage. Finally, a ring was set up. The local press again featured him on television. It made everyone look good—he was a model prisoner who worked hard, got the attention of others, and in turn, kept tensions low with a viable and exciting boxing program.

Catherine Holmes of the *Michigan City News Dispatch*, unlike Hurley, discovered a more contrite Kevin; he was no longer the reclusive and angry man he once was. She asked him about his future and what he hoped to achieve. At ease with the young female, he explained his dire home situation. Holmes saw a very focused man with sad eyes who was vulnerable, soft spoken, and respectful. This was a complete change from the time he had entered the facility. Holmes's commentary on Kevin's achievements again made the local news, and soon, more donations started coming in to support the boxing program. The warden personally congratulated Kevin after the good press.

Kevin's moves—from proper form in jumping rope, sparring, leg stances, ducks, and upper and lower jabs, coupled with some advice—made him a star. He showed some of his moves to Holmes while the camera was rolling. Kevin loved the attention. Knowledgeable about the history of the sport, he mentioned his favorite boxers—Ken Norton, Muhammad Ali, Smokin' Joe Frazier, and George Foreman.

He was able to persuade Matos to subscribe to *The Ring*, the leading boxing magazine. In addition, he knew the rules of boxing as outlined in the Marquess of Queensberry rules. He explained the rules to the inmates in his program and what a good fighter should expect, telling them that the moves on one's feet, jabs, ducking, and confidence meant nothing if one did not have a strategy. Kevin would insist that the person training stand tall, never slouch, and look his sparring partner squarely in the eye, with no fear. "I learned from the best in Gary—Joe Montalvo," Kevin explained. Within a short span of time, Kevin became a recognized leader. The positive attention made the once reclusive and moody young man a star among his fellow inmates.

Having experience in the ring, he explained the art of intimidating his opponent by eyeballing. "You got to do your homework and look at some boxing tapes. Especially your opponent's last fights. Get to know his style of boxing. Study his moves, his feet work, his jabs—is he a southpaw, traditional, or orthodox fighter? Look at them until you're comfortable. Only then, are you ready." Kevin knew his trade. He credited his trainer, Joe Montalvo, whose dogged determination never wavered.

Kevin, having learned from his trainer in Gary, motivated the serious guys who gravitated toward him, and it showed. A few from Gary mentioned that they hoped to join him in the boxing gym once he was released. This always brought a smile to his face, knowing his history and that corresponding with fellow former inmates would mean he would probably be banned.

The day before he was scheduled for release, a cake was provided by the mess hall chef Dan Donatello and his assistant, Marge Bellau. Donatello, a boxing fan, kept telling Kevin, "Get the hell out of here and hit the gym. I've seen you work with those hands. Quick jabs. Keep it up, and you'll go far—real far."

Donatello prepared a big chocolate sheet cake for Kevin. Donatello had become a fan of the good-looking young man. Kevin had worked in the kitchen for a period of seven months, getting to know the entire staff.

Donatello, the fifty-four-year-old, second-generation chef of Italian immigrants, also had a cousin who boxed, Frankie Aiello. Aiello later opened up a popular bakery in Indiana State and got his cousin Dan interested in baking. "It kept me out of trouble," he laughed, adding, "but I ended up in jail." In reality, Donatello had no criminal record and applied for the well-paying job having gotten an endorsement from a patron of his brother's bakery, who was a correctional officer at the prison.

Dan Donatello's specialties—cakes, cupcakes, muffins, and chocolate chip cookies—were a real treat to the staid and routine menu that was followed at the prison. His time at his cousin's bake shop got him started. He never looked back. Customers came from a distance just to buy his goodies. Soon, he got noticed in the local press. One of his customers was the warden at the jail. When asked if he'd like a job as chef with good benefits, he jumped at the chance.

Hired by the state of Indiana, Donatello became the chef in charge of menus at the prison. Versatile and imaginative, his cakes became his trademark. His other specialties were also a hit—veal and chicken parmigiana, meatloaf, roasted vegetables, and salads. Even the staff would come in to eat. "I eat better here than at home," Officer Larry Watkins remarked to Donatello one day.

Each Sunday, he would have his best desserts—usually cupcakes, chocolate cake, and tiramisu—as a special treat to both inmates and correctional officers. His specialty was his chocolate cake. To no one's surprise, he prepared a special one for Kevin. It was Kevin's favorite—chocolate-layered sheet cake. The icing had a clear message: "To the Future Champ." Donatello and his staff made sure that the sheet cake would be large enough for staff and inmates eating at the 1 p.m. mess call. With permission from the warden, the cake would serve as a going away send-off.

Often, Kevin had managed to get an extra slice of the delicious chocolate cake at mess hall. As Donatello explained, "Kev would smile at me, give a wink, and put his index finger to his lips." The message to Dan couldn't be clearer—don't tell anyone else. Donatello played the game, knowing full well what would transpire.

Kevin got extra perks from the chef. If Kevin knew that one of the inmates was celebrating a birthday, Kevin would give a heads-up to Dan and have a nice surprise for the unsuspecting man, whose birthday might otherwise go unnoticed. Whenever Kevin would ask the staff at the cafeteria to send a message to Donatello, the staff knew to be quiet, letting Kevin stand aside while Donatello sent the extra slice of cake, pizza, chicken, or whatever the menu highlighted. The correctional officers found it to be an innocent game that they ignored, knowing no harm was done. Other inmates wouldn't tell, as they benefited whenever their birthday came up or on other rare occasions, such as the birth of one of their kids or passing the GED occurred. It worked out for all.

The cake prepared that day was, indeed, special. The chef, smiling, needed two assistants to carry it out to the large table set up with a paper tablecloth. A labor of love, he had two of his best assistants help him, giving them a three-hour overtime approval by the warden, Jack Molton.

The cake was placed at the center for all to see. Dan Donatello proudly added, "I know we're going to hear from him. Wait and see." The two cafeteria staff members, Mabel Watson and Arthur Wagner, had helped carry the large, flat sheet cake to the center of the table. As other inmates shouted and clapped, Watson, a fifty-seven-year-old veteran, bowed. Known at the prison, she was a star—a fixture at Indiana State—having worked in the kitchen preparing meals for thirty-four years. A tough, religious woman who doled out advice, whether solicited or not, she knew who was real and who was a phony. She knew which of these motley crew inmates would be returning and which would make something of their lives.

Watson took a liking to Kevin. At first suspicious of why Dan Donatello let him in the kitchen when it was usually off-limits for inmates, Mabel Watson soon warmed up to the young man from Gary. Everyone called Mabel "Mama," and Kevin was no exception. She waited for him, usually on Thursdays, as the aroma of the desserts permeated beyond the kitchen. "Oh yeah, Mama, the joint smells great. Whatcha gonna do when I'm not here no more?" By this time, Kevin had come up to her, tugging on the strings of her white apron and giving her a hug.

Mabel Watson loved it. Like Donatello, she found a soft side to the young man. "He just needs a lot of tough love, and he'll be okay." Other inmates, seeing the perks that Kevin got, would ask *why him*? Why was he so special? But, they knew he would emerge with goodies. They benefited, and that would be the end of any issue.

He would smile, reach out, and dole out an extra trayful of cupcakes or cookies or slices of cake that Watson put together. The other inmates knew that Thursdays were special, and, before long, the tray of goodies became known as Kevin's trays. The guys lucky enough to have that extra perk would shout and slap the table. It made Mama Watson's day.

Ana Matos was on hand the day of the big cake send-off. Kevin was presented with a large, homemade poster card by one of the inmates, Jamal White. It was more of a large poster than a card. It reminded Matos and the other staff members of the colorful graffiti cartoon art that graced urban walls of bodegas and subway cars in New York. Garish, gritty, yet homemade with a sincere message, it was signed by the inmates who worked out in the yard with Kevin. It was also signed by correctional officers, kitchen staff, and the warden himself.

White depicted Kevin in boxing attire as a cartoon figure akin to Batman—complete with golden trunks and red gloves, replete with a good backdrop facsimile of Madison Square Garden. The Garden, completed in 1968 at its present site on West 33rd and adjacent to Penn Station, was the main venue for boxing before Vegas started to expand beyond the casinos. The art said volumes. White, the prison artist, was a man of few words, yet felt obliged to speak as others were eating cake. Standing up and displaying his masterpiece artwork for all to see, White said, "This is where I see you ending up—in New York at a world championship at the Garden. This is one White guy who has what it takes." This comment brought about resounding applause from the correctional officers stationed in the mess hall and the prisoners who were lucky enough to have their lunch at that designated hour.

White, proud of his creation, was symptomatic of many of the young inmates—a twenty-four-year-old from Fort Wayne, he had served three years of a four-year sentence for robbery. Coerced by peer pressure, he was in a getaway car that had robbed a Kentucky Fried Chicken takeout in suburban Indianapolis. While in prison, like Kevin, he found himself, and it showed that day with his gift to Kevin. Kevin, who was sitting to the right of White, gave him a high five. Kevin was in the moment, and yet he knew things would be different once outside the prison walls.

Kevin was deeply touched. More importantly, he was ready to go back to Gary. He wanted out, however dire the circumstances in his hometown. The two years in jail had changed him, giving him the confidence to excel and overcome the most emotional scars in his life. The mandatory rap sessions every Friday had proven to be a healing process. He had not really come to terms with his mom's death when he first was imprisoned. He was angry. He needed to grow up and face reality. Withdrawn at first, he eventually opened up, becoming a vocal advocate for other inmates. A good listener, he soon started to open up, speaking of his own problems in Gary.

Hearing other inmates explain their concerns, fears, and family issues, he realized he was not alone. He started to speak more often. At one session, one of the inmates, Frank Bianco, asked Kevin what he wanted to do once released. Without hesitation, he responded, "Become a pro boxer." No one took him to task, and he added, looking at Frank directly, "You see me in the yard. You know how intense my workout is with the others. I'm helping them stay focused and train. It makes me feel good, too."

Nodding, Frank chimed in, "Yes, I see how fast your fists are, and I don't want to come near you." Once the laughter died down, Frank added, "He's helped a lot of guys just by showing them some good moves. And, yeah, I wouldn't be at all surprised to see him as a champ." This response brought about a round of applause from the six others in the group.

These sessions proved to be seminal events for Kevin. He took a leadership role, gave advice to others, and felt that he had a purpose. The visiting weekly moderator, an assistant to Dr. Aaron Baker, Dr. Ari Shapiro, took a liking to Kevin, noticing his progress. Kevin also brought up issues that others were concerned about, such as extending time in the yard, asking for more books about African American history in the library, and requesting more tests in the infirmary when an outbreak of flu sidelined many inmates.

He also had time to hone his skills, not only in boxing but also as a student. Matos and others in the program had instilled in him something that he long needed—that self-confidence that was sorely needed and a sense of pride. He liked himself better, slept better, and was ready for whatever challenges lay ahead. He would soon be on a bus to take him home.

He was indeed ready. The bus ride wouldn't be long. It was just twenty-nine miles from Indiana State Prison to Gary. His confidence, tried and retried, once again ate at him. "I don't have a place. Where the hell am I going to stay in Gary?"

Yes, he knew things would never be the same. Events at home had made his future seem bleak. No longer angry, he came to terms with his sister's departure to Texas. Others had asked about his lodgings. Despite the inquiries by Matos, Brown, and others, Kevin didn't want the officials at Indiana State to know he had no place to stay. He knew no one was at his last known address. He knew the parole board would probably follow up with a visit and find the building vacant. Right now, he didn't care. He wanted out. He didn't know where he was heading in life, but he knew something would evolve. Deep inside, he felt a sense of relief in getting out, and he also had the confidence that he could rise above. Life gave Kevin Bolton a reality check. He would be tested, and he would emerge a better person, having gone through so much in his short life. Still a bit too proud, he was released by the authorities and was then on his own.

Released early on good behavior, he returned to Gary—his hometown. "Had no place to go," he remarked. It was the only town he had ever lived in. His world was Gary—he grew up there, went to school there, and never had the chance to leave the state.

The two-year stint at Indiana State was now over. He knew he had to make some hard decisions. *All this for a stupid act by my messed-up self.* His thoughts kept his mind preoccupied by that fateful day. Shaking his head in disgust at his stupidity, he remembered, "I was set up. Bitch! Just left the gym after punching the bag, jump roping, and sparring for three rounds. Wanted some smoke—some downtime after a full sixty minutes of sweat. It's time to forget and move on. I got bigger fish to fry." It was not meant to be.

Fortunes turned sour when Kevin encountered someone as he exited the gym. It was in the past, but it haunted him as the bus got closer to Gary. He wanted to forget about the circumstances, but he couldn't get it totally out of his head.

On that fateful day, the plainclothes rookie cop, Steve Cominski, came up and started a conversation that proved disastrous for Kevin. His backup was in an unmarked patrol car. The trap was set. "He saw me. He knew I just got out of the gym. He was standing there, acting like he was interested in my workout. Started asking about my boxing routine. Yeah, acted liked he cared. Told him I was thinking of being a trainer if I lost more than two consecutive fights. He then asked if I boxed. Told him that I had a few good amateur bouts. Never lost the three amateur fights. My trainer, Joe Montalvo, wanted me to go pro. Then this bullshit. He caught me at the worst moment. I should have just said nothing. Bastard."

Kevin bought a few grams of marijuana, and the result was an arrest by Cominski followed by plea bargaining. Indiana law in 1971, the year of Kevin's arrest, the purchase was a felony because anything over thirty grams and up to ten pounds was a Level 6 felony and subject to two and half years of prison. Cominski had enticed Bolton to buy more, thus elevating it to felony. This was the reason why Kevin's lawyer asked him not to plead guilty and instead was going for entrapment, knowing full well that Cominski wanted a felony arrest.

Even though it was Kevin's first felony offense, due to amount that was purchased, the climate in Gary, and the national opinion, the result was a movement to push hard against any users or sellers. It was the 1970s, and the push from the Nixon White House to the states was to be tough on crime. States started to pass laws that stiffened penalties. The three-strikes laws would later become the rallying cry for politicians running for office. It helped many conservative, albeit tough, laws to be passed in the statehouses in the nation. Indiana was one of them.

Despite the fact that the arrest was nonviolent, Kevin was not immune to the justice system. He was known to the Gary Police Department. His reputation had preceded him. He got into scrapes at bars, even though at nineteen he was not of legal drinking age. With a weight lifter's physique and looks that intimidated many whenever he was angered, he was known as someone to avoid. This was especially true after a few beers.

His manager, Montalvo, had to restrain his volatile personality on several occasions in the gym, telling him, "You have a quick upper punch, but cool it. Don't bring your attitude into this gym. I'll throw you out just as fast as you came in—got it?" Joe Montalvo had seen the furrowed brow, squinting eyes, and tight-lipped Kevin on several occasions that resulted in a shove match. Montalvo would not tolerate breaking the rules of the house. He ran a tight ship, knowing full well that many of the amateur, young kids coming into the gym came from dire circumstances. They had relatives in jail, other family members on drugs, lived in abject poverty, and didn't trust authority. He had lived it all himself, having had a brother killed in a drive-by. Montalvo became the only person who gave them the attention and respect they craved. It was no small undertaking.

Kevin Bolton was his star but had much baggage. Montalvo knew he had to reach out to him. Kevin fit the profile—angry, young, and from a dysfunctional family full of problems. With an alcoholic father who abandoned his family and sisters who ran the streets, Kevin was symptomatic of the problems of urban America. White, poor, and destitute, he definitely could fall through the cracks. With Montalvo mindful of his circumstances, it didn't mean a thing. He had seen it all.

In one tense sparring session, Kevin wasn't focusing on his opponent. Montalvo stopped, getting in Kevin's face, and shouted, "You think you're the only one with problems? Bullshit! Stop the nonsense and take this place and the routines seriously or leave!" Kevin knew he had to fess up but almost lost it. Again, out came the furrowed brow and the squinted eyes.

Later, an incident in the locker room almost sealed his fate and nearly put an end to whatever hopes he had to make it as a boxer. His dream almost died that afternoon.

What started as a shouting match quickly escalated into a shoving match replete with curses and threats by backup units. Soon, other boxers intervened, lest there be a fight outside the ring. Kevin had reacted the only way he knew how—by shoving the other person and set to use his fists.

On that occasion, Montalvo pleaded with the owner, Frank Owens, to allow his trainee to stay on. "The kid is a pain, but he'll listen to me. Believe me when I say he has talent. I've seen boxers come and go. With Bolton, we can sharpen his skills and get him somewhere. Yeah, I don't like the fact that he broke the rules by pushing that Carter kid. But let's give him a chance."

Kevin had pushed a fellow boxer in the locker room after a snide comment about Kevin's long hair. The fact that he was a White minority in a largely Black and Hispanic environment and could floor any boxer made some of the trainees both jealous and angry. Some of the boxers had experienced outright racism from all aspects of society, and the fact that Kevin—the blond, White kid—stood out ignited their hostility. Others just didn't like him because he was White. Montalvo knew Kevin was a powder keg, but he also saw a raw talent that seldom comes and knew he could, with time, mold him into a fierce fighter in the ring. He first had to reach out and gain his trust. Montalvo became a mentor, trainer, teacher, and somewhat of a psychologist. He had no choice. Kevin was a person in need.

Acting quickly, his attempt at assuaging the owner paid off. Owens remarked, "I don't need these guys pissed at one another. Take care of it, but if that Bolton kid acts up again, he's history. Got it? Johnny Carter didn't shove Bolton; it was Kevin who did it." Called into Owens's office, both Carter and Bolton were told the consequences. Both would be thrown out and never come back. The scare tactic worked. Before he excused them, he made them shake hands. "You don't have to love each other, but, dammit, you'll respect this gym and my rules. Got it?" With that, he dismissed both fighters, sat down, looked at the dusty floor, and called his wife.

Owens himself came up the hard way, working odd jobs as a dropout in the 1950s. He eventually ended up at the boxing gym and going a few bouts on the amateur circuit. When offered the chance to buy Southside, he jumped at the chance. Getting a minority business loan in 1968, he helped transform Southside into a respectable boxing venue. It was, as he often said, "a secure place for some of these kids who have seen too many shootings and misery." The fact that he had strict rules made it all the more challenging for some of the most hardened individuals who came inside the door. His tacit capitulation to Montalvo to give Kevin a second chance said volumes. Owens, looking at Joe Montalvo, could see that he had a lot going on with this young White kid. Owens decided to give in.

A nodding Montalvo, relieved that his best boxer could stay, now was aware that he had to be on guard with the volatile Kevin Bolton. As fate would have it, just a day later came the encounter with Officer Cominski and the arrest of the aspiring young pugilist. Kevin hadn't cooled down much. He was still pissed about the incident with Johnny Carter. That didn't help when he was confronted by Officer Cominski. When Owens heard about it, he went up to Montalvo and remarked, "You've done enough for that rat. I knew he was trouble."

The incident outside Southside Gym ended Kevin Bolton's short but remarkable stint as a boxer. He was targeted. The parking lot outside the gym was a known after-hours hangout for drug deals. Yet, that day Officer Cominski, in civilian clothes, was determined to collar someone. Unfortunately, the person he approached was Kevin. What happened was a farce and a miscarriage of justice in a tense America out to punish any violator. Kevin was arrested for a nonviolent crime that should have gone nowhere, save a fine or probation or counseling. But that was not to be.

Kevin Bolton pleaded guilty. He ignored the repeated wishes of his court-appointed attorney and his trainer to go to trial. "I was stupid not going to trial. Should have listened to Kyle Anderson, my lawyer. He knew I was entrapped by agreeing to buy more than six grams. Didn't know or care about the law on weed. I was so pissed at everything. I was pissed at that little punk, Johnny Carter. I got into a spat with Montalvo over Carter. Almost was thrown out. The gym was my life. I didn't want to get the boot. But, I was pissed big time. I didn't give a damn. Yeah, stupid; real stupid." Given a mandatory two-and-half-year sentence at Indiana State, he now had a criminal record. He had no one to blame but himself. And now, wiser and older, he was out and free. Or was he?

Two and half years in jail. Now, free and nowhere to go. Big deal! Now a free man, he had to make some decisions. Hard decisions.

Coming back to Gary would not be easy. Alone and with no address, he had no family and no support system. With the few dollars in his pocket given to all parolees, Kevin was a stranger in a city he had called home. He lied, giving his old address to the prison officials. He didn't want to be assigned to a shelter.

The hard, lonely streets looked the same—the urban blight a bit more apparent from the abandoned row houses along what was once a tree-lined street. There were more boarded-up houses. "The stench sucked." Even the rain the previous night didn't take away the stench. The pools on the pavement attracted a few pigeons that were thirsty for some water. There was little sign of life. The vacant lots that a few years earlier were homes had been replaced by fields of weeds and overgrown grass. The neglected sidewalks had large cracks and assortments of weeds, dandelions, and other wildflowers growing through the pavement. Added to this were the feral cats scavenging for food. When they got lucky, they occasionally had the luxury of cornering a rat or mouse.

The few people who passed gave no eye contact and quickly walked on. "It's like a dead zone here." The few storefronts—once a bevy of activity with candy stores, laundromats, liquor stores, and storefront churches—lay vacant. "Man, this is insane. In just a few years, the place has become a ghost town." In some spots, the rotted-wood, boarded-over broken windows of houses gave it an eerie, almost surreal aura. The unkempt grass in front of the once proud and now empty houses looked like a scene from a horror film.

The foul smell from the rotting-wood buildings was matched by the billowing, acrid smoke still spewing from the nearby US Steel plant in the distance. The tall, brick smokestacks gave the area a permanent haze and an added malodorous stench. And, on this once busy street, little was left. It had given way to the Rust Belt reputation. It was a scene devoid of the sights and sounds of a once-proud city neighborhood. Gary was the victim of outsourcing from big business to find cheaper markets abroad while neglecting the rank-and-file union households. Gary's problem was emblematic of the once thriving Midwest cites that stretched from Buffalo through the Ohio Valley and into Indiana, Illinois, and Michigan.

Like the city he called home, Kevin was also down and out. Life, the prospect of a job, and living quarters were the most important things on his mind. "I won't go back to the joint, no way. If I have to, I'll dig ditches. Ain't gonna go back!" His dogged determination was matched by a restless desire to do something positive.

He remembered what his jailhouse GED instructor, Matos, told him; "You have potential—use it!"

He also remembered how angry his boxing coach was when he gave up and copped a plea. *Bet he doesn't want to see me anymore*, Kevin thought. But the sendoff by Donatello and his staff and White's poster reminded him that he was not a loser. His drive was there. Yet, he was proud. He wanted to visit the gym and see both Montalvo and Owens, but he knew the priorities that stood in the way.

He had given the parole board his old address. He once lived there with his elder sister, Laura. It was the only address he had. He had stayed there after the death of his mother, Norma Baranski Bolton, for four months before he was arrested. But now, no one was at that address. He knew that Laura had left. The last two letters that he sent to her were sent back, indicating a return to sender. He knew there would be a problem. Laura left no forwarding address.

No address. No home. He was now an ex-con with no place to stay and no family who cared. Running his fingers in his full mane of thick, blond hair, he shook his head, wondering, *What the hell is going on? I got nothing—nothing.*

The landlord had evicted his sister for not paying. Owning three months' rent, she absconded with no forwarding address. She had lived on welfare but failed to show up for a random drug test. She would have failed the test. With too much marijuana in her system, she isolated herself, occasionally venturing to a local dive that sold cheap beers and hung out with a few so-called friends.

Laura fled to Texas with her new boyfriend, Frankie Ortiz, leaving her brother to fend for himself. Laura's continuing issues with her drug use made her very vulnerable. Her relationship with Ortiz only exacerbated the distant and acrimonious tension between her and Kevin. Ortiz manipulative, lustful, and noncontributing to her needs—used Laura, moving in until she was evicted. She didn't write to her brother, save once when he first entered Indiana State Prison. Once Ortiz entered her world, it was all downhill.

Kevin was often argumentative and short-tempered during his stays with Laura. "She's lazy and doesn't even clean up. I hated living with her after Mom died, but I couldn't pay the rent since I only worked part-time at the gym."

His relationship with Laura, such that was left, further deteriorated once Kevin was forced by financial circumstance to move to Laura's drug-infested building when their mother died. His mom wasn't financially secure, and he barely had enough from the insurance policy to bury her. While he was doing time, Laura—a lonely, depressed, and lazy pothead—met Ortiz. It would prove to be a disaster for Kevin.

She decided to leave with Ortiz. Ortiz was in Gary for a funeral of an aunt. His aunt was also his godmother, who had left Texas to live in Gary with her late husband who worked in the steel mill when jobs were plentiful during World War II. His cousin, Milagros Perez, paid for him to fly into O'Hare from San Antonio and met him at the airport for the short ride to Gary.

Frankie Ortiz and Laura were eventually matched. A drifter from San Antonio, Oritz met Laura at a karaoke bar one cold November night. They connected. They started hanging out together, and their relationship evolved into a sexual one. Soon, they were living together. Ortiz, who had his roots with an ex-wife and kid in Texas, used his new girlfriend. He had a place to crash. He didn't want to return to his dead-end job in San Antonio, delivering takeout at the local Mexican restaurant. His aunt's family, knowing his sordid history, didn't invite him to stay on once his aunt's funeral was over.

Both had issues. His included a failed marriage and wife and kid to support. Laura's situation was no better, featuring a history of bad relationships with the men in her life. She owed back rent. Her welfare checks dried up as her pot smoking got worse. She hustled men in bars for money, sometimes sharing a night or two with them. Seldom did it extend beyond that. When Frankie Ortiz came on the scene, he gave her what she needed—someone who had a few dollars in his pocket from his aunt's estate. He also liked Laura, seeing himself as her alter ego.

Despite his own craziness and pot smoking, he listened to her. At thirty-four years old, he was tall and slim. His dark, piercing eyes complemented by a pencil mustache were initially what attracted Laura to the handsome Latino. Soon, they were an item. The dysfunctional, misguided, petite, brunette woman and the machismo Latino got along well. When he suggested she go to Texas with him, she jumped at the chance. "I can get out of here with all these problems, get a new life, and maybe even a job or start a family." It was an offer too good to pass up.

Ortiz was the perfect escape. With her finances and drug-related dependency, she told no one about Ortiz's offer. As fate would have it, she had a new issue and reason indeed to leave Gary: she was expecting his child. Now three months pregnant, she took her chances with him and left town in the middle of the night. What was left for her brother, Kevin?

With no place to call home, Kevin needed help. With his elder sister gone, he knew he would be in trouble without a place to stay. Getting off the thirty-minute bus ride from the prison, he headed to his old neighborhood. He stopped by his old address. The apartment was still vacant. "The place is more messed up than when I left it. Knowing my crazy sister Laura, I'm not at all surprised." He didn't like what she did to him. She ate at him as he walked by the building she had lived in.

Shaking his head, he wondered, *Damn! Laura didn't have the decency to tell me where the hell she was going. All I know is she went to San Antonio with some lowlife drifter named Frankie who knocked her up. She started hanging out with him, allowing him to stay with her. Bitch!*

There was one glimmer of hope in this whole episode. He had received a letter. It wasn't from Laura. Why would it be? It was written by an old school buddy, Claude Evans. He had explained it all. The information about his sister and Ortiz was the focus of the letter. Claude lived just a few blocks from Laura and wanted to give Kevin an update. He had friends who hung out at the bar that Laura and Frankie frequented and who bought their pot. Claude wrote that Ortiz's funds were drying up. His aunt had left him $1,000. He spent most of it with Laura getting high, hanging out, ordering takeout from Domino's and McDonald's, going to the movies, and buying a new television.

Laura, a manipulator, got Ortiz in her orbit. Laura mentioned that she was behind in rent. Ortiz decided it was time to act. The one time she had mentioned the possibility of getting evicted, Ortiz's cryptic remark was, "No problem. Move to San Antonio with me." She also told Ortiz she was carrying his baby. He didn't give her any money for rent. That was the only time she had asked him for help. And now, she was pregnant. What to do? He gave her an offer to start anew in a location far from Gary. She felt it was her only option. Ortiz told Laura he would take care of her and the baby. He also stopped buying pot, started taking the pregnancy seriously, and wanted Laura to be well. As for Kevin, he was the left out one.

Claude Evans proved to be a decent, stand-up guy. He felt for Kevin. He knew he had had a rough life, and he had been witness to his older sister's behavior. Claude wanted to make sure that Kevin knew what he was up against once released.

The letter he sent to Kevin changed everything. Kevin really had no intention of staying with his older or younger sister. He hoped that he could get a job and get an apartment. The letter drove the point home that he, indeed, would be in trouble once released. The information Claude Evans conveyed in his letter to Kevin was not totally foreign to Kevin. He expected something like this from his sister. He knew how unstable Laura was. It didn't, however, make his living situation any better. He needed an address. The ex-con now had to make a decision.

Upon being released from prison, he got an early-morning bus at 8:00 a.m. Knowing his dire circumstances, he had those decisions nagging at his mind. The decisions would determine what his future would entail.

The endorsement from his jailhouse teacher kept nagging at him: "You have potential." A smile came over him as he recalled how well he performed on his GED. He took out a comb, brushed his thick, blond hair, and placed the black, plastic comb in his breast pocket, letting out an audible sigh. The uncrowded bus meandered along, and Kevin nodded off for a brief ten minutes. The trip was short and uneventful, and he soon arrived in Gary.

Kevin looked out the window when he awakened from his brief nap. He tried to clear his head about his home situation. "As the brothers in the joint used to say, 'What happens, happens.'" He saw the signs of life from the passing cars, trucks, and a motorcyclist who waved at him. It was a natural surrounding—life—complete with trees, grass, roadside restaurants, and people walking to and from their cars in parking lots adjacent to suburban malls along the highway. These signs of life gave him a much-needed uplift.

The bus arrived on time at the Greyhound station in Gary. Navigating his way from the back of the bus, he proceeded to exit. A few people in the front had already gotten off. Glancing out the window, he let out a sigh, not knowing what would ensue.

Noticing that an elderly woman sitting a few rows in front was struggling with her medium-sized suitcase, he instinctively decided to help. He walked up, having just a light duffle bag, and smiled at her, saying, "Let me help you with your bag." The gray-haired woman, about sixty, gave Kevin a friendly nod. He removed the black suitcase from the overhead bin and placed it on the sidewalk.

Turning to Kevin, she smiled, thanking him and asking, "Do you live here?"

Embarrassed to tell her he was homeless, he nodded, adding, "Yes, this is where I grew up."

She casually mentioned that she was going to see a sister when a midtwenties man approached and took her bag, saying, "Hello, Aunt Mamie." She gave him a kiss on his cheek, and he smiled at Kevin and took his aunt by the hand.

She turned and again said, "Thank you, young man. You take care." Kevin waved to her and her nephew and picked up his faded-green duffel bag and walked in the opposite direction. He thought of the people who made a difference in his life at the prison. "I won't let them down, because I know I can make something of my life. Wish I could go back to the boxing gym. Ms. Matos should see me now; she might think a little differently."

He wanted to return to the boxing gym, Southside. Yet, he was reluctant. His trainer Montalvo sent a few letters and a Christmas check of twenty-five dollars the first year he was incarcerated. Too proud to write back, he had given up, thinking, *He's being nice but knows I'm a loser*. Kevin never wrote even a thank-you for the correspondence and money. Now home, he deeply regretted it.

He never mentioned it during his time at Indiana State. Still proud, he felt it would show his weakness. He realized now what a mistake it was not to write back. "Yeah, I'd love to go back, but I know Joe Montalvo would probably call me a loser and throw me out." Kevin, alone and homeless, knew he was left with few options.

Where was he to go?

The homeless shelter had to be avoided. "I'll get into trouble the minute I get there. I won't go there. Hell no! I'll be in a fight before the night is over. I know what a hellhole it is. I'll be surrounded by people with problems, and they'll test me worse than in the joint. No way!"

Shelters could be dangerous. The inhabitants would have been a recipe for disaster for the young parolee. He knew that churches and community groups did a lot, but he was young, cocky, and independent, and wanted to stay clear of any potential problems. He didn't want any help. At least he thought so. It took the confinement of a prison cell and a life-changing event in the form of a dream to transform Kevin Bolton into a serious, mature, caring individual. His dysfunctional, rebellious, and self-centered life quickly changed once his mom's dream took hold. His reentry into society was about to shake him up. And it was about to impact the boxing world.

CHAPTER FOUR

Gary. The Steel City. Kevin's hometown. As he walked around the old neighborhood on the cool, dank, cloudy day, the dreary weather seemed like an omen to him—he was a person in need. Kevin knew that the shelter would be the last resort. He wanted to avoid it. "Maybe I can get a job at the boxing gym even if I have to clean up after everyone. Don't know they'll allow me there. I know I disappointed my trainer, who was all set to see me fight again and go pro. Me, who should have turned pro. What an idiot I was not listening to the people then."

Would he be treated like the biblical prodigal son? Returning to Gary was a mixed blessing—for one, he was free and had the chance to move on. On the other hand, he was a felon with a record. He had disappointed his former trainer who had expected so much from him. He pondered how to approach Montalvo. He was not good at being humble, and the time spent behind bars was a reality check. He had to fess up and be responsible. He was ready to swallow his pride and move on. Yet, he was still uncomfortable at the prospect of seeing his old boxing gym.

The humiliation of his incarceration plus the added fact that he let people down weighed heavily on his mind. It ate at his every fiber. Deep inside, he knew he belonged back in the world he knew—boxing. "It's my meal ticket, and I just hope that they'll let me in the door. I can train and spar with others. I'd love to be in the ring. I doubt they'll let me."

His thoughts and anxieties were swirling in his head when he noticed someone walking briskly up to him, then running toward him, winded and waving his arms. It was someone he had hoped to see—his old homie, Claude Evans. Kevin immediately felt like a weight had been lifted off his shoulders. "I thought he just wanted to forget about me, like everyone else." Kevin, in his last letter to Evans, had recounted the problem of getting released with no place to stay. But Evans knew all the sordid details about Laura. And he knew what date Kevin was scheduled for his return to the old neighborhood. He had been waiting for Kevin's bus, having placed a call to the prison to find out the arrival time of his friend by Greyhound. Kevin's release went smoother than expected, and he boarded an earlier bus that arrived a full hour before Claude expected.

Claude wanted to surprise his old friend when he arrived. Claude, waiting for Kevin, watched as seven passengers got off at Gary. The Greyhound's next stop was Chicago. Kevin was not on this bus.

Claude, suspecting that something had gone awry, quickly picked up his pace and proceeded to a nearby street phone booth. He placed a call to his wife's cousin, who, fortunately, was working the morning shift at the prison. After a few minutes, he was able to get the information on Kevin. The release papers were checked, informing him that Kevin had departed an hour earlier than anticipated. Claude knew where to go. "He'll head either to the old neighborhood or walk near the gym." Claude was certain that Kevin, a creature of habit with no family or place to stay, would get back to his own 'hood.

Claude's hunch paid off. He knew Kevin and felt certain that he would encounter Kevin. "He most definitely would gravitate to his old neighborhood—I got to hustle to get to him."

Without a cell phone in those days or any other means of communicating, Claude rushed to Kevin's former home that Kevin had once shared with Laura. It was a ten-minute walk from the Greyhound station. Claude wasn't worried once he was notified of Kevin's earlier release. He had given Kevin his home phone number. He knew that Kevin would probably call his home, only to find no one there. Yolanda was working, and her one-year-old son was with her mother, Mamie Young. Yet, he knew that once Kevin didn't see him at the bus station, he might have decided that Claude didn't want to go the extra mile. And he knew the old Kevin.

Kevin was stubborn, suspicious of authority, and didn't like taking orders. It was as simple as that. Pride. "He probably figures I gave up on him." Claude, shaking his head, knew he had to move. But, as luck would have it, he spotted his old buddy walking aimlessly around the street he once called home.

Approaching Kevin, Claude's broad smile said it all. Getting his wind back, he went up to Kevin. It sent the right message to Kevin. Claude's appearance at once gave Kevin some cause for hope. Claude was relieved that he had located his friend.

Deep down, Kevin knew Claude Evans to be a stand-up guy who would go the limit for a friend. He was very grateful.

Claude gave Kevin a once-over look that caused him to shout, "Damn, bro, what have you done? Looks like you been working out four hours a day." The sight of his buff friend brought a laugh from Claude. The former inmate had indeed buffed up, adding twelve pounds of solid muscle to his already in-shape self.

"Hell, with so much time on my hands, I spent two hours a day in the yard lifting, sparring, jump roping, and jogging," Kevin added.

"And it shows!" Claude, delighted to see his friend, gave him a pat to his hard right arm. It was evident that his friend had utilized his time behind bars to harden his already buffed self. Seeing Kevin in such shape made him envious.

Claude Evans was the complete opposite of Bolton—a bit shorter, a few pounds overweight, Black, and married. Kevin was White, Catholic, and of Irish, Polish, and German heritage. Claude had a good job. Though they were never in trouble, Claude and Kevin had bonded in high school despite their differences. Claude was the product of a single mother with strong values. "She expected a lot from us—made sure we got our homework done, got to school on time, did the chores, and went to church." Claude credits her for his stable upbringing, completing high school, and going to Indiana University Northwest College in Gary.

What drew the opposites was a mutual respect. Claude saw in Kevin a troubled friend who had a lot of talent. He was aware of Kevin's mom's struggle with breast cancer and the constant attention needed as her condition worsened over a period of eight months. He witnessed a softer side of Kevin in attending to her needs in her final days.

Claude once stopped by Kevin's house unannounced after Kevin left his wallet on the locker room bench.

It only held $4, but Claude suspected that Kevin might assume it was lost or stolen. Walking into Kevin's mom's small, two-bedroom apartment on the third floor, he noticed the graffiti on the wall leading up to the second landing. The apartment was located in an area that was undergoing urban blight.

Kevin answered the door and was surprised to see his teammate, Claude, smiling and showing him the wallet. Claude said, "You left this on the bench in the locker room."

Kevin thanked him as his mom asked in a faint voice, "Is that Mary Collins?" Collins was the assigned health-care worker who came every two days to ensure that proper medication was administered. When Kevin told her it was a friend from school, she told her son to let him in. Kevin, not wanting Claude to know that he was a caregiver, reluctantly told Claude to come in. Claude felt that he should come in, as Kevin's mother had invited him in. Claude was ushered into her bedroom. He saw the emaciated woman in bed, who managed to smile.

Kevin mentioned that Claude was returning his wallet. This gesture made Kevin's mother smile, and she added, "I'm so glad you have a nice friend you can trust."

Claude, before excusing himself and leaving, observed Kevin preparing a meal for his mom on the kitchen stove and checking on her meds. A softer, doting son who loved his mother, Kevin didn't inform anyone of his mom's deteriorating condition and the attention demanded by it. Before Claude left, he shook Kevin's hand and said, "Your mom is lucky to have you."

An uncomfortable Kevin, not used to attention, nervously smiled and replied, "I appreciate you bringing the wallet back."

The unexpected visit had an impact on Claude. His gesture cemented their bond in trusting one another. He witnessed a softer and more humane side of the rough kid who was on his football squad. Indeed a dutiful son, Kevin spent his mother's final hours attending to and assisting the aide sent by the hospital. This was quite a contrast from the Kevin everyone knew. He only shared this part of himself with Claude after his visit.

Claude asked if he needed anything. Claude felt for his friend, knowing he was going through such tough times.

Kevin, a taciturn and unassuming, brooding individual, never let anyone else know about his home situation. It became a secret between Claude and him. Kevin didn't boast. He wanted to be there for his mom. "Kev's the real thing—he just had issues with his sisters."

Claude felt for Kevin, who of his mom's three children was the closest to her. Claude could relate to his friend. Claude's own mother had cared for her father after she worked long hours at the steel mill. Claude's grandfather, Franklin Longworth, had lingered a year with lung cancer. Claude could appreciate Kevin and wouldn't let others on the football squad or in school bad-talk his friend. He also related to this side of Kevin in his experience with his mom and the sacrifice he made for her.

Kevin didn't tell anyone or let on how much time and effort and love were given. Claude appreciated this quality in Kevin yet never mentioned it to him. He knew better. Yet, he knew Kevin was vulnerable and would need a network to help him. When Kevin's mother died a few months later, Claude started a donation drive that raised $300 toward his mom's funeral. He also attended her funeral Mass at the old Polish church, St. Hedwig's on Pennsylvania Street, with several football team members. This was the church that his mother's Polish parents attended and where his mom was baptized and attended the parochial school adjacent to the church.

Claude was also a loyal person who possessed an affable manner that made him popular as a school athlete. His loyalty to Kevin raised eyebrows. Some remarked, "You know he's a loser. Just White trash. Always in fights." Claude would hear none of this.

During Kevin's confinement at Indiana State, his loyalty was unchallenged. He corresponded with Kevin with a few letters and an occasional phone call. Claude felt that Kevin was someone who needed attention. Kevin had, in last his letter, told of his problems with his two sisters and the prospect of living in a homeless shelter. It was one of only two letters he sent to Claude. But it did wonders. This plea for help, however subtle, touched Claude.

At age twenty-two, Claude was a young father of a one-year-old boy, Khalid. Claude had also gone through rough times, having to leave college after a car accident left him with a permanent injury to his left leg. It ended his sport scholarship. He still walked with a slight limp due the accident. But he had stability. He married a local girl named Yolanda Young. He had a steady job as a dispatcher for the city of Gary's bus line and a wife who worked weekends at the local Target to supplement their income. Claude proved to be the perfect person that the vulnerable Kevin could rely on. He had taken the day off from work to meet Kevin at the bus terminal he knew so well, as his office was in the same building.

Claude and Kevin had gone to the same high school—Theodore Roosevelt. They were just one year apart, and both were on the football team. Kevin dropped out of school in his junior year, telling everyone that he was going to join the army. Everyone, from his guidance counselor to the football coach, tried in vain to change his mind. He would have none of it. His mind was made up. It might have happened had his mom's condition not worsened.

They became instant friends and always got along well. That

day, coming in contact with Kevin wasn't a surprise. Claude tried to get in touch with Kevin the previous few months but hadn't heard from him. It was Kevin's fault.

"I may be down and out, but I ain't gonna ask anybody for a handout." Too proud to ask for a favor, he ignored the last two letters from Claude. "Just don't want to be in the way." Evans, however, knew the date of Kevin's release, which was a public record. Plus, he had put in a call to the prison where one of his wife's cousins worked. His wait at the bus station showed his loyalty. When Kevin failed to show, Claude, ever responsible, felt for his old buddy. The call to his wife's cousin confirming his release earlier than expected caused him at first to panic. But he knew Kevin. Sure that he would gravitate toward the old neighborhood, he set off and found him.

Kevin Bolton was a man in need. The recent events with his sister's abrupt departure changed everything. Now on the street that they knew so well, the sight of Claude immediately brought a smile to Kevin's face.

Seeing Kevin, Claude knew he had to get some information from his old buddy. Aware of Kevin's dire situation, Claude said, "It's good to see you, Kev. I was hoping you would call. I knew the date. Don't be so damn proud, bro. My wife's cousin Darryl told me what bus you took. Didn't know you got out earlier and took an earlier bus. I knew you would head to the old 'hood to see what's going down."

The crestfallen Kevin took a deep breath and replied, "Wanted to call, but—"

Claude quickly interjected, "But nothing. I gave you my phone number, right?"

"Yeah, but I didn't want to . . ."

Claude, a bit annoyed, shook his head and brushed aside his arm, saying, "You too damn proud to get a little help? There's a phone booth right outside the terminal."

Claude looked at his friend, who looked a bit older but fit. Kevin's sad eyes, evident despite the forced smile, gave Claude a chance to ask about Kevin's lodgings.

"Where you staying?" Claude asked, gently touching his friend's right shoulder. He knew that Kevin had no permanent address with the sudden departure of his older sister. He needed to hear it from Kevin.

"I guess I'm gonna go to a shelter until I can find a job and a place." Kevin looked at the ground, his body language sending a message that clearly intended to resonate with Claude. He was uncomfortable and didn't want to tell his buddy the truth, but knew he had to. "That's the last place I wanna go to." It was a topic he wished he could have avoided. Claude Evans knew the deal. It now gave him the chance to intervene. He already had a plan.

"Wait a minute. When I last wrote you, you told me you that your sister Laura was living at your mom's place. Then, I found out she up and left. I know what happened with some guy she met."

"Yeah, until she hooked up with some idiot a few months back and they left high and dry and didn't pay the rent. Pregnant, too." Clearly angry, his voice rising, Kevin added, "She cares about herself. Never even got but two letters from her or my kid sister, Charlene. She never wrote me one letter, anyway. Charlene has her problems, too, now living in Fort Wayne. I'm thinking of just hanging out in Gleason Park—"

Claude interrupted, "Oh shit, maybe you should think twice about going to the shelter. And you can't stay in a park. You know what goes on, especially in the shelter. You're tough, but . . ."

Claude's voice trailed off. "I've heard stories of guys getting rolled there." Claude's sympathetic gaze caught Kevin off guard.

"I know but—"

"You got no place to crash?" Claude, knowing the situation, was ready to make a proposal to his friend. A smile on Claude's face at once made the harried parolee feel better.

The ex-con knew he had to make a change now that his parole ended. He didn't want to go back to his old 'hood, but where was he to go? In prison, he made up his mind. "I don't know if I should even stay in Gary. It's too much for my head to absorb. I love the few friends I had, but they're probably gone or don't want to see me. Can't blame them. I know I got to give an address and have some place to stay. I know I'm supposed to be in Gary. The temptations are there to do bad—hell, I can't end up in that hellhole cell again. I want to keep the promise I made to myself—once I leave the joint, I'm not looking back." He also remembered the dream he had of his mom when he first arrived. It haunted him, forcing him to make changes. Now, this was a new episode. He was grateful to have Claude here today for him.

He thought of leaving his home—Gary, Indiana. It was the only home he knew. Gary had been a good place for him growing up. Despite its problems—urban blight, loss of jobs, and soaring crime rate—it was still home. He liked the parks. He liked the gyms. And he had a good friend in Claude Evans. Yet, he needed to change.

Kevin just couldn't go back to his old neighborhood—what remained of it. He also had a bad reputation. "That kid has a short fuse." People who avoided him and his family—what was left after his mom died—weren't ready to take him back. He had several barroom brawls, resulting in his eviction from his favorite sport bar, Clancy's. The bartender, a burly, bearded, overweight badass named Pete Hastings, liked nothing better than to get rid of the troubled Kevin. He also knew that at age nineteen he was underage to drink, despite a bogus ID stating he was twenty-one. "He has a few drinks, gets high. If anyone looks at him the wrong way, his attitude takes over, and the fights begin."

At six-foot-two, the blond, handsome, muscular, former defensive-end on his football team was someone to avoid. Despite his good looks and athletic prowess, he was suspicious and distrusted most people. No doubt, this resulted from the treatment by his father. His own family had abandoned him for their own pursuits before his mom's death. But, he did have some talent—using his fists. It came from many hours in the local boxing gym.

Often challenged, he got into fights. Worse, he was also known to the local precinct. His mom's passing plus his older sister's erratic behavior only added to the mix. His mother's rather sudden illness and death made matters worse. He became more reclusive, losing his job as a packer for UPS as a result of a verbal spat with a coworker who was trying to hit on him. "She's wasn't my type—overweight and constantly in my face." An angry young man, he was destined to get in trouble, and the encounter with the plainclothes cop two years earlier capped it all.

His older sister, Laura, had two daughters with James McNamara by age twenty-six. McNamara, a local guy, had had enough of Laura's binges with alcohol and drugs. Having been together for eight years but unmarried, he left one night after a fight that resulted in Laura getting a bad bruise to her left shoulder. She never reported the incident and filed for welfare as a single, unemployed mom. McNamara often drank too much and didn't have steady employment. He also had a short fuse and a criminal record for cashing fraudulent checks.

McNamara was said to have gone to Oklahoma, where a younger brother had relocated. Working in Tulsa, McNamara's brother Michael quickly found him employment in an oil refinery. When James told him of the ongoing troubles with Laura Bolton, he suggested the move to Oklahoma.

Now, once again an expectant mom, she and her two daughters relocated with Ortiz to Texas. Kevin understood her desire to leave Gary and relocate. But he couldn't come to terms with the fact that she wouldn't correspond. Once she started a relationship with Ortiz, a promise of a better life in Texas seemed a good way out for her. She wanted something good for her kids. "I know that her life wasn't good with a lowlife like James." McNamara had left and wouldn't return. It was best for her and her two daughters that he stayed away. He had had enough of her mess. Unemployed and having too much leisure time, she started smoking more pot. Her kids were missing school too often, and the truant officer was ready to take action just before Ortiz arrived on the scene.

Ortiz's arrival filled a lonely void in her life. She was more than happy to take a chance and move on. She didn't know or care where her common-law husband, McNamara, was. And Ortiz found in Laura a vulnerable, lonely, and miserable woman. Ortiz liked to control his women. He jumped at the chance of moving in and having a good time with someone he could use. Jobs were more plentiful in Texas. Three months before Kevin was released, she left with her two daughters, aged five and seven. Already living in San Antonio, Ortiz was able to get her a part-time job as a maintenance worker. Since she spoke no Spanish, she couldn't get a counter job in the largely Hispanic city.

His other sister, Charlene, had her own share of problems, from the abusive men who controlled her to health issues of obesity and drug use. At twenty-four, she also had moved from Gary to Fort Wayne after her boyfriend, Tony Adolfo, walked out on her. "I knew she wanted out. I think she's staying with our cousin, Bobby Langford, and his girl, Marlene."

Charlene and Laura had their own lives and a host of issues. Kevin was on their radar. They loved him, but they had their priorities. But Kevin also had little to show.

Once arrested, he was determined in the solitude of his cell to start anew. But how? A place to crash, even in Claude's basement apartment, would be better than going to the men's shelter downtown. What was he to do? The encounter with Claude, however unexpected, was a godsend. "I've got to stay in Gary until I get this parole off my chest. Maybe then I'll move on."

Claude clearly knew he had to intervene. "Look, you're staying with Yolanda and me. I won't hear otherwise. And I'm not taking 'no' for an answer. It's all arranged, anyway. We got a place in the basement. It's not much, but I use it to watch the games and have a few buddies over. The pullout couch isn't the greatest but . . ."

Kevin was at a loss for words. He looked up at his old friend, interrupting, "It won't matter. I'll be quiet. Claude, thanks, I do need a place." Claude noticed the drab, navy blue, standard prison-release zipper jacket and matching pants and black shoes. It was late October, and winter would soon be setting in. Claude had an older cousin, Khalid, in a state prison and knew what it did to the family. He felt for his old buddy.

Kevin looked up at Claude, nodding as if to reassure him, and told him, "They, the board, wanted me to go to a shelter until I found work and got a place on my own. But, that's not for me."

Before he could continue, Claude, the easygoing, black-eyed, close-cropped–haired man, smiled and said, "Tell your parole officer you can stay downstairs in our basement apartment. He or she can come visit if necessary. Like I said, it's not fancy, and there's no great plush carpeting—"

Kevin took a deep breath and interrupted, "I don't care if it's the damn boiler room, I just need a place to stay. But, your wife and kid . . ."

"No need to worry. She knows. She's okay with it. I have that extra couch bed, and you can stay till you get back on your feet." Kevin was overwhelmed by his friend's generosity. Not one to show emotion lest it cast a perception of weakness, he raised his right hand, giving a high five met by Claude. Determined to ultimately leave Gary, he, nevertheless, had to report for two months to the parole board. They would have the power to approve of his stay at Evans's home. Knowing that Claude had no criminal record, it should have been no problem. But the city of Gary was not the problem. The problem was Kevin Bolton. But, like the once thriving city, he needed a boost.

Kevin Bolton was symptomatic of the problems of the Midwest. He had to change. Change would start by getting out of the city he called home. But where to go? With the GED he obtained at Indiana State Prison, his skills were limited. He could look for work, but where? Gary, like the ex-con, needed help. Yet, he did possess a great skill that often got him in trouble—fighting. And the job market wasn't good. The big industry US Steel was laying off its workers. So, the offer by Claude would show parole he had a viable address.

Young Kevin had looks, youth, and a drive to get on with his life and leave behind the lure of drugs, the occasional loose women, and being a deadbeat. Yes, he would have to leave his hometown, Gary. But, he knew the city. It was still home. The two months he had to report to the parole board afforded him the opportunity to search for work elsewhere. "Perhaps California or even New York. I was brought up here, but it's not the same. Got to get out, recharge my batteries, and get a new chance on life."

Kevin had impressed the parole board. He was a one-time felon. Despite his strength, he never was arrested for assault. The incidents at Clancy's were usually the result of some jerk who had challenged him after sizing him up. Minor snaps and it was over.

It was the '70s, a time in America when throughout towns big and small the crack epidemic was taking hold. Pressured by voters, state legislatures started to pass tough, often repressive measures for even first-time offenders, and Kevin got caught in the mix. Even though he had no cocaine, the marijuana bust satisfied the local prosecutor's desire to show he was tough on crime. With an election the next November, he endorsed the Nixon-era "Tough on Crime" mantra.

Kevin was never in serious trouble before his arrest despite his volatile temper that didn't help him win over friends. The Gary Police Department knew him as a kid who liked to challenge others after a few beers. The climate wasn't good for anyone when it came to drugs. The irony was that Kevin, ever conscious of his looks and physique, seldom smoked a joint. That is, until his encounter with Officer Cominski.

Troubled at the prospect of a long sentence, his court-appointed attorney performed a miracle and got him a limited sentence. Yet, he now had a record. Now he wanted out and was ready for a change.

"Claude, you sure it won't be a problem?"

"Hell no. Yolanda knows you and asked about you. She knows what happened and doesn't like the fact that you had to face the music in that shithole in Michigan City. She's a good, churchgoing woman so don't think twice."

"Don't you think you should ask her first?"

"Stop worrying, man. It will work out. Besides, she knows the deal."

"I'm only on parole for two months, and then I want to get out of Gary. Need to make a fresh start."

"Stop it, man, before I give you a knuckle sandwich."

Laughing aloud, Kevin, much larger and stronger, nodded his head. "Don't hurt me, man." They both hugged briefly, and Claude sensed that his friend was indeed a person in need. At last, he had reached out to the jaded Kevin Bolton.

Claude, seeing that the question of having a viable address was a major issue, reassured him, patting him on his shoulder. Claude said, "Come on." Looking at the faded-green duffel bag, he asked, "Is that all you got?"

"Yeah, my life's in a ripped-up bag, but it's a start."

"Right." Claude smiled and asked, "Your sisters—do you know where to find them?"

"They've moved."

"Yeah, I know about Laura. And your other sister? What's her name?"

"'Crazy Charlene.'" Kevin smiled at the mention of her name. "She's in Fort Wayne. Bad all around," Kevin added, sighing and looking away. "I could live with Charlene if I push it. But, like I said, she's in Fort Wayne. I don't get along too well with our nerdy, beer-drinking cousin and his girlfriend. She lives with them. My cousin Kyle's girl tries to hit on me every time I see her. Don't know if the parole officer will okay me living here. And, hell, I would never go to that place."

"No," Claude quickly interjected. "Not a good choice. It'll all work out."

"I got to get myself together, man." Kevin looked at Claude and could see what was about to unfold. "But you got family."

Kevin's nervousness was apparent in his voice and gave Claude the chance to say, "Stop it! My wife knows you—knows all about your situation."

"Just don't want to re-create a problem."

"Won't be a problem. Let this die." Claude needed to reassure his crestfallen friend. For Kevin, running unexpectedly into Claude and being given the opportunity to have a stable place was a godsend. For someone who had been locked up for two years, Kevin's invitation from Claude was right on. Kevin knew he had to prioritize his life, given the errant and often on-and-off relationships he had with family and friends. Claude's offer couldn't have been sweeter. "I don't care. Right now, I need to show parole and myself I'm not a loser. Hell, up to now, I've been a bum. Starting today, I'll get it together." But, deep inside, Kevin Bolton knew, however promising the offer from Claude, it would be temporary. Claude was a family man with a young son. Kevin realized his stay at Claude's would be a short stint. And he didn't want to be in the way of his wife and kid.

"I've read so much in the joint, I know I have to get out in the world. Maybe even back at the gym taking out my messed-up attitude on the punching bag. Who knows, maybe I'll try boxing or at least coaching the young kids there." One thing was certain—he had to make changes. Those changes would indeed change his life. His mom's wish for him to excel would exceed expectations and surprise everyone who thought the rebellious, bellicose young man was destined for failure. He would prove them wrong.

CHAPTER FIVE

Like Kevin, changes were occurring in Gary. Changes that would have lasting impacts.

City after city along the vast stretch from Buffalo through the other Great Lakes cities of Cleveland, Toledo, and Detroit witnessed a steady dwindling of its population. Jobs, once plentiful and attractive for immigrants from Europe and Black people escaping Jim Crow in the South, had been outsourced, leaving many without a job. Inland industrial centers like Youngstown and Pittsburgh, which once spewed out the nation's supply of steel, were also not spared. What was once a reliable, steady employer had given way to abandoned factories with little hope for revival. The resulting departure of many of its now unemployed citizens added to an overall feeling of abandonment. People who had lived and toiled generation after generation in the sooty and often dangerous mills looked elsewhere. The once-familiar belching smokestacks that lined the landscape with the rising malodorous smoke in Homestead and other Midwest centers gave way to the shutting down of once-proud factories. The mills that once attracted both

European immigrants and poor, Black Southerners to go North were now part of a changing landscape. It wasn't pretty.

Once-thriving and -proud neighborhoods were now places to avoid. Boarded-up houses on blocks of empty lots that once boasted mom-and-pop convenience shops, barbershops, hair salons, liquor stores, banks, churches, and restaurants of all varieties became lost. Gone was the sense of neighborhood and the security of steady employment. The people in Detroit and Dearborn who toiled in the steamy automobile industry now became a symbol of the decline of a once great industry. What would the future hold? Would the Big Three—Ford, Chrysler, and General Motors—go under, too? The nickname "Rust Belt" became symbolic of a big stretch of the United States that once thrived. Day laborers who turned to their union for help found little. Leaders, some of whom ended up in jail or dead, further added to their woes.

Fear of the loss of a job coupled with the uncertainty of finding a viable replacement drove many out of the city. Spreading itself like some unavoidable virus, the same malaise was evident in the Pennsylvania and West Virginia coal mines, with an equal erosion of laborers. The dangerous mine jobs with a once-strong union had also been outsourced as cleaner alternative fuels supplanted the coal industry. A feeling of despair left the inner cities and parts of Appalachia with needs that both the state and federal governments didn't grasp until it was too late. The workers and their families were left to fend for themselves. Like the Dust Bowl of the 1930s that ravaged the soil, forcing many in the Great Plains to go west, the elimination of factory jobs led to another great movement from towns like Gary.

Nowhere was this exodus of industry and people greater than the Lake Michigan city of Gary, Indiana. Kevin's hometown.

Founded in 1905 and named for Judge Elbert Gary, the former swampland and dunes had been transformed into a massive eight thousand acres that eventually became the gigantic US Steel mills along Lake Michigan. With nearby iron ore from the northern reaches of Wisconsin and Minnesota and coal from West Virginia, Ohio, and Pennsylvania, the city of Gary grew, attracting many Eastern and Southern European immigrants and as well as southern Black people in search of jobs. It was the place to go. Schools, hospitals, churches, and homes, along with a variety of ethnic stores, attracted both immigrants and Blacks who were escaping the segregated South to the lakefront city. Blacks started the trek up north as had many poor Europeans from mostly Poland, Lithuania, Italy, Russia, and other parts of the European continent in search of a better life. Gary soon became a city that welcomed the newcomers with the prospect of the American dream—good jobs, housing, and schools, coupled with a promising future for their children.

Gary, like most of its Rust Belt neighbors, witnessed its share of labor problems from greedy owners who resisted change. Gary and other Midwest industrial centers had endured struggles before and came out stronger. The unions started to organize, and the workers demanded reforms. Workers, sweating in the hot steel mills and working long hours, wanted part of the pie that was the illusive American dream. Rising early and working late—up to twelve hours—they demanded increased wages to provide for their families, giving them a sense of pride and a stake in the American dream. But, these demands fell on deaf ears. The movers and shakers wanted nothing to do with these agitators. So, it all came to a head in 1919. The result was the Great Steel Strike. It would occur with devastating results.

The strike ended only when the powerful bosses who controlled the factories got the government and public opinion to go against the workers' modest demands. The great strike was crushed with the arrival of some four thousand federal troops led by popular World War I General Leonard Wood at the request of Indiana Governor James Goodrich. The bosses were determined to stamp out these "communist foreign workers" and their supporters. World War I had ended just a year prior, and the nation was awash in getting rid of dangerous immigrants. Unions were deemed a threat to the owners, and the owners successfully got the public, with the aid of friendly newspapers, to go against the workers' demand for better working conditions.

Unions were to be crushed at the behest of the steel managers, intent on profit over work reforms. The troops sent a message to the average Joe who was struggling: work or be fired. The strike had begun in Pittsburgh. It became part of a massive strike that threatened to stop the nation's production of steel needed for the building of skyscrapers and railroads. It soon spread to Gary.

The strike began with a simple request by miners. The miners in nearby Western Pennsylvania weren't allowed by the owners of the mills to simply meet and discuss working conditions. It was, indeed, a simple request. Discussing grievances was not in the cards. To the owners, it was a threat. The request was ignored by the powerful mine owners. What resulted was a devastating strike that spread throughout the Midwest.

The strikers' demands were nothing extraordinary: a raise in wages and improvement of working conditions. Up before sunrise, the workers in the steel plants, like the miners, endured long hours in the hot, dark, and dangerous plants. They wanted their just due. But the owners refused. It was too much for the bosses, who preferred to keep their workforce under a tight rein, knowing that some powerful, corrupt politicians could be bought off. With a sympathetic press squarely in managements' corner, the strike was doomed from its start. Americans, tired of the recent involvement in World War I, feared the large, uncontrolled immigrant groups coming into the factories in need of work. Unafraid to speak their minds and appealing their grievances to the people, the leadership of the unions were labeled as anarchists and a threat to American values. Their appeal to the American public, which was tired of war and wanting to get back to prewar isolationism, fell on deaf ears.

By 1919, the Red Scare also allowed the bosses in conjunction with state and federal officials to further frighten Americans into thinking that communist Bolsheviks in the newly formed USSR had a hand in the strike. Many of the immigrants working the mines in Pennsylvania and Ohio were from the regions that brought about the Russian Revolution in 1917, scaring capitalist moguls in the railroad, steel, coal, and iron industries. Workers from Russia, Poland, Lithuania, Romania, and the former Austro-Hungarian Empire were suspect.

To further drum up anti-immigrant feelings, Attorney General Mitchell Palmer, with the support of President Wilson, deported suspected immigrant agitators in the labor movement. In New York, Palmer had federal agents round up and deport Emma Goldman, a strong Russian, Jewish, immigrant spokesperson for the worker's rights. She was considered too popular and drew crowds in densely populated New York City. Palmer wanted this agitating anarchist out. Management looked to her as a threat to the largely Jewish and Italian women who worked in New York's sprawling garment industry. They would have none of it. Owners, managers, and bosses would win the day. The lunch-pail laborer didn't have a chance.

The strike in 1919 was a real test for the worker who toiled long and hard and wanted to help his family. Times were changing, and technology was advancing. The workers, afraid of the loss of jobs to mechanization, asked only for a just wage. A loss of job, jolting and chaotic to the breadwinner, was the last thing he wanted. But a strike was the clearest message to send. It was the only tool they could use to effectively send a message to America and the recalcitrant owners. The ensuing strike, spreading across the Midwest to Gary, would have disastrous effects. And Gary became the focus.

As a result of the magnitude of the strike, martial law was declared in Gary, and General Wood, fresh from his victories in the trenches in the Argonne Forest during the World War I, was able to quell whatever chance the poor workers demanded. Nothing was gained. The union—Amalgamated Association of Iron, Steel, and Tin Workers (AA)—was weak in numbers. It had declined from twenty-four thousand in 1892 at the start of the devastating Homestead Strike to a mere eight thousand members nationwide by 1919.

The Homestead Strike had epitomized the weakness of the unions. In that strike, which resulted in several workers' deaths, Andrew Carnegie's private force of strikebreakers crushed the strike. No one was surprised that once the striking steel workers were out, the press fed upon Americans' suspected fears of anarchistic immigrants and the collusion between owners and the often-corrupt politicians. What resulted were the deaths of workers, the hiring of strikebreakers, and the futility of trying to unionize.

Homestead became a rallying cry for the workers, but to no avail. With the national papers on the side of management and the state government in Harrisburg, as well, the poor strikers had lost. Much would be the same in Gary in 1919. The strike, with little public support, was doomed. Workers were given a choice—work at the behest of the bosses or be fired. Left with little power and no friends in government, the jaded steel workers in Gary—like their counterparts in Youngstown, Akron, Pittsburgh, and Detroit—went back to their daily, laborious jobs. It would be a long time before their demands were met.

More than a decade later, in the New Deal of the 1930s, the federal government finally fought for the hard-pressed workers to get recognition from management to be a full partner in labor negotiations. That would have to wait until FDR signed the National Labor Relations Act, known as the Wagner Act, in 1935, which finally gave workers the right to unionize and bargain collectively.

As bad as the 1919 strike was, the real decline started decades later in the 1960s, with steel mills closing as a result of global competition. Unlike their forebearers in 1919, the workers of the 1960s feared changes that would prove lasting. The world was getting smaller as companies looked to overseas markets to make profits. Unable to keep up with lower-paying jobs in overseas companies that exported steel, the hardy workers at the plant who had given so much of their time, sweat, and loyalty to the mills were now left in the cold. What resulted was the gradual closing of the factories that had given so much to the country.

The US Steel plant and the nearby BP Refinery in Whiting started to lay off workers beginning in the 1960s. Overseas competition was to blame. The sense of continuity that US factories had provided for each generation had suddenly ended. No longer would the young, high school graduate or dropout look forward to a good-paying union job that his father and grandfather had enjoyed. From a peak of thirty thousand workers in 1960, the erosion of jobs in Gary saw a mere six thousand factory employees in 1990 and 5,100 by 2015. With the decline came problems. Families and relationships eroded in some cases. Depression, a loss of self-esteem, and a general feeling of malaise added to the misery. People began to refer to a "misery index" when discussing the plight of the Rust Belt worker. Gary became known as an "urban desert." And with it came other issues.

Added to the problems were the increases in crime, housing vacancy as former residents left the city, and political corruption. A shrinking tax base resulted in diminished city services, which affected the quality of life from the schools, to garbage pickup, to replacement of city streetlights. Despite the fact that the city enjoyed the distinction of being the birthplace of the internationally famous pop group The Jackson 5, Gary—like another, larger Rust Belt city, Detroit—became symptomatic of the hemorrhaging of the outscoring of jobs abroad.

Like a cancer, the erosion spread. Homes were abandoned as the White flight to suburbs or to other areas ensued. Blocks of once tree-lined neighborhoods became vacant lots. Formerly safe neighborhoods became crime ridden, with desperate people looking for jobs. They were places to avoid. Dilapidated and crumbling buildings added to a surreal, eerie atmosphere. Gary, once proud and booming, had joined the ranks of America's cities that had fallen victim to the progress of international competition. With cries for help falling on deaf ears in Washington, little was done to assist the cities and the people. The damaged and abandoned landscape did attract some producers who saw an opportunity to make a buck and exploit the situation.

With its stark and foreboding landscape, the History Channel later used the city of Gary as a prop for one of the episodes in its uniquely riveting series of *Life After People*. Eerie and surreal, the popular episode displayed the extreme effects of urban blight without people. With the abandoned homes and businesses, the scene did indeed seem like a futuristic Armageddon and wake-up call to rest of America. It was a call to face its problems of urban neglect, crime, and despair.

Gary, the city shown in the History Channel series, was the same lively city that had been highlighted years before in the Broadway musical *The Music Man*, with its catchy tune "Gary, Indiana" in the 1950s. Gary had given America so much, and now, when it needed help, it was neglected. The city had contributed much to the country, not only in its output of steel but in notable personalities ranging from astronaut Frank Borman to twice-middleweight boxing champ Tony Zale and the preeminent group of all: The Jackson 5. A proud city was soon to join the litany of other urban centers hit by factory closings and increased crime with a futile cry for help from the federal government.

So it was that by 1974, a city that had done so much for the growth of the country in its Gilded Age of industry had fallen on hard times. It was a city that wanted to succeed. Like a child in need of love, Gary suddenly found itself the center of what was wrong with urban America. With its residents fleeing. The city, the population started to fall after its 1970 peak of 175,000. It was a mini-Detroit that was not given the federal assistance it so needed. The White House, with Richard Nixon in the Oval Office, was too preoccupied with grappling with the worst scandal in US history—Watergate. His major troubles would force his resignation in August, 1974, as a result of the investigations by both the House and Senate of the subsequent cover-up that sealed his fate. Impeachment and conviction appeared real, and Nixon, absorbed in his own messy scandal, had little time to attend to other issues, such as those facing Gary.

In 1950, with 133,000 inhabitants, the city along the lake was second in size only to Indianapolis, the Hoosier capital to the south. All seemed to be well, but it wasn't. Ten years later, Gary would start to become a victim of the outpouring of jobs as companies started to downsize. Changes would soon occur.

Gary did hold the nation's attention when it elected Richard Hatcher, one of the nation's first Black mayors of a medium-size city, in 1968. Just a year prior, Cleveland elected Carl Stokes as mayor, making history as the first duly elected Black mayor of a large city. Hatcher's wasn't an easy election. He had challenged the incumbent Mayor Martin Katz, beating him by just 2,300 voters in a contested primary.

The Lake County Democratic Party, suspicious of having a Black man in power, confronted Hatcher. They demanded that they have the power to select the police chief, city attorney, and other administrative offices to shore up their support. Hatcher knew the ploy. If he agreed, he would be only a symbolic leader with little power. He refused, causing a rift when the county leadership endorsed his Republican opponent, Joseph Radigan.

Confident and competent, Hatcher epitomized the new power in the city—a successful Black man whose rise to power attracted the national press. Time and again, the voters of Gary went to the polls and reelected Hatcher. He became one of the longest-serving mayors and was in power 1968–1988. A spokesperson for civil rights, he gained national attention in the 1980s when he served as vice chair of the Democratic National Committee.

Hatcher's election showed the strength of the Black vote, which, by 1970, was a majority of the population in Gary. Hatcher's Gary resulted in a resurgence of pride in the embattled city. He targeted cleaning up corruption in the police department and appointed officials based on merit. His election gave hope to the citizens who had witnessed abandonment by top federal government officials. Events, however, would soon catch up with the new mayor and the city along the lake. The city was about to go through a difficult period that tested its very fiber. Gary had been through tough times before. Most felt it would overcome as its troubled history witnessed. It was not to be. With the neglect from the Nixon administration, cities like Gary declined further. Emigration from the city ensued, crime rose, and once-thriving neighborhoods were now abandoned. Like other cities throughout the region, Gary suffered from loss of jobs, factories, and aid from both state and federal governments.

It's little wonder that the cities of the Rust Belt, from Youngstown to Detroit—which were mostly Democratic, largely union based, and overwhelmingly minority populations—were not a priority. Put on the back burner, the abandoned cities cried out for assistance but were largely left on their own. Cutbacks in federal funding, an increase in crime, and an administration mired in scandal resulted in cities having to fend for themselves. This was the city that Kevin Bolton knew and grew up in—a once proud city that had seen hard times and was now trying to readjust.

Its people still had to cope with the daily challenges of life, from providing for their families to preparing for any eventuality. Not everyone could or wanted to leave. Families who still had jobs and kids in school chose to stay and hope for a new dawn for Gary. Free time was a luxury. Burdened down with heavy mortgages, high rent, and a constant fear of losing their jobs as factories closed, no wonder their gatherings usually centered around sports. Yet, even the most jaded, hardworking lunch-pail crowd still rooted for their teams, be it football, basketball, or baseball.

Getting together with friends at the local bar to have a beer or two and a pizza was the closest thing to a night out. But of all the sports, the most challenging and the one that aroused the most emotion was boxing.

Events have a way of changing one's outlook. Kevin Bolton thought he was a loser. His chance encounter with his friend would forever change his fortune. And it began with a world spectacle in far-off Zaire that would change Kevin's luck. It was a boxing event. Not an everyday boxing event but the World Heavyweight Championship. It was the event that would change Kevin Bolton's fortunes.

CHAPTER SIX

The Rumble in the Jungle, as boxing promoters called it, dominated the sports world in October, 1974, the same year and month that Kevin Bolton was released from Indiana State Prison. While much of Gary and the rest of the country—and, indeed, the world—was eager to see whether the former loud and raucous Muhammad Ali could withstand the formidable reigning champ, George Foreman, Kevin Bolton had more pressing issues on his mind. But, the much-hyped boxing match couldn't be avoided. "Everyone was talking about it—betting on it—and I got wrapped up into it, too." Kevin related to and was inspired by Ali. "He's coming back after being banned, and he's not afraid to speak his mind." Kevin liked that. Like Ali, Kevin was ready for the change, too.

Ali had a very cozy relationship with the city of Gary. He visited often. One night, he noticed a very curvaceous and beautiful woman at a cocktail lounge. He soon found out her name—Sonji Roi. At the time of their introduction, he was still known as Cassius Clay. It was July 1964, and, although Cassius was to convert to Islam and change his name to Muhammad Ali, Sonji was told he was Cassius Clay.

Roi had a tough life. At the time she met Clay, she was going through hard times. A part-time singer and model, her job as a cocktail waitress helped sustain her. She had lost her parents at a young age and worked in neighborhood nightclubs as a cocktail waitress in Gary to pay bills. It wasn't easy. Taking abuse from intoxicated and often vulgar patrons, she struggled on. She had no choice. Life had been a struggle for her, and she was caught in a changing Gary that offered few incentives for the young female.

She was a vulnerable young woman, trying hard to keep herself solvent. Working at the club offered her a paycheck. Concerned for her welfare, her financial stability always an issue, she had little chance to find a different source of income. The very attractive woman caught the eye of the young, up-and-coming boxer. Fate would intervene that night that would change her life. Working one night, she met someone who liked what he saw and was intent on meeting her. He wouldn't take "no" for an answer. She was introduced to Cassius Clay, the handsome, cocky, and proud young pugilist who would soon embrace Islam and change his name to Muhammad Ali. At the time of their meeting, he was still Cassius Clay and allegedly couldn't take his eyes off the beautiful, curvaceous cocktail waitress.

It is rumored that Ali was so smitten by her beauty that he proposed marriage the night they met! That happened in July. It worked. Within a month, they were married. For Sonji Roi, it seemed like a dream come true. Clay was a meal ticket for her to release herself from the Gary nightclub. Married to an up-and-coming boxer on his way to glory, it was the perfect match, or so it seemed. He was an escape from the long hours with drunken, foul-breath sorts who tried to hit on her. They demeaned her with sexist taunts and treated her like some rag doll.

Meeting Clay was an escape from her drab and monotonous life, a way out of a dreary, dead-end job. She wanted out of this unappreciated life. She didn't like her job and jumped at the chance to leave. Who wouldn't, with such a prospect? Meeting Ali, for Sonji, became a transformative moment. Ending her nightmare of working long hours and coming home dead tired, she jumped at the chance to make a significant life change. Events that sounded promising soon turned sour. It would not be pretty. It soon got her in trouble.

Sonji became Ali's first wife. Ali's marriage to the local girl is little talked about even today. She was a tragic figure who ended up badly. Indeed, most people can't recall his brief first marriage. Sonji's past life in the fast lane didn't sit well with her new husband, who took his newly adopted faith seriously.

Within a few months, Clay became Muhammad Ali. His embrace of his new faith proved to be the undoing of a marriage that was destined for failure from the start. So few people knew that the dominant fighter of the age met and married a local Gary girl. For Sonji, what seemed like a promising and comfortable life took a very different turn. Tough and uncompromising, Sonji Roi Ali proved to be nobody's fool.

The marriage, it turned out, was too much for Roi once Ali became a Muslim. As she explained to a friend, she couldn't accept Ali's demands. "I wasn't going to take on all the Muslims. If I had, I probably would wind up dead." Used to the nightclub circuit, she became a lonely and reclusive figure who wanted out.

As with many episodes in her life, the thought of marrying a renowned personality, however appealing at first, soon turned sour. They were in a no-win situation. Their personalities conflicted. She was a nightclub hostess and outgoing and gregarious. She liked being around people and getting noticed as the center of attention. And the religious issue came to the forefront. Like many converts, Ali's life centered around his newfound faith. He became absorbed and devoted to his faith. Soon, it caused problems. Their marriage was, indeed, doomed from the start.

A childless couple, their disagreements escalated. Roi and Ali filed for divorce in early 1966. Ali was angry at Roi's behavior, which he considered going against the dictates of Islam. Ali said, "She didn't do what she was supposed to do. She wore lipstick, went to bars, and dressed in clothes that were revealing and didn't look right." To Ali, the habits of his wife were unacceptable. Sonji wasn't about to make the drastic changes he demanded. She had her own set of values, like it or not. She was not going to give in. They were two tough personalities that clashed with no chance of reconciliation.

With little communication and more disagreements, the marriage ended. She and Ali had obtained a marriage license in the nearby suburb of Crown Point in 1964. But, because of her refusal to adhere to strict Islamic code, whatever romance that initially attracted Ali to Sonji soon eroded. It quickly became a loveless marriage. Unhappy and feeling alone, Sonji realized she couldn't match her famous husband's demands. She wanted out.

A Gary native, she decided to stay in her hometown. Sadly, at age fifty-nine in 2005, she preceded her former husband in death when she was found unconscious on the bathroom floor of her Gary flat. She died later that afternoon. Her death was due to natural causes. A relative believes she died of a heart attack.

The marriage that had lasted only a year and a half was a sad chapter in an otherwise stellar career for the world champ. The marriage officially ended in 1966. Ali, a native of Louisville, Kentucky, had often visited Gary. Despite his failed marriage with Sonji, he liked coming back to the city, and he continued to visit Gary.

One visit was especially noteworthy. Back as a now-famous world champ, he made a special trip to Gary in 1975. He came to Gary to campaign for the reelection of incumbent Mayor Richard Hatcher, one of the first successful Black candidates for mayor of a medium-sized city. He stopped at Lew Wallace High School and was received with a standing ovation despite a few protesting dissident White students who were still angry about his conscientious objector status and refusal to be drafted when it came to the Vietnam War. Gary had indeed remembered Ali, and just a year prior, most residents were cheering for his comeback into the ring.

It was in 1974 that the global pugilistic event would take place in the early morning dawn along the Congo River in far-off Zaire. It became a must-see, historic event in the annals of boxing history. And it sent the boxing world on its toes. It catapulted Ali's fame beyond expectations. Fans and the curious tuned in to the much-hyped event. The people of Gary were no exception. One of those listening and watching was a newly freed inmate—Kevin Bolton.

Like most Gary residents, the new parolee was rooting for the Louisville boxer. "If he comes back and is champ, maybe I can do it, too." The boxing event took on a more significant meaning for Kevin. His thoughts went back a few years to when he was destined to go places in the boxing world. Right then, like millions of others, he was just a fan bent on witnessing a historic bout.

In the former Belgian Congo country of Zaire, today known as the Democratic Republic of the Congo, reporters flocked to the capital city of Kinshasa to Stade du 20 Mai, the stadium built by the strongman dictator of the country, Mobutu Sese Seko. With Don King as promoter, the fight, dubbed the "Rumble in the Jungle," soon took off, becoming one of the most talked-about bouts of the twentieth century.

Don King, no stranger to controversy, made it an event that is still talked about today. The Cleveland-born promoter and former convicted felon (pardoned in 1983) known for his trademark hairdo would soon get the publicity to further line his pockets. King was looking for a venue that would provide the maximum exposure. With Ali and Foreman as the main event, he knew the bombastic young Ali would attract an international audience.

There was another reason for Don King to get into the mix. King, who was strapped for money at the time, searched around, getting the attention of the feared dictator Mobutu to guarantee each fighter a purse of $5 million. King was ready, and the public, eager to see an Ali comeback, jumped on board. Mobutu would have a world audience to showcase his country.

In addition, flocks of worldwide reporters and spectators would guarantee a big payoff. Hotels, restaurants, airport limos, and television crews would help inflate both King's and Mobutu's pockets. The two renowned pugilists—Ali and Foreman—would face one another for the heavyweight world champion belt. It would be held outside in a hot stadium along the Congo River in the stadium that would be filled to capacity with sixty thousand fans.

That was what Mobutu and King wanted—a standing-room audience to augment the hype. Scheduled for 4:30 a.m., the unusual hour would be prime time in the United States, drawing a crowd of betting fans from Vegas to Atlantic City and across the globe. Money was to be made or lost on the questions—did Ali have what it takes? Could he stop the steamroller Foreman?

The television crew had a herculean task at hand. Added to the mix was the fact that the TV satellites were transmitting the event to some 450 US theaters for maximum exposure. It was more money to be made! Reporters and writers, such as Norman Mailer and George Plimpton, were also on hand to witness and record the historic bout in the hot stadium.

To hype up the crowd, like a Broadway impresario, Don King negotiated a contract with the leading salsa bands of the United States—the Fania All-Stars, a band with a mix of Cuban-Afro roots that by 1974 had a clearly distinctive Puerto Rican influence. Such notable Latino musicians as Eddie Palmieri, Willie Colón, and the salsa-loving Jewish musician Larry Harlow had a great following. They attracted fans, onlookers, and the curious over the years at the famed Corso Nightclub on East 86th Street in New York City's Yorkville neighborhood. With the additional appearance of the renowned and flamboyant James Brown, the stage was set for a unique mix of music and boxing. The crowd, whipped up in a frenzy of music and dance by Brown, was ready. The iconic sporting event would forever be recorded in the annals of boxing history. The fact that the two African American fighters were on the soil of their ancestors made the event ever more significant.

Ali, stripped of his heavyweight belt for refusing to report to the draft board, wanted it back. He was hungry. He wanted to strut his stuff, and King provided the logistics. It had been a long, seven-year stretch after the New York State Athletic Commission had stripped Ali of his belt for refusing to report to the Selective Service Board. The strongman dictator Mobutu, who had seized power in 1965, wanted to sponsor the event, showcasing his country and displaying his power in the impoverished country.

Foreman, the undisputed champ, had a solid record of thirty-four unbeaten bouts. He was the favorite. Foreman had beaten two great heavyweights prior to this bout, Joe Frazier and Ken Norton.

He was seven years younger than Ali and was eager to retain his belt. His red robe was emblazoned with the words *World Champion*. He was confident that the older Ali could and would go down in defeat. With Ali's forced absence from the boxing world, many were ready to write off the loud, iconoclastic Ali.

Determined to stop Ali, Foreman came to the ring prepared to win and win big. Ali's three-year absence from the ring was seen as a major setback for a comeback. The absence was the result of the boxing commission's decision. But, it had recently been overturned in the nation's highest court. In the landmark 1971 decision, *Clay v. United States,* the Supreme Court, in a unanimous decision of 8–0 (one justice recused himself), agreed that Ali's First Amendment right as a conscientious objector to the Vietnam War was violated. The decision allowed him to return to boxing. When asked why he refused induction, in typical Ali fashion, he boasted to the press, "No Viet Cong has ever called me a n—." He had no desire to go to some far-off, Asian jungle and fight for a cause that he felt was unjust. Many Americans agreed with this assessment. Like the nation, loyalties were largely divided between Ali and Foreman based largely in part on Ali's belief not to serve. So the fight took on a life of its own.

His cause became a rallying cry for a very unpopular war that, by 1971, saw demonstration after demonstration against what the protesters called an "unjust and poor man's war." The fact that the draft had sent some five hundred thousand men to the jungles of Southeast Asia, resulting in the deaths of over fifty thousand Americans and thousands more Vietnamese, made the American public war weary. College students, in the meantime, could avoid being drafted. Given a status of 2A, a professional deferment, upon graduation, many started teaching and retained the 2A status to keep from going off to the jungles of Vietnam. The weary nation took note. In the halls of Congress, reflective of the nation, many liberal lawmakers sided with Ali. With congressional hearings and more elected officials wanting out, the war had become the most unpopular in American history.

The war, the nation's most controversial involvement, divided America. Many were tired of the protracted and seemingly endless conflict. They wanted out. So, it was with great relief that the court decision allowed the flamboyant and profane boxer to return to the ring that had given him international acclaim in 1964. At age thirty-two, most professional analysts felt that Ali would have a tough go against Foreman who, at age twenty-five, was at his peak. Ali had been on the outs for a long period when stripped of his boxing belt. With an unbroken record, George Foreman went into the fight the clear favorite. Yet, Ali drew a crowd wherever he went or spoke. No one could match the rhetoric and vitriolic shots at his opponents. He was theater, and he loved the spotlight.

As a dethroned champ out for a long stretch, the gambling public was taking a long-shot chance in hoping for an Ali victory. Many hoped for just an upset. A victory would be one for the history books, as Ali would be only the second former champ to regain the title. The war-weary nation wanted a diversion, and the boxing world provided the venue for escape. On that historic day, in the sweltering African heat, Ali would once again turn the boxing world on its head.

History would be made there and also in far-off Gary, Indiana. On that same day, Aida Manfredy, a young, Puerto Rican resident of Gary, had other things on her mind than a popular boxing event. Her attention was on her newborn, not on a fight. She gave birth to a son who one day would become a lightweight and junior lightweight champion. Her son was named Angel. Little did anyone know that her infant born the same day of the fight in the jungles of Africa would one day make his mark on the boxing world.

For the moment, most of the attention of many was in the remote jungle of Zaire. Ali vs. Foreman. That was the deal. Everyone was talking about it, making wagers legally and illegally, and tuning in on their televisions in their living rooms, local Gary bars, or in the theaters and casinos throughout America and the rest of the world.

Foreman, unlike the flashy Ali, remained secluded away from the throngs of eager fans. Ever the showman, Ali basked in the affection of the adoring throngs. He was their hero. Mobutu had angered Foreman. The strong-arm dictator insisted that Foreman, who had sustained a cut to the eye, remain in Zaire rather than seek treatment elsewhere. As a result, the fight had to be rescheduled six weeks later, allowing for the eye to heal. His eye, in need of medical attention, took a good deal longer to heal. The searing heat didn't help. The cut was deep as a result of sparring hard. Mobutu's insistence that Foreman remain in Zaire lest he never return added to the drama. Mobutu, in control, made his decision—Foreman was to stay. As the day of the match drew nearer, the world was ready. Ali had boasted to reporters, "Mobutu's people are going to put Foreman in a pot and eat him!"

Mobutu, not amused at this reference to cannibalism, went public, adding, "We are not cannibals." Yet, Ali had the affection of the masses.

George Foreman was the expected favorite coming into the ring. He was the champ, was younger, and had a record of 40–0. Undefeated and in great shape, Foreman was ready for the kill. It was not the same for the challenger, Muhammad Ali. While Foreman was undefeated, Ali was not.

Ali had, after the court decision, been defeated by Frazier in 1971. Coming into the hot, African arena in that early hour, Ali, despite his braggadocio, was the underdog. And he resonated with many people. As a "comeback kid," many hoped for an upset.

All the major players in Vegas felt that Ali, as an underdog and having been away from the action, would fall to the canvas. Just what round would he fall? Could he go the distance? Most boxing experts and followers, however enamored of Ali, predicted his defeat. How wrong they were. No one was more confident than the loquacious Muhammad Ali.

Aware of the United States' trauma from the recent Watergate Scandal, he remarked to the American press, "If you think the world was surprised when Nixon resigned, wait till I kick Foreman's behind." The underdog never lost self-confidence. Ali had devised his own path to victory, and it would be classic Ali surprising even the most jaded pundits. The fight is still talked about and discussed today.

Aware of Foreman's strong and steady pushes, Ali backed up on the ropes to give his fans and the boxing world the now famous rope-a-dope strategy. Simply put, he leaned back on the ropes and allowed Foreman to pummel him until he tired. Take the punches and tire your opponent—it was a brilliant strategy. And Foreman did tire.

By the end of the fifth round, a clearly weary and exhausted Foreman, sweating profusely in the equatorial heat, was confronted by his challenger. "Come on, George, show me something! Is that all you got?" Taunting Foreman became Ali's mantra in the ring. Foreman, clearly uncomfortable, tired, and still healing from his eye mishap, met his match. The strategy by Ali was about to come full circle. Ali continued to evade Foreman on the ropes.

That is, until the eighth round. That's when Ali came full circle.

Sapping the strength of the formidable Foreman, Ali allowed himself to take and evade punches until the eighth round, when it was clear that Foreman was slowing up. At the eighth round, Ali finally got away from the ropes and sent Foreman to the canvas. George Foreman was down. He didn't get up. The crowd roared.

Across the globe, many who had never given up on Ali made good on their bets. No doubt the next day the discussion across the globe centered on the comeback kid. Everyone likes the fact that an underdog can, with hard and resolute determination, overcome an overwhelming obstacle. Ali became a metaphor for the little man who struggles and triumphs—a come-from-behind champion who never lost confidence. Like it or not, his victory made others feel proud of his triumph. It was indeed a boxing event unlike any other. His victory is still analyzed by the boxing world.

It was an upset victory—one of the greatest comebacks from a challenger. Foreman, more exhausted than hurt, became the victim of Ali's rope-a-dope. The knockout victory in the eighth round no doubt meant that the gambling public who invested in Ali would reap the benefits of putting their faith in the comeback kid.

Arguments among friends must have ensued from thousands of miles away in Vegas casinos and nightclubs and in smaller towns like Gary, where people challenged their neighbors as to who would triumph. For the Ali followers, it became a seminal moment in the annals of boxing history. Many would lose money, while others would defy the Vegas odds-makers and add to their bankroll. Arguments over who had the fastest jabs or who would outlast the other would become the topic in post-fight analysis from pros and amateurs alike.

The fact remains that this bout's outcome made boxing history, catapulting Ali to claim his rightful place in the International

Boxing Hall of Fame. It was a fight that lived up to the hype and, as mentioned, is still analyzed by pro and amateurs alike. In towns throughout the United States, those who had watched in the theaters, bars, casinos, or at home witnessed history and a legacy that still endures. Yes, bets were won and lost, friends argued, but the fight would go into the history books as one of the greatest comebacks in boxing history. It also had an effect on young Kevin Bolton.

CHAPTER SEVEN

Boxing has it own magic. As one faded boxing poster on a New York City Times Square boxing gym boasted, "You don't play boxing!" It was a clear message to anyone seriously dedicating himself to the sport—asking, "Are you ready for it?" In what other sport can a person attain a world crown with one historic encounter? A sport where long hours of training all come down to a one-time professional match? Often, in a do-or-die scenario where one can soar to fame or be floored to the canvas with life-threatening, bloody injuries, ending it all. A sport that has seen its share of tragedies in the ring. And for the victor, a ticket to international fame and fortune. Alluring, suspenseful, and unpredictable, it remains the most controversial sport.

Of the one-on-one sporting events, boxing is paramount. Brutal, often bloody, and sometimes difficult to watch, it's the sport that has been most highlighted on stage and screen. Love it or hate it, boxing remains an in-your-face event for all to see. Bringing drama and theater coupled with the challenges of the often-brutal rise to the top of the competitors, a champion boxer is in a class by himself. Recognized for his skills in the ring, one can enjoy instant fame or rejection, depending on the outcome. Indeed, no one "plays" boxing.

Boxing is unique, drawing crowds of admirers and equal amounts of distractors. Witness the fictional portrayal of Sylvester Stallone's popular *Rocky* movies and the gory, graphic, and gruesome time that the fictional Rocky Balboa had to endure. The audience, rooting for the underdog Rocky, is mesmerized by the indefatigable Rocky. His triumph in the end is representative of struggles of life against the most challenging odds. On the screen, others such as Will Smith's great performance in *Ali* as well as the *tour de force* performance by Robert De Niro in the Academy Award–winning role in *Raging Bull* of legendary Jake LaMotta are among the more recent and notable entries.

Dating back to ancient Greece and Rome, boxing, despite its gore and brutality, remains a sport that still attracts millions. Watching the boxers dance in the ring, the occasional antics and upset victories provides the public with suspense, awe, and drama. Americans have always had a love for the sport. Bets are won and lost. Families, too, are often divided as to which boxer is better. Friendships are sometimes strained, and arguments as to who had the best jabs, who is better on their feet, and who is the best fighter can lead to divisions among both family and associates.

In the end, it's the drama in the ring that matters. Boxers go through the rigors of incessant training, dieting, and changing strategies whenever a hungry challenger wants to win the coveted world champion belt. Boxers witnessed famous bouts that are now forever enshrined in the International Boxing Hall of Fame in Canastota in upstate New York.

Like the gladiators in ancient Rome fighting for freedom, boxing became a big business that makes a heavyweight an overnight celebrity. The art of boxing endures. Much of America tunes in to a world championship fight.

Today, Las Vegas, the showcase of the nation, has replaced New York City's Madison Square Garden and Atlantic City as the Mecca for the boxing world. Throughout America, young men and women in gyms aspire to be the next world champion. That love of the sport was also felt in Gary.

Gary, like much of America, was no exception. It was attracted to the sport as evidenced in the boxing gyms scattered in the city. The down-and-out kid who made it, sweating and sparring in the ring, spending long hours devoted to his craft, kept hope alive.

These kids, not only in Gary but from all parts of the country, wanted to make it to the ring. Hungry and intent on getting a piece of the American pie, they spent hours in the gym in hopes that one day a promoter would recognize their talents after a win in an amateur bout. It would be their meal ticket to fame—getting a lucrative contract and a chance to shine under the lights, with-cameras and reporters present.

Getting fame and acquiring respect and hopefully that coveted contract from a promoter made the sport all the more competitive and alluring. Those long hours spent in the dusty and often malodorous gyms became a second home for many youngsters. Many just wanted to escape from the poverty and dangerous streets, rife with allure of drugs and quick money that landed so many in jail or the morgue.

Kevin Bolton—poor, with little education, and lacking skills—had to gravitate toward some purpose in life. The gym became his life till that stupid decision he made outside the gym. He had it all—youth, looks, boxing skills acquired through the hard work of his trainer, and a killer instinct. He let it all go away and regretted it. Yet, the dream in the jail and the desire to make something of himself motivated him to excel. He wanted to prove to others—his former trainer, his friends, and most of all, himself—that he could make it. He was ready for whatever fate had in store for him. Time and again, eating away at him was the desire to prove that he had what it takes.

Getting bruised while hoping for a chance at the Golden Gloves in Vegas or New York was the dream of kids not only in Gary but throughout the United States. Those dusty, damp gyms were often in need of repair. The chipped paint often laden with lead and asbestos meant nothing to a hungry young man in search of the big prize. To the anxious young fighter, it was a palace. Boxing—magic, indeed. The dream remained—the goal for a world title kept the hungry youngsters off the streets and focused on the dream.

In 1974, Gary, like the rest of America, looked to a distant African country, where a worldwide match attracted millions. It would take place in Zaire. Dubbed the Rumble in the Jungle, it matched two of the best boxers in the world—Muhammad Ali and George Foreman.

If a poll was taken in Gary, the results would show that most people rooted for Ali. Ali had connections to the Gary area that would continue beyond the iconic fight in Africa in 1974 and his failed first marriage. Indeed, in 1975, he came to Gary to campaign for the reelection of Mayor Richard Hatcher. He stopped at Lew Wallace High School and was received with a standing ovation despite a few dissident White protesting students. But it was in 1974 that the great pugilistic event would take place at dawn along the Congo River in far-off Zaire.

In the former Belgian Congo country of Zaire, today known as the Democratic Republic of the Congo, reporters flocked to the city of Kinshasa to Stade du 20 Mai, the stadium built by the strongman dictator of the country, Mobutu Sese Seko. With Don King as promoter, the fight dubbed Rumble in the Jungle, soon took off, becoming one of the most talked-about bouts of the twentieth century. King, at the time strapped for money, had gotten dictator Mobutu to guarantee to both fighters a purse of $5 million each.

The two renowned pugilists—Ali and Foreman—would face one another for the heavyweight world champion belt. It would be held outside at the stadium in the African heat along the Congo River in the stadium that would be filled to capacity with 60,000 fans. Scheduled for 4:30 a.m., the unusual hour would be prime time in the United States, drawing a crowd of betting fans from Vegas to Atlantic City and across the globe. Added to the mix was the fact that the TV satellite was transmitting the event to some 450 US theaters for maximum exposure. Reporters and writers, such as Norman Mailer and George Plimpton, were also on hand to witness and record the historic bout.

Kevin watched the events in Africa from far away. Like the other patrons at the smoky corner bar, the twenty-one-year-old, who was a fired former packer for UPS and now a convicted felon with a record, was drawn to the grainy television set above the bar. "At least here I can be with my buddies and enjoy the fight."

Kevin gave serious thought to a boxing career. "It's what I do best—hurt people. I'm not proud of it. Why not make money for it?" His thoughts went back to when he was a youngster. His mom Norma Baranski Bolton told him of his birth during one of the worst snowstorms in Gary's history. His mother told him of his entry into the world on that fateful night in January 1953.

She remarked, "You're a born fighter. Your entry into this world is a story in itself." Smiling at him, she said, "You made sure that your entry into this crazy world was noticed." Kevin knew his dad, James Bolton, was not in the mix. An absent father the night he was born, he played little role in Kevin's life.

His mother told him what happened the night he came into the world. "The snow was so thick. You couldn't see in front of you—a real whiteout. Everything was closed. There was no way I could get an ambulance. We didn't have 911 then; you just called the fire department for an ambulance. The firemen told me that they couldn't help, as most of their men were stuck and couldn't get to work. They suggested I call for a cab or the police."

When Norma called the Gary Police Department, she was on hold and eventually hung up. "They were busy trying to get drivers out of snowbanks, and I guess there were a lot of accidents. I remember that the streets were already in need of plowing. The snow came down so fast that it was a whiteout within a few hours. I thought you were going to be born in the house, but I needed to be in a hospital. I didn't want to have to call a few neighbors. I called the doctor, and he advised going to the hospital. The closest was Methodist Hospital."

Kevin knew he was born during a bad snowstorm. He didn't appreciate the efforts until he was told the details as a teenager. Methodist Hospital—it's where Kevin Bolton came into the world. He never asked much about his entry. Why should he? All he knew was the fact that his mother's Uncle Harry almost didn't make it to the hospital with his mom in labor.

His father was another story. It was typical of James Bolton to check in on his wife after leaving his job at the steel plant. In fact, his dad was too busy to care. He was getting soused at the local gin mill, called Shorty's. Norma Bolton called the bar, only to be told they were closing early due to the storm and that John Bolton left at least two hours prior with his coworker Al Kurich. Frank Gordon, the owner of the bar, had Al's number and told Norma she should trying contacting him there.

As the storm progressed, his errant dad had indeed crashed at Al's nearby house, never knowing that his wife was about to give birth to his only son. Call after call to Al Kurich's home was met with a busy signal. "I knew he was tanked and staying at his friend's house, Al. They took the phone off the hook and nodded off, never knowing that I was in labor."

What she had to do was to act fast. "It was up to my Uncle Harry to think fast and get to the hospital. Thankfully, Methodist Hospital was open and ready despite the storm. As for Kevin's father, he was not in any condition to help, even if he were around. This was a pattern with him—getting drunk on the weekends and neglecting his responsibilities as a father and husband." In just a few months, Kevin's dad would desert the nest and stay out of his young son's life. James Bolton didn't take responsibility well. When Kevin was twelve, he finally left his poor wife with three kids and never looked back, heading out west. They never heard from him again.

Kevin never talked about his dad. "I never knew except that he would come home and then go to the bar. I don't want to know anything about him; he put Mom through too much." Indeed, Bolton's abuse was known, and friends of Norma always wondered why she endured so much pain from him. When he abruptly left, most people were relieved, hoping that poor Norma Bolton could get on with her life. Whenever anyone wanted or needed information about his dad—from school officials to applications to play high school football—he left the block blank when asked his dad's name. "He wasn't in my life. Never asked how I was doing in school. Never was there for my sisters and me and, most of all, mom. She had to do everything—cooking, cleaning, shopping, taking us to the doctor. No, he was a drunk and someone I hope to Christ I never become. Don't remember him even at Christmas being nice, and don't want to. If he's dead, I really don't care. Don't want to know, period."

Kevin Bolton came into the world without the joy of having his dad present. His mom was fortunate, despite the storm and neglect of her husband, to deliver a healthy, eight-pound, seven-ounce boy at 4:34 a.m. The staff at Methodist were amazed that she and her Uncle Harry could make it to their hospital. Before the storm ended, an incredible thirty-two inches of snow descended on the Midwest, and Gary got the brunt of it.

Harry Sporta ended up staying at the hospital as the streets were impassable. A tough, Polish immigrant, he wouldn't let the worst snowstorm in decades stop him. One of the nurses, Miriam Gibson, got him a cot on the main floor where he got a few hours of sleep, rising at 8 a.m. Norma and her uncle were grateful to the staff on duty and the three doctors who made it in. Kevin was delivered by Dr. James Watts, a young resident assisted by two nurses, Cora McNamara and Carol Costello.

Priding itself as a modern, all-service hospital, Methodist Hospital was and still remains an important institution for the people of Gary. The hospital, a facility with 634 beds, has served the people of Gary and surrounding communities in Lake and Porter Counties over many decades. Cited by the American Heart Association, it proudly displayed the Gold Plus Performance Achievement Award in its showcase. In addition, the American Diabetes Association singled out Methodist as a facility of excellent care. Additionally, its Breast Center for Women also won a choice award for excellence for four consecutive years. The maternity ward, the largest in Northwest Indiana, was second to none. For his mom, this choice hospital was a welcome site. Here is where she knew she would receive the best attention.

He smiled when he recalled that his mom told him that even the ambulance dispatcher told her to try to get to the hospital on her own. They had set out with an ambulance crew but got stuck in drifting snow. Stuck! She had called her brother Harry. Luckily, he had good winter tires. Despite the whiteout conditions, Harry, a former bus driver in nearby East Chicago, knew the streets and was not overstressed. He was, with some difficultly, able to navigate his way to Methodist Hospital. Shoveling out his driveway with the ever-increasing accumulation of snow with his young son, Mike, he finally had enough clearance to get the car on the street. And he set out for his niece's house.

Harry was able to navigate his way to the hospital, ten blocks away. It was a short distance, but with the whiteout conditions, it took thirty minutes, having nearly gotten stuck in the blowing and drifting snow. It was a feat that only an astute, measured, and calm person in charge could maneuver. Harry rose to the occasion.

"Mom said that the staff was stunned to see her arrive—some doctors couldn't make it, and others were stuck for the night. If it weren't for my Uncle Harry, who knows what would have occurred." The snow, coming down at one more than one and half inch an hour, paralyzed the city. By the time Harry was able to get his niece to the hospital, twenty-six inches had already accumulated, isolating the city for the next two days.

In the end, an incredible thirty-two inches of snow would cripple much of Midwest for nearly a week. "Good old Uncle Harry saved Mom from a home delivery. She said the three doctors on duty kept telling her, 'You are strong to make it here, and your kid will have a story to tell.'"

East Chicago, Indiana, where his Uncle Harry Sporta worked, was close to Gary but much smaller than it. Kevin vividly recalled good times at his great-uncle's house. "It was just a block away. Uncle Harry and Aunt Sophie lived on second floor, above the small grocery store. I think it's now a bodega of some sort. Aunt Sophie was my great-aunt; she was the twin sister of my grandmother Barnanski. What I can recall is that it was close to my school. Since my uncle worked at Inland Steel and worked part-time as a bus driver, he had a good job, and I liked going there. He would tell us stories of how difficult it was growing up."

Born in 1930, he was a child of the Depression, leaving school in seventh grade to provide for his single mother and her five other kids. "It was crazy, but thanks to Inland Steel, I was able to get a job. Part of my job was to drive parts to a loading zone. Soon, I was making some decent wages and eventually got hired part-time for East Chicago as a bus driver. That's what I loved to do as a kid—drive a bus and feel good."

Kevin remembered his great-uncle as a gregarious family man with an infectious smile. "Whenever I was with him, it was great. He wasn't a lush like my dad and took me and my sisters to the beach and into Chicago to the zoo or a Cubs game. He always felt proud of his jobs as a bus driver and at Inland."

Inland Steel, founded by financier Philip Block in 1893, grew from 250 workers to 2,600 by 1910 and had a staggering workforce of over 25,000 at its peak in 1969. It became the largest steel mill in the country, surpassing the behemoth Homestead plant near Pittsburgh. The work force, much of it immigrants, Black people, and poor White people from the South, toiled long hours in the early twentieth century in an era before strong workers' right and union reforms. That was the way it was for Kevin Bolton's family and for much of Gary and East Chicago.

Much was expected of the workers. Jobs were expendable, and if a worker was lax or late, without strong unions, firings were common. It would take actions such as the 1919 strike and ensuing worker-friendly federal laws such as the New Deal's Wagner Act of 1935 to cement the rights of the working class.

Looking at the black-and-white television screen above the bar, Kevin smiled when he thought of his great-uncle. "He told me I could be moody and to channel my anger into being a trainer—a workout fitness trainer before it was fashionable. Funny how these memories come back, looking at the fight. Maybe, just maybe, I'll stop at the PAL boxing gym and see if they could hire me. The least I could do is clean or even spar, if they let me."

He turned to Claude as Ali floored Foreman and the raucous crowd responded with a deafening cheer. He blurted out, "I'm definitely going to the gym."

As the roar of the excited crowd at the bar subsided, a frowning Claude let out an audible sigh, adding, "Why the hell not? What have you got to lose? I used to have a cousin that worked out at Carr's Gym, but he got tired of the routine and wouldn't stick with the program. A shame—he could have gotten somewhere. With you, it might be a different story. I mean, what have you got to lose?"

Kevin, psyched at the prospect of the possibilities, decided right then and there to take up the challenge. He knew Gary had given much to the sport of boxing. He recalled reading about the boxers who put Gary on the map—Tony Zale, "The Man of Steel" and former World Middleweight Champion. Also, Charles Adkins, an Olympic Gold Medalist in the 1952 Helsinki games who went on to become World Light Welterweight.

Kevin wanted to join this elite group among the pantheon of famous Gary boxers. Deep down inside, he knew he had a different and more humane outlook on life as a result of the time he did at Indiana State. He had finally dealt with the death of his mom. He knew it was time to fess up and move on. Having messed up before, Kevin was intent on showing the world that he was ready. More important, he knew he had the drive inside. He had to get back in the ring. He was willing to start at the bottom at the gym and work his way up by sparring, competing in amateur bouts, and finally going pro.

Kevin looked at his Mom's Book daily and realized that the entry for that day was *get back*. Getting back would become the mantra that would catapult him to success. He knew he had what it would take. The fight with Ali and Foreman solidified it. It was a call to action.

Watching the fight in far-off Zaire indeed would change the once-angry and disagreeable man. Now, it was different. He wished his great-uncle Harry was still alive. Unlike his drunken and abusive father, who made life miserable for his mom, sisters, and himself, he knew his uncle would approve. "He was there at my birth, and my mom was always grateful for the struggle he endured to get her to the hospital during that storm." He had to get back. Most definitely!

Events change our lives. Life is about making changes and moving on. From his time served in jail, Kevin, at long last, had come to terms with himself. Taking responsibility and being loyal to a cause or a movement or a friend was important. He was grateful to have Claude Evans as a friend. Kevin wouldn't disappoint his friend, who had confidence in his quest to get back into the ring. More importantly, Kevin, his head now focused, would dedicate his energy and his skills in the ring, remembering the dream from his mom that he experienced in prison. "I'm not going to let her down; I'm ready to show the world I can do it." He had youth, strength, and, yes, a killer instinct that made others pause before getting into a fight with him. Those days were over.

With the fight on TV over, he glanced at his friend, Claude. He gave a wry smile to him that suggested that he might just surprise himself. That night, thinking of his late great-uncle, his mom, and Coach Montalvo, he knew what to do next. Watching the comeback of Ali became a seminal moment for Kevin Bolton. It was a life changer. He definitely knew what he wanted—"I'm going in the ring. Yes, I can do it, too."

Kevin, realizing quick opportunities may pass him by, decided he had to plunge headfirst in the boxing world. What the future held remained to be seen. Right now, inspired and motivated by the Ali win, the young Gary boxer decided that he had to try. Kevin looked at his friend Claude, a broad smile on his face.

Claude knew what that meant.

Claude Evans raised his left arm in a fist-like gesture. Claude didn't need to say anything to Kevin—he didn't need to. That night, as the world watched the return of Ali, Kevin got ready for his own return. And what a return was in store! Soon, Claude, the city of Gary, and the rest of the boxing world were in for another big surprise.

CHAPTER EIGHT

THE DECISION TO ENTER THE BOXING WORLD. Could it be possible? A formerly angry, crass, ex-con with no source of income just suddenly appears and walks into a gym, deciding he wants a shot at boxing. What would others think? Was he too rusty, having been in prison for nearly two years? What if Montalvo decided he was a loser? Kevin prayed that Joe Montalvo was still around and would accept him back. "If he tells me to get lost, I'll understand. I was such a disappointment. Should have listened to him. Stupid me! Lord, please let me get a shot at this—Montalvo's tough but fair. Please, let me get in that friggin' gym."

It had been two and half years since Kevin Bolton had stepped into the ring—a lifetime in boxing. Yet, he thought again of Ali's forced absence from the sport due to his refusal on religious grounds to go to Vietnam. But he was Ali, the Champ. He had a following. It was easy for Ali. He had the connections to make a comeback. "Could I do the same?" Motivated by the Ali win, the young man had his mind made up. "Ali was away because they took away his belt. I was stupid and did time 'cause I was too thick-skulled to listen to reason. It was my stupid, hard-headed attitude that did me in. I'm focused now. I'm ready now. But I'm going to use Ali as my model. If he can make a comeback, who knows. Maybe I can do the same."

Watching the Rumble in the Jungle sealed the deal—it was a turning point for the former promising boxer. Watching the event unfold in the noisy bar a few blocks from Claude's home, Kevin, turning to his friend, asked, "Do you think I got what it takes? I mean, I've been working my butt off in the jail yard for two years just to stay in shape."

Claude knew where this conversation was going. Looking at the screen and then tuning to Kevin, he put down his mug of Budweiser and said, "I know you can. Do you need me to encourage you? Search your soul, man, and if you think this is what you're cut out for, go for it."

This reaction brought a smile to Kevin's face. He needed the reassurance in a neutral setting—a bar away from Yolanda and the baby Khalid—to get this issue off his chest.

Events shape our lives, from global natural disasters such as earthquakes and hurricanes to man-made events such as the comeback Ali fight. Our lives, too, are shaped by events that seem to overpower us. Good or bad, we fess up to them and deal with the situation. Changes are made, and we move on. Sometimes it takes a major event—the bout in Zaire—to seal the deal. That hot, steamy night in remote Zaire became that kind of moment for Kevin Bolton. He knew it all along. Like a punch to his gut, he reacted to it. Kevin just needed an extra push. Claude's presence and his faith in his friend were an added boost.

With the upset Ali victory, Kevin had a new purpose in life—he would get back in the ring. His self-confidence never wavered.

He didn't care what others may say. He had made a difference in other people's lives at Indiana State Prison. He had what a leader needed—a calm and steady hand under pressure and poise and confidence in himself. He got to know himself during his incarceration. Now, it was his turn. He knew his true calling. "Hell, I might as well make money. It's the only legit way I can. My body is my meal ticket. Don't want to be on the street selling and dealing; I already got screwed by buying a nickel bag. Even if I screw up, at least I know I gave it my best shot."

True to his word, he got up the next day after his first night in Claude and Yolanda's basement and went upstairs. Kevin was determined to make changes. He looked at his Mom's Book and entered his word and aim of the day: *confidence*. It was time.

It was 8:15 a.m., and Claude was getting ready for his day shift. Claude sat at his kitchen table and sipped a cup of coffee. He was waiting for his friend to come up.

Kevin had the luxury of a stand-up shower and toilet that Claude installed downstairs. Off to the side was a small linen closet with a washer and dryer beneath. This allowed Yolanda to wash and dry clothes any time in all kinds of weather. This was Claude's birthday gift to her once he realized that she needed time with Khalid. It saved her from going to the laundromat several blocks away in a neighborhood that had seen better days. It also gave Yolanda some independence.

Claude, proud of the work done downstairs in the once-musty and drafty basement, remarked to Kevin, "When Yolanda gets tired of me watching basketball, football, baseball, and boxing upstairs, I retreat to my little fiefdom downstairs. Then, she can watch all those shows on television without giving me that look." This remark brought a nervous smile to Kevin.

Yolanda, not missing a beat, remarked, "Yeah, it's good for both of us. I can watch what I want without Mr. Claude here taking over. Now, at least, he'll have company and quit bothering me." The little banter eased whatever tension Kevin had, and the exchange brought a laugh from both Claude and Yolanda.

The basement of Claude Evans's home was a lifesaver for Kevin. Over the next few months, it would serve him well. With a small, black-and-white, eighteen-inch television and the amenities for showering, a toilet, plus a small linen closet and adjacent old bureau, he had everything he needed right there. On the walls, several posters of past sport heroes like Joe Louis, Jesse Owens, Floyd Paterson, and Rocky Marciano were on display: the Wall of Fame. "Gee, Claude even put up these posters of famous boxers. Is he trying to tell me something? Whatever—this place is a palace compared to the cell at Indiana State." Claude had collected several posters of the famous boxers and posted them on the wall adjacent to the pullout sofa bed that Kevin would sleep on.

Kevin was grateful to have Claude as a friend. "I'll repay him back somehow when I get on my feet again. He was there when I needed him the most—the only one who was there." He valued his friendship with Claude. He was indeed grateful but knew that he would have to bounce soon, as it wasn't his place. "In times of need, you know who your real friends are."

The relaxing shower eased the pent-up tension he experienced at his new quarters. He reached into his duffel bag and placed a razor, aftershave, and lotion on the small shelf below the mirror in the bathroom. "Yes, this is a palace compared to what I've been through."

After showering and shaving, Kevin heard Claude shout up, "I hear you. You're up. You coming up for some chow?"

Kevin, opening the door leading up the flight of stairs, shouted back, "I'll be right up. Thanks."

Yolanda, who knew him as a former buddy on the football team with her husband, smiled at her new tenant, walked over to the door leading to the basement, and asked, "So, what do you want for your breakfast?"

Kevin, smiling and wishing them a good morning, said in an almost inaudible reply, "Whatever you're preparing. If it's no trouble."

Yolanda, with her one-year-old in a high chair, had already finished feeding young Khalid. She answered, "There's coffee and cereal. I can make you a few eggs with toast."

Kevin, not wanting to be intrusive, quickly interjected, "No eggs, thanks. Don't got to have all that. Coffee and cereal are good."

This remark brought a smile to Yolanda. Looking at her husband, she replied, "I really think he's lucky to have you at this point in his life."

Glancing at the sports section of the local paper, Claude smiled and added, "I just want him back on his feet. We all need help."

"Don't I know that," Yolanda added as she poured a cup of coffee for their soon-to-appear guest.

Claude was finishing his coffee and put down his newspaper that highlighted the fight they saw on TV with Ali and Forman.

"Claude?" Yolanda gave him that look that suggested that she was about to make a point. "Put down that paper. I know you're reading about the fight."

"Right. I am," Claude said, putting down the paper. He dutifully responded, "Yeah, you're right. I can read about the fight later."

"Everybody is talking about it. It's all over the news. It's Ali's comeback. Maybe, just maybe, Kevin will be inspired and realize he can go back to boxing." Yolanda looked at her husband and added,

"Kevin will be coming up any minute. You might want to ask him if he had any plans for his future. He can stay here until he gets back on his feet—you know I don't mind."

Claude realized that his wife's concern was genuine and that his friend needed to make choices. His thoughts were interrupted by the footsteps coming up from the basement level.

Kevin climbed the narrow cement stairs and entered into the kitchen. The aroma of fresh-brewed coffee and toast permeated the kitchen. "It's been a while since I didn't have to look over my shoulder and stay in a chow line. This is better—most definitely better." Yolanda and Claude looked in his direction. Yolanda had just taken the bib off her baby and was set to pour a cup of coffee for Kevin.

Claude spoke up first when he saw his friend inviting him to sit at the table. "Good morning. Was there enough hot water for the shower? Did you sleep okay?"

"Yes and yes! It's a whole lot better than what I've slept on for the past two years." This comment brought about a laugh from Claude. Claude gave Kevin a friendly pat on his shoulder. Kevin sat to the right of him with the empty chair ready for Yolanda, who had just finished getting Kevin's breakfast. The small talk worked, bringing a smile to a somewhat nervous Kevin.

"Thanks, the shower was great, and the bed is comfortable. I had a good night's sleep, thanks." Kevin, looking at the baby Khalid, liked what he saw and thought, *A stable family with no drugs and tension*. Looking at the one-year-old relaxed him. He smiled at the baby. He hadn't seen a baby or young child since his release. As on instinct, one-year-old Khalid let out a gurgling laugh at this attention. Winking at Khalid caused him to laugh aloud again.

"I think the little one likes the attention you're giving him," Yolanda said.

Kevin wanted to show his gratitude as he sat down to the hot cup of coffee Yolanda placed in front of him. He didn't know where to start, but knew he had to say something. She had placed sugar and a creamer containing 2 percent milk nearby for Kevin.

"Yes, that mattress is very comfortable," Kevin remarked, noticing the smile on Yolanda's face. By this time, Yolanda had also placed a box of Cheerios and assorted fruits consisting of blueberries and prunes and some nuts—almonds and pecans—near him.

Without missing a beat, she said, "I know you're hungry. You sure the cereal is enough? It's not a problem to prepare some eggs."

Kevin wasn't used to the attention. He even glanced again at one-year-old Khalid banging a plastic toy that looked like a bear. The baby, getting attention as a result of his theatrics, let out some more gurgling sounds, causing a smile on Kevin's face. For the first time in a long time, he felt relaxed and at peace.

"The cereal is great." Kevin added some almonds and pecans and milk, and proceeded to add two sugars to the cup of coffee placed in front of him by Yolanda. He raised his spoon in the direction of Khalid, causing him to let out another gurgling laugh. This brought a smile to Kevin and Claude.

"I see you have a new friend," Claude said, looking in the direction of his infant son.

"Yeah, it's great. He's a very fun-loving kid." Kevin, not knowing how to react, proceeded to sip his coffee after placing two more sugar cubes and some of the 2 percent milk in his cup. Kevin, the recipient of such attention and hospitality, knew he had to speak up. "I just want you to know how much this means to me." With his head looking at the bowl of Cheerios, he struggled to continue.

Picking up on this, Claude, who had put down his paper after his wife's reprimand, added, "Don't be silly, man. You can stay as long as you want."

At this comment, Kevin looked in the direction of Yolanda, who smiled back at him. "My husband's right. You can stay. I know you've been through a lot, and we're glad to help."

Kevin wanted to set things straight. This was not his family. Yolanda and Claude were a hardworking couple raising a child. They had given him what no one else had—hope and a welcome mat.

"Thanks, but I will get on my feet and hope I can get a job and—"

"That comes later," Claude said. "Right now, you're our guest."

"Okay, but I'm serious about stopping at the gym and seeing if they could hire me." Kevin's voice rose.

"My cousin Charles knows the manager. They have a new guy there since you've been gone, so he doesn't know you. I think Montalvo is still there." This remark that his old coach was still at the gym gave Kevin some hope. Claude wanted to help Kevin get started at the boxing gym, adding, "Maybe I can introduce you to the new owner and manager? They already know you're out. Maybe you going there will be a nice surprise for Montalvo."

After Claude mentioned his former trainer again, Kevin frowned, knowing that Montalvo might not be so happy to see him. Claude continued, "Kev," Claude stopped as if to emphasize what he was about to say to have an impact, "are you sure you want to go there? Will the parole board like it? Think about it."

Knowing that the adjacent parking lot is where he was arrested might send the wrong message to the parole board. But, Kevin thought, *What have I got to lose? It's the only place I really know I can do something*. Taking a sip of coffee, Kevin had made up his mind. "It can't do any harm trying, that's for sure. Right, Claude?"

A sympathetic nod from Yolanda gave cause for Kevin, who up to this point sounded unsure and in need of support. Yolanda's comment brought a smile to his face. Kevin added, "Yeah, if it's okay by you, Claude, I'll walk over and see my old stomping grounds. I appreciate the offer of your cousin, but . . ."

"Can't do any harm as far as I can see. But they'll probably ask if you've been training when in the joint. Like I said, Montalvo is still there, and you probably should see him. Just be ready for any eventuality. But, I think you got nothing to lose, Kev."

Kevin appreciated the frank discussion, knowing that his entry might set off controversy. Claude was right. To do nothing and not show up and meander around the old neighborhood with no means of support would only land him in territory he swore to avoid. Kevin's mind was made up—he would show up at the gym and see what evolved. "I know. I'll tell them the truth. If they don't like an ex-con coming in, I'll just cut my losses and look somewhere else." Kevin knew that despite his boxing record, others might not gravitate toward him, especially parents of young people enrolled in some of the boxing venues. The stigma of having a record was apparent; he knew he would probably have to explain himself to others in the gym.

"Okay, but don't be down. Maybe they'll even hire you to do some cleaning to compensate for training. But you're a boxer, and they know it. Can't put a man down for trying, right?"

"Right." Kevin put down the coffee cup, looked up with an audible sigh, and added, "I'll give it a shot. By the way, this coffee is great." Smiling at Yolanda, he breathed in the aroma of the fresh, vanilla roast cup of morning Joe and looking at Claude. He added, "I'll tell the truth. I'm sure there's a few dudes that are there who I know from the street or the joint, anyway."

"After you left, a new owner took over, replacing Owens—Frank Ramirez. He worked with some of the boxers in the area and was given the chance to manage the gym."

"Do you know this guy, Ramirez?" Kevin's curiosity was aroused. He wanted to get back to Southside but knew that managers could be a problem. "Is he a good guy? I hope that he'll let me in," Kevin said with a smile.

Claude found out that Frank Ramirez was as solid a guy as they come. He came up the hard way, working his way from a kid in a Chicago gym to a trainer and now manager. Claude also knew that Frank was looking for new blood in the gym. He wanted to make Southside a place that would be proud for the city of Gary by getting a state or world competitor.

A realist, Ramirez knew the hard fact that the city of Gary, tough and suspicious of outsiders coming into a local boxing venue, would pose a possible problem. But he wanted the chance to make Southside proud and produce a pro in the ring. Methodical and introspective, Ramirez ran Southside after the mercurial Owens left when he felt that the gym wasn't supportive and the city started on a downslide. Ramirez knew he had to gain the respect from the staff, the patrons from boxers, and the curious people who would come in to watch aspiring pugilists strut their stuff with a few sparring rounds.

Frank Ramirez was a middle-aged Puerto Rican whose family had settled in Chicago in the 1950s. He had a good track record, having managed a small, suburban Chicago boxing gym in Evanston. When Kevin was released, Ramirez had been managing Southside for the previous year and a half. Already, he had been noticed.

Serious, tough, and a stickler for rules, he dismissed a few staff and would-be boxers who didn't adhere to his code—be on time, clean up, no cussing, and have respect for fellow boxers. The changes at Southside he implemented raised the tone of the gym. His moral compass was the result of a devout Catholic grandmother who raised him after his mom died when he was nine.

He wanted to make a change. He knew cosmetics and appearances made a difference. As a result, a fresh coat of paint, plus new lockers, bags, and gloves earned him the respect of the people who used the gym. Gary was undergoing serious urban problems, and Ramirez knew that the gym was a safe haven for the many dysfunctional youth of the city. It was a real challenge but one he embraced. The visionary Ramirez gave Southside a much-needed shot of adrenaline when it most needed it after Owens's sordid tenure. And it showed.

Ramirez helped sponsor youth programs, gave young boxers a chance at Golden Gloves, and had one boxer go pro—Tyrone Dawson from Toledo, another tough town in the Midwest not far from Detroit. Dawson was the perfect catch. A known boxer with a great record, he fit the bill for Southside's resurgence.

Dawson fought at Madison Square Garden after winning four pro bouts in the Midwest and two fights overseas—one in Berlin that resulted in a victory and another in London, which he lost by decision. His opponent in the Garden fight was Jamal Chambers, a former street gangster who turned his life around and became the pride of his hometown, Camden, New Jersey.

Chambers was the favorite, with a pride and swagger some considered arrogant. Facing a hostile, large audience that came in two busses to New York from Camden to root for the Champ, Chambers, the young fighter from Camden, had a hard time focusing. He had split up with his girlfriend, and it stayed with him when he entered the ring against Dawson. Yet, Chambers triumphed despite his personal dealings. The fight went the entire fifteen rounds, which was still the rule at that time.

Losing by a close and controversial decision, Dawson again lost in a rematch with Chambers in Atlantic City five months later. This time, there were a lot of nearby Camden fans cheering on Chambers. The hostile atmosphere didn't help Dawson, who was roundly booed entering the ring. On that very humid August night, Dawson lost badly. His career really ended with the loss. It was a technical knockout in the sixth round. "There were no promoters after that. I had lost the last three fights; I wasn't getting younger, and I started to slow up."

Dawson, ever the realist, had won enough fights to live comfortably, having saved frugally with his wife, Keisha, who was in charge of finances. He knew he couldn't compete anymore. With no sponsors and a bad cut to his eye, Dawson's doctor recommended that he give up the sport lest he end up blind in one eye. Dawson decided to retire at age thirty-four. He'd had a stellar career and was a stand-up fighter who saw the future and knew he had to give up his beloved sport.

Dawson, now retried from the ring, was offered a job as the lead trainer for up-and-coming fighters in the Gary area. The new owner was none other than Frank Ramirez.

Ramirez was given a chance to run the leading boxing gym in Gary. Getting on in years, he knew he wouldn't find another Tyrone Dawson. Ramirez reached out to Dawson. He wanted his former fighter there.

Hesitant at first, knowing how tough the city was, Dawson decided to take the job, knowing it would be a notch down for him. But it also kept him in the game, impacting and training up-and-coming young pugilists. Now, with some money, the former contender looked upon Southside as a real challenge. Dawson felt he could train a future champ and, with the right contacts, go all the way to the top. He took the job just a few months after his loss to Chambers and arrived in Gary ready to train. Both Frank Ramirez and Joe Montalvo were ecstatic that the former world champ would attract some new prospects.

Coming to the gym in Gary, Dawson was greeted by the local boxing gym for having gone the distance. A local newspaper, the *Gary Crusader*, ran a feature article on the Toledo-born boxer. Dawson, liking the reception from the people of Gary, also spoke to young people at school assemblies, churches, and civic organizations. He demonstrated a soft side to the much-maligned sport, and it showed. Liked the bruised city, he reached out to the people and got respect. He may have lost the biggest fights, but he found his calling in assisting the needy youth of the city of Gary.

Ramirez, a local from nearby Chicago, knew the city and showed Dawson the good and bad parts. Tough but straightforward in his approach, the balding forty-three-year-old Ramirez also had been in the trenches and felt for his young protégés. And especially for Dawson. "He made us proud. He was a great fighter, who got matched with the undefeated Chambers. But he rose to the occasion." Loyal to the core, he knew the agony of defeat lay heavy on Dawson. He decided he had to act. Dawson had to fight one more fight in his contract, losing once again in Chicago with a purse of $600,000. He indeed knew it was time for him to hang up his gloves.

Retiring at age thirty-four, Dawson became the pride of Southside Gym. Young upstarts looked up to him, asking him for advice. He started mentoring up-and-coming boxers. Ramirez assigned him to train the best boxers. "He knows the ropes! Literally and figuratively," Frank remarked to the reporter, Marie Brown, who had interviewed Dawson for the *Crusader* article.

"This joint may not be the Taj Mahal, but it molds young kids to stay out of trouble and stay the course." This comment brought a smile to Brown, who was impressed at the intensity of the young men at Southside that morning. A few looked her way, smiling and waving when she asked about their future. Sweating and sparring with their partners, the boxing in the three rings at Southside was theater of the highest order. Young teens were in one ring. The second ring consisted of amateur boxers and anyone who wanted a few training sessions to tone up. The third ring belonged to Chambers and the two boxers he was currently training for the upcoming Golden Gloves.

The dedication, intensity, and hard punches impressed Brown. A recent graduate of Northwestern in nearby Chicago, she was a journalism major fresh out of college. She landed the job at the *Crusader* after the editor, Percy Mullins, read an article she had written about job loss in Gary. Impressed, Mullins hired her on the spot just a few months earlier as a result of the article that addressed the problems of urban blight in the city of Gary. When asked to get an interview from Dawson, the product of a single mother brought up in a Toledo project, she jumped at the chance. The resulting article gave the gym, Dawson, and the city something to think about. She summarized her interview with a good commentary, adding, "Tyrone Dawson makes Gary proud. The Toledo native is now a die-hard Gary fan. A hard life, yes, but Dawson rose to the top, making it as a professional boxer. His current dedication to his former trainer and gym owner, Frank Ramirez, is evident the minute you step into the unpretentious surrounding. With little fanfare, the aura of a vibrant and exciting venue like Southside is a plus for the city of Gary. Keeping the young pugilists off the dangerous streets by showing them rules that have to be adhered to, a rigorous schedule, and a daily sermon from Ramirez make it a great refuge from the scary streets."

The article was published just a few days later, once the editor made a few changes. Getting the recognition that he hoped would result in a few donations, Frank Ramirez was a happy man. He had his best ex-boxer now training a few serious contenders. Yet, he really wanted someone to walk through the door and say, "I'm interested in getting started and going even further than Dawson." "Someone who will go the distance, that's my dream. Getting another Dawson to the Garden."

But, Ramirez, Chambers, Marie Brown, and, in fact, the entire Southside Gym had no idea that their gym would indeed again make the news. For soon, events would catapult a young ex-con with no address or family to speak of, a destitute and down-on-his-luck, vulnerable ex-boxer.

That day, November 2, 1974, just a few days after Ali's victory in far-off Africa, Kevin Bolton entered Southside. It was his reentry back to life. Like his hero Ali, this was his reentry into the world of boxing he loved so much. He had excelled once. Could he do it again? He had no idea what to expect. Would Montalvo want him back? Would Ramirez, the owner and manager of boxing programs, let him back?

He took a deep breath and decided he had nothing to lose. And he was confident, young, in great shape, and still able to try his luck in the ring. He had done it before; he might be a bit rusty, but he was no quitter. He walked up to the door, ready to enter his former gym. That would be the start of a new phase in his life.

Like Ali, he was destined for bigger things. At the moment, however, he was just a down-on-his-luck ex-con looking for a purpose in life. Looking at his Mom's Book, he again read the entry for that day, *confidence*. Picking up his gait, he sighed, taking a deep breath, and entered Southside. That day, November 2, would change his life.

CHAPTER NINE

Kevin Bolton stood outside Southside Gym and took a deep breath. He had walked the seven short blocks from Claude's home, turning down his offer to drive him to the site. The ten-minute walk gave him the chance to clear his head. Invigorated by the crisp, cool, November morning, he took another deep breath as he stopped, looking at the one-story gym. Standing there, he was ready for whatever eventuality would occur. He fidgeted. He looked around to see if anyone was looking at him.

Reaching into his duffel bag, he pulled out his Mom's Book and read the entry for the day—*responsibility*. He felt the need to bond with his dead mother. His entry today was to the point. He had written it down that morning but needed to give it another look. Kevin didn't know if he should even be here.

He quickly brushed that thought aside as he again saw his daily word in his Mom's Book. "Yeah, like it or not, I got to face the music. Responsibility." He picked up his pace as he drew near the place where so much had occurred. "Could it all happen again?" Mixed emotions swirled around. "I just need to go there. If I can, I'll work there. If I can train, I'll do it. If they see that I still have the mojo to get back in the ring, that would be my goal." He knew that he had to fess up for his past. Yes, he would be responsible.

But, he also wanted to restart and redirect his life.

Staring at the outside of his former refuge with a smile on his face, he again paused. Going inside meant that he would meet up with people he had disappointed. "Yeah, I'll be responsible. If they don't want me here, maybe another gym." He again looked at his word of the day in his Mom's Book. Ready, indeed, for any eventuality, it was time to face the music.

To Kevin, the gym before him was a palace. To a passerby, the faded gray exterior with the sign *Southside Boxing Gym* would not even draw a second look. It was another aging building in a run-down part of Gary. Or was it? To Kevin Bolton, the once-vulnerable and now more confident person, it was an awakening. Not just a gym, but a chance at renewal, a place that could change his life.

Life is about making changes. Kevin Bolton had shown the officials at the prison that he could make a difference in other people's lives. Now he was prepared to redirect his life on his home turf and show his former trainer and others he was ready. Southside was not just a gym; it became a metaphor for this change. Like the city he grew up in, Kevin needed to prove he could change and redirect his life despite all barriers that he had endured. Gary, the symptomatic symbol of urban blight, had nowhere to go but up. And like the once-proud Steel City trying to rebound, Kevin, too, was ready to make changes in his life.

The gym. It had indeed been a refuge for him just two years earlier—a home away from home. It held so much hope for a better future. It also served as an extended family that he craved after his mom's death. It was a special place. It held such promise for him.

Being angry at his former self wouldn't help. Yes, he was his own worst enemy. He knew he had let down so many who had invested in him: his trainer, the city of Gary that rooted for him, and his loyal friends like Claude Evans. This is where it all came apart. And this is where he wanted it to fix it and come together once again.

Kevin's once hopeful future had been dashed in a nanosecond with his arrest. He hesitated once again. He looked at the small, diagonal parking spot where he had encountered Officer Steve Cominski. Shaking his head, he reached into his green duffel bag and took out his Mom's Book. That day's entry, unlike yesterday's *confidence*, was replaced by the entry of *responsibility*. "Sounds stupid, I know, having this notebook, but it motivates me. If Montalvo lets me in, I know I can make something of myself. It's different now—I'm so ready. Lord knows, I am." He had mixed feelings about coming back. He was apprehensive, unsure, and didn't want to be rejected. His hope hinged on Montalvo and the owner, Ramirez. "Maybe, just maybe, he'll look beyond the moment and see that I've changed." Kevin walked up to the door.

Entering Southside Gym, one would be immediately greeted by the malodorous stench common to gyms and locker areas. Despite the efforts of the full-time maintenance men, Frank Cummings and veteran Lloyd Hopkins, the smell of dirty socks seemed to permeate the gym. The single-level gym was an unpretentious space devoted solely to the art of boxing. If visitors came in looking to lift weights and use the treadmill, they were told politely to leave. With a few weights, loose dumbbells, and an assorted array of boxing gloves, jump ropes, and headgear, one knew Southside was exclusively a boxing venue.

One side wall was dedicated to past and present world boxing champions. This was side that had the weights. The opposite wall was devoted to the Rules of the House, which included: No spitting on the floor, no littering, no cussing, clean up after you finish, hang up gloves and other equipment, and keep the locker area clear.

Southside had seen its share of wannabe boxers come and go. Most of the young men who came in couldn't endure the regimen that was demanded of them. As Ramirez, a devout Evangelical Christian, quoted the Bible, "Many are called, but few are chosen." He expected much for the serious prospects as deadlines for amateur bouts and Golden Gloves crept up. A strict daily diet, exercise focusing on jumping rope and outside runs of two miles, plus the sparring for three rounds were part of the regimen. For the not-too-serious, curious young men venturing into the gym, they soon faced a reality check. Focusing on a goal that took too long in the making for many, they quickly left after witnessing those who were more serious, sweating, and enduring insults and shouts from trainers.

Ramirez, never one to push someone who he felt didn't feel boxing in his mind and heart, politely advised them to quit. Indeed, not seeing instant results resulted in most leaving. Giving up leisure time, staying home, avoiding friends and girlfriends, and getting up early to be at the gym by 7 a.m. was too much for most. But, for the few dedicated, committed young men who were hungry to get in the ring, it was a ticket to success and possible fame and fortune. The dream stayed alive, and it showed with the regulars who hoped to go pro. Determined to make something of themselves and hoping to get a chance to leave a life of poverty and hard times, the dream kept even the most jaded coming back. The hard, scrappy life of many in Gary kept the gym abuzz with activity.

With three rings, Southside was a constant whirlwind of activity. As with any boxing gym, the rings took center stage. The players had the spotlight on them, and those lucky to hone their craft got recognized by the occasional scouts who stopped by to write up a contract for the up-and-coming boxing events. Southside was no exception. It provided a nonstop sparring atmosphere with boxers from teenagers to adults.

Trainers, such as the now-retired fighter and respected champ Tyrone Dawson and Joe Montalvo, were at the ready, shouting instructions. They demanded much. Like a stage director, they wanted the best performance. Shouting orders, they expected their protégés to work it to the max. Going over strategies, they had their protégés perform until the right jab was executed, the right leg moves coordinated, and the ducking and dancing in the ring became an art.

Boxing routines were executed over and over again. They held center stage, and their every move, micromanaged by their trainers, molded them in a fierce warrior who, like the actors they were, would soon be recognized. A slice of the American dream hinged on their thirst for getting to the top. It was a climb that filtered out most. Their hunger to excel, on display for all to witness, motivated them. They ate, drank, and slept boxing, thinking little of anything else. It was a total commitment, as evidenced by the action in the ring. By the time they made it to the arena to the cheers of the crowd, the road taken had been long and arduous. They were there for all to see, holding center stage with devoted fans intent on seeing theater in the ring. And, like the stars on Broadway, one bad performance could end their career. But, the desire to make it made it all the more enticing. As one jaded ex-boxer who was no longer recognized by the crowd that once made him king said, "You don't play boxing."

The young boxers, eager to make their mark, sweat dripping down their face, kept up the dance in the ring until the bell rang.

With the added weight of protective headgear plus the mouthpiece and boxing gloves, their desire to perform was not diminished by occasional breakdowns in the air conditioning. They were there for the long haul. Bruised and hit too often despite the protective gear, the regimen became an endurance test. Who would last? Who would quit?

Those lucky enough to withstand the blows and who learned to duck and jab at the right time would go on. They would learn the art. It was a contest of will and a performance unlike any other. Capturing the unsuspected onlookers, it provided an atmosphere that demanded attention. The boxers, like the Broadway actor, got attention. Every move, hard to watch at times, mesmerized the crowds. Like a successful smash hit, the boxers' theater also drew a dedicated and loyal audience.

The often-gory spectacle, like the ancient gladiatorial combats in Rome, became a sport that was hard to shun. Once hooked, the boxing fan craved for more. Crowds packed local and large arenas to see their favorite pugilist in the ring. And it made for great theater, catapulting a young, talented, and determined figure into a superstar.

Southside was one of the hundreds of boxing gyms in the country. Unpretentious and in need of a painting, it served the Gary community. A small locker area in the back, to the right of the one bathroom, and a tiny office for Ramirez at the other end completed a tour of the facility. To the right of the rings, posters of past pugilists up to that year—1974—were displayed. Included in the pantheon of boxing greats looking down on the fighters were Muhammad Ali, Ken Norton, George Forman, Rocky Marciano, and Joe Frazier. They no doubt motivated the young prospective boxers and any visitors. *The Heroes of Boxing* was scrawled on the top of the posters. The opposite wall displayed the Rules of the House, along with a fire extinguisher.

A wooden bench with an assortment of neatly piled, clean towels was next to a water cooler adjacent to the tin trash receptacle for the used plastic cups. Iron hooks for coats and jackets also lined the wall. Not a fancy place, the gym served its purpose as a no-nonsense venue. The manager had tough rules. Frank Ramirez, known for his temper if anyone violated any of the rules, was otherwise a fair, albeit tough, manager. He had to be. It was a tough environment in a city that was going though rough times.

Ramirez ran a tight, no-holds-barred ship along with a few trainers, a maintenance man, and a few volunteers along with an array of occasional street drifters. Most of the visitors who descended on the gym were relatives and friends of the boxers, giving them much-needed support.

Ramirez ran the gym on a shoestring budget. He relied on getting some donations from the public, especially when local officials, including retired police officials, the mayor's office, and the public, knew of upcoming bouts. Gary liked the sport of boxing and the fact that the gym, despite the financial challenges, proved to be an asset to the community. This fact was not lost on city hall. The mayor was a supporter and brought a few of his staff to publicize and give donations to the gym. "It's a refuge and keeps a lot of young men off the streets." Elected officials knew it, often enhancing funding during election season.

Seven years earlier, Ramirez, the former winner of the middleweight division in the Golden Gloves with hopes of going pro, sustained a serious injury in a car crash and had his hopes dashed. That crash on a rainy, slippery road in early December left his shoulder permanently damaged despite two surgeries. He could no longer fight. Depression and a period of withdrawal with pain killers ensued until an offer was made to manage a small boxing gym in the suburban Chicago town of Evanston.

Ramirez enjoyed the gym at Evanston but was distracted by the upscale clientele who didn't take boxing as seriously as he knew it needed to be. A product of a tough upbringing on Chicago's southside, he jumped at the chance of going to gritty Gary. "I can really concentrate on getting a pro into the ring." He had stayed in Evanston for six years until Southside was offered. He wanted to train a prospective champ. Evanston didn't produce a boxer despite a few prospects. When the opportunity to manage Southside was offered, he didn't take much time to make a decision.

At Southside, he would be in his niche—surrounded by fighters who wanted to excel and make a life of the sport of boxing, who were serious and motivated. In addition, he wouldn't have to endure the petty complaints from the upper-class and not-so-serious boxers. "My humble upbringing made me want to leave. They were nice people, good people, at Evanston, but I needed the grit, the sweat, and intensity of a place that stank and yet was a real home for boxers."

When the opening at Southside was offered, he jumped at the chance. Many thought he was foolish and would regret it. Gary? It was a crime-ridden city with little tax base to expand abandoned neighborhoods, and it had lost jobs and people. He knew what he was about to do would test his resolve. But he visited Southside twice. Despite the reputation of Gary and the downslide it projected like many Rust Belt cites, he felt he could make a difference. "Who knows? I may even have a world champ come out of Southside with the right trainer and boxer."

Ramirez also knew Joe Montalvo. He had seen him at several Golden Gloves venues. Dedicated to the core, Montalvo would be a reliable, sensible, and loyal trainer. Montalvo's reputation as a tough trainer who produced several Golden Gloves champs was an additional asset for Ramirez. Ramirez also wanted to be near Tyrone Dawson, whom he admired in the ring. "A great local fighter who had a few rough opponents. He'll be there at Southside. I know he'll make a difference." Ramirez felt for Dawson, having had a bad break with his own accident many years earlier. Dawson had done Indiana proud but was ready to help others. This clinched Ramirez's decision to come to Gary.

Yes, Southside would be a challenge. But it would be the challenge he wanted. He felt he could hire more trainers. He had a former pro with Tyrone Dawson. He knew he could motivate and get results. Hungry boxers intent on going professional were here, not in the suburbs. This is what he wanted. And he was ready for a change.

With his dream of going pro long gone due to the car accident, Ramirez had devoted his time to helping others. It was his way of staying in the game. His right shoulder, never the same, was always a reminder of what could have been. Yet, he was a realist and didn't want to work in any other venue. He was looking for raw new talent now that he was the man in charge. Southside would have several local prospects.

He had no idea that a young, former prospect named Kevin Bolton standing outside that early November morning was about to change both their lives. No notice was given. Kevin never wrote to the gym. He was too embarrassed and felt he had let his trainer down. "Even though I changed once I was in the joint, I was too proud to admit my stupidity. If I were Joe, I guess I'd think twice before letting me just walk in off the streets like nothing happened."

Like many remorseful people, he had gone through a transformation and now needed some support. Would Montalvo and the new owner let him in? What about Dawson? He may feel that Kevin had had his chance and blew it.

With thoughts swirling around in his head, Kevin needed some downtime. The walk to the gym helped clear his head. He strategized. What was he going to say once he encountered Montalvo? He thought of what Claude had repeated to him—confront your past and move on. Grateful to have an understanding friend, Kevin wanted desperately to be back in the gym, not as a worker or trainer but as a contender. "I'm young, stronger than I was before all this, and I'm ready. Please Lord, let me have this chance to redeem myself."

This silent prayer reinvigorated the erstwhile boxer. He wasn't afraid to enter. He felt guilty for having let down his trainer and fans. Like the prodigal son returning home, he was torn inside. Wanting to be part of the boxing family, he waited for what seemed a long time in front of Southside. Claude told him to have faith in himself. Claude was a churchgoing Baptist and believed that Kevin deserved a second chance. Yet, he wouldn't interfere with Kevin's dilemma.

Claude knew a few people who worked out at the gym for recreational purposes. Two of his friends, John Taylor and Mike Azarro, were not aspiring boxers, but they enjoyed the sport and did some sparring. Told of Bolton's imminent release, Mike Azarro, a former fan of Kevin's, said he would approach Montalvo, telling him the news. Claude indicated that this might ease the tension of Kevin's abrupt return being a cause of concern.

Mike, an ex-firefighter, remarked, "I know Joe Montalvo. He's tough as nails, but he's fair. I know he was pissed that Bolton dug a hole for himself and landed in jail, but who knows? Maybe, just maybe, he'll let him in, and that'll be great."

Claude was too busy working and raising a family to get immersed in the gym. He didn't want to be an interloper. Besides, deep down, Claude knew it was Kevin's choice to do what he wanted. The statement by Azarro seemed to help.

Kevin once again looked at his Mom's Book. He read the word over and over again: *responsibility*. Yes, he was ready. Ready for any eventuality, be it total rejection, a tepid acceptance with a reluctant Montalvo allowing him to enter, or an embrace like the prodigal son returning. He didn't know what to expect.

Walking into the gym, Kevin immediately noticed the changes in the two and half years since his arrest. It was busy—busier than his last visit. The constant action in the three rings was complemented by shouts of the new trainers in each of the rings to the sparring young pugilists. Kevin smiled. He felt like he belonged here. He liked what he saw. The constant, loud commands from the trainers drowning out the noise of each punch was a welcome reminder of his past. "Damn, I missed this so much."

CHAPTER TEN

Without any advance notice or expected fanfare as a returning ex-boxer, Kevin Bolton entered Southside Gym. Almost as if on cue, Joe Montalvo looked in his direction. Montalvo was training a new prospect, Gerard Holley. At nineteen, young Holley, a southpaw, had a quick left jab that had already gotten him noticed. He was Joe Montalvo's hottest prospect since Kevin. Like Kevin, he was a native of Gary and was talked about in the local press as a hot contender.

Montalvo, looking at Holley, told him to stop sparring with his partner, John Aquino. Young Gerard Holley had not expected this action. Joe Montalvo, focused and in control, expected much from his trainees. To Holley and Aquino, something strange was happening. "Why stop sparring?" Holley asked, curious if he had done something wrong.

"You want me to stop?" Holley again asked Montalvo, receiving a nod from Montalvo, who didn't take his eyes from the figure at the door.

Holley, not aware of the new entry to the gym, suddenly looked in the direction of the door. At once, everything seemed to stop.

The trainers, the maintenance staff, and the loud, crushing noise of repeated poundings on the bag ceased. An eerie silence took over, as if an omen of something about to occur. Holley, like the rest of Southside, looked directly at the sole entrance of the gym. Holley knew immediately that Montalvo's directive to stop was due the presence of the huge, hulking individual at the door. When Holley glanced at the figure in the door, he, like all the others in the gym, knew the reason why Montalvo told him to stop sparring.

What Holley and everyone else saw was a large White guy with a thick mane of blond hair. "Maybe he's a scout and checking us out." Holley, unaware who the stranger at the door was, knew it had to be someone big to make Montalvo stop him from sparring.

His partner, Aquino, gave Holley a quizzical look. "Must be somebody, bro," a casual Aquino said, looking at Holley. Montalvo by this time had dropped the towel he had for Holley. It was apparent that the stranger at the door had gotten the normally focused and programmed Montalvo's attention. The other boxers in the two other rings suddenly stopped. One of them was getting ready for a three-round spar.

Kevin's entry put a halt to everything. Looks went in his direction. The older regulars who hung out and were hitting the three bags suspended from the wall also stopped. Kevin was recognized by one of the longtime regulars, Tony Izzo. "I don't believe it! it's Kevin Bolton," he said almost in a whisper. The mysterious visitor drew stares. Kevin looked around, saw a few familiar faces, smiled, and nodded in their direction. Looking down, Kevin, not knowing the reception he was about to get, felt uncomfortable and vulnerable as the center of attention.

Soon, a few others recognized the former upstart boxer. Not knowing what to do or say, Kevin remained motionless, saying nothing as he looked up at Montalvo, who was now coming in his direction. All eyes were on Montalvo. He was the main trainer. The former champ, Dawson, was second to him. They called the shots. But Tyrone Dawson was out that day at a much-needed dentist appointment to get replacement caps and a crown.

Montalvo grew nearer. Kevin stood there, waiting to see what fate would ensue. It was Joe Montalvo's call. What was he going to do with the edgy, nervous young man just inside the door? A few of the regulars and newcomers were aware that Kevin once had been a hot prospect who had let Montalvo down. And now he was here. What was to happen? The suspense was about to end. Montalvo knew he had to act.

Within a minute of Kevin's sudden and unexpected arrival, Joe Montalvo left the ring where his prospective boxers, Holley and Aquino, were sparring. When Montalvo stopped the sparring match between Holley and Aquino, it quickly attracted the others in all three rings. "Someone big must have come in for Montalvo to stop Holley and Aquino," a young, eighteen-year-old Mark Stomper said to a fellow boxer hitting the other bag. Stomper, a very focused and well-built track star from nearby Hammond knew something was going on.

The other boxer, nineteen-year-old Jerry Turner, remarked, "He must be somebody."

Soon, the normally busy and noisy gym fell completely silent. Montalvo approached Kevin. All eyes gravitated toward this anomaly—a young, White kid looking so out of place, standing just inside the wooden, faded-green entrance door.

Montalvo knew he and the young man at the door were the center of attention. He decided to end the drama. Montalvo turned to the entire gym and shouted, "Stop everything! Everybody, listen up and give me your attention." Most had already done just that. Turning to Holley and Aquino, who were still not used to having their sparring stopped in the middle of the round, Montalvo nodded to the puzzled young pugilists. For Holley and Aquino, the nonverbal communication was obvious: something was happening. Expressionless, Joe Montalvo continued walking briskly toward Kevin, who had moved just a few steps from the creaky wooden door.

A nervous Kevin, knowing all eyes were upon him, looked down again at the floor and scanned the gym, feeling suddenly very alone. "About to get screwed by my old manager."

Kevin Bolton indeed did not expect what was about to unfold. Inching closer, an expressionless Montalvo moved his right-hand fingers into his thick, wavy, speckled, black-and-white hair. Joe looked directly at the crestfallen Kevin, whose uneasiness was apparent to all.

Kevin was ready for a disappointing dressing-down by his former manager. *Please don't make him get so pissed at me, Lord.* Looking up as Montalvo approached, Kevin had no idea what would happen next.

Stretching out his arms, Montalvo grabbed a startled Kevin and said, "About time you got here! I knew this day was coming, Kevin. Get your ass in the ring!" Montalvo, giving the former boxer a big Latino *embrazo*, turned to the now-curious upstarts in the ring, who were still wondering what the fuss was all about. They were further surprised at the reaction of Montalvo, who was normally taciturn and strictly business when it came to boxing. This was an unusual greeting.

Montalvo, holding center stage, took a deep breath, extending his arms wide saying, "Boys, I want you to meet the best boxer I ever trained; he's back and going places—this here is Kevin Bolton. Some of you may have heard of him. He's back, and that's all that matters." Looking at an awed Kevin Bolton, he added, "He's a local Gary boy. And yes, like I said, you'll be hearing from him."

This response was initially met with complete silence until Holley shouted, "Welcome back." Following this, a few applauded, and then most causally returned to their daily boxing routines, glancing back to get a better look at the new prospect. A few continued looking at Kevin, trying to figure out what the fuss was all about. Not knowing what to expect next, Kevin looked at Montalvo. Surprised by the sudden attention given him, Kevin wanted to show his gratitude yet didn't know what to say. He, like everyone at the gym, was surprised by the reaction of Joe Montalvo.

Taken off balance, Kevin, speechless and smiling, looked at Montalvo. It was time for him to respond. In an almost inaudible whisper, more like a penitent in the confessional, he whispered, "You mean I can come back and start over after what I did?" Kevin, the prodigal son, had returned, and it was time to move on to the next level. What was next?

Montalvo, aware of the drama unfolding, decided he had to again get everyone's attention. In a loud, booming voice for all to hear, he shouted, "Yes, Kevin's back. He's here, and we're here for him, too. You new guys maybe don't know him, but you will. Pay attention to him. Like I already said, he's going places. He's bound to be heard."

By this time, the young Gerard Holley, John Aquino, and the other boxers cast additional glances at both Kevin and Montalvo.

Kevin, not knowing what his fate would be with this new turn of events, knew that Montalvo held all the cards. Montalvo, a good judge of character, shouted, "Don't worry. Kevin's not about to intrude on any of your goals. Like you, he's a team player. You do your thing, and he'll do his. But once I get this hardhead in the ring, I want you to learn from him. Yes, like I said, he's the real deal—the real deal. Yes, he sure is."

Not expecting such a welcome, Kevin remained mostly silent up to that moment. Montalvo had heard a very sensitive side of young Kevin. Up to then, Kevin hadn't gotten much respect except in the joint. Without family, he knew that Montalvo was extending himself and putting his reputation on the line. Not knowing how to react, he pursed his lips and decided to speak up. He looked at Montalvo, tears welling up, and said, "I screwed up so bad and didn't listen."

Montalvo, gently grabbing Kevin by the arm, said, "That's in the past. Let it die. I was told you were released. I knew you'd come here. This is your home. Felt it in my bones."

Still caught off guard, Kevin nervously asked, "Was it Claude Evans who told you I was out?" Kevin wanted to know who gave the information to Montalvo. He had had no communication with the gym, Montalvo, or anyone else who worked there. Kevin now regretted not writing to Montalvo. Too proud, too angry, and too ashamed, he had shunned any correspondence from most.

Montalvo, ever the realist, came right to the point, "No, don't even know a Claude Evans. One of the regulars here whose brother is in the same place you were told me. I have a few contacts at that jail. Know a few who used to be here before they got busted." Kevin looked at Montalvo with a sheepish smile, wanting to say the right thing. Montalvo knew what to say next. Kevin's awkward presence was augmented by the continued stares from the rest of the boxers, who had stopped sparring and working out. Montalvo indeed knew what to say next. He continued, "You're back. I also know about your dire home situation, too. Sorry about that. You got a place to stay?"

"Yeah, Claude, the one I mentioned, has a nice basement. I have my own bed and shower there. I'm lucky to have him as a friend."

"That's good. Otherwise, I would have gotten a cot here for you."

Unaccustomed to the generosity extended, Kevin thought of his mom and his entry for the day, *responsibility.* This brought a faint smile to his face. Welcomed back despite his past, he felt at once relieved. "I should have kept in touch with Joe while I was locked up. Just too proud and stubborn, I guess."

Kevin, still in shock at this homecoming, indeed felt like the biblical, errant prodigal son. The son who had come home after leaving without a word and later returning to a grateful father. In Kevin's case, his pride had done him in and caused his incarceration. His stubborn refusal to accept good legal advice landed him in the jailhouse.

Returning now, he, like the prodigal son, didn't know what reception he would have. He looked at Montalvo and added, "I can help you with maintaining this place . . . I mean, I can work here for the training." Kevin was at a loss for words, and the suggestion that he could work for his training hit Montalvo. He saw in Kevin an evolving, penitent young man. Montalvo liked what he saw. It was time for him to respond to the vulnerable and needy Kevin.

In an unusual display of profanity, he looked Kevin squarely in the eye and said, "Forget that bullshit! I'm offering you a spot here to train with Dawson and me. Dawson the pro. The pro! Tyrone Dawson knows all about you and is eager to assist you. T has had a rough life, brought up in the projects—on the West Side—the Dorie Miller homes."

Kevin added, "Yeah, I know where they are. I lived not too far from there, near Burr Street."

Located in Northeast Gary, the project was named for the Black hero at Pearl Harbor who was later killed in action. Projects such as the Miller houses, Delaney West, and Concord had gone into disrepair as the city experienced the outpouring of jobs. The resulting closing of factories led to whole sections of the city being abandoned. Joe Montalvo knew the dangerous, drug-infested area where Kevin ended up after his mom's death. It was far from the Miller houses.

Montalvo added, "Like I said, I had contacts. I kept tabs on you during your stay at Indiana State Prison. I knew you would be back, and yes, I'm glad you're here. My wife's cousin, Rafael Soto, is a correctional officer at Indiana State. He told me that you were leading and organizing a boxing session. Got the attention of the warden, too."

Kevin smiled at this response. He knew Officer Soto as a solid and fair correctional officer, who often asked about his neighborhood in Gary. Soto never mentioned that he knew Joe Montalvo. Kevin often wondered why Soto inquired about his plans post prison. Now, he knew; it all made sense. Joe Montalvo never gave up on Kevin.

Montalvo continued, "Rafael also said you were working out hard—sparring and jump roping and keeping up with the weights. He was impressed by the intensity of your workout and the fact that you helped others. Looking at you, I see the results for myself right now. I'm looking at you and offering you a chance. Either you take it or leave it. But, I tell you one thing: if you go this time, don't come back!"

Joe Montalvo had indeed hit the right notes with Kevin. Realizing that this was not only a meal ticket to possible fame and stardom but also a chance to redeem himself, the dressing-down that Montalvo gave him set the standard. Kevin knew he had just one chance now. He could blow it all. That wasn't about to happen.

Kevin knew that he couldn't let Joe, the ex-champ Tyrone Dawson, and most of all, himself, down. Indeed, opportunities like this come once in a lifetime. The young, teenage future boxers stared at him, wishing to hell they had the same offer. No doubt envious and perhaps a bit angry, they realized that Kevin was someone whom Joe Montalvo would invest his reputation on. Kevin also knew this was a seminal moment.

To reinforcc his argument, Montalvo added, "Yes, we both think you have what it takes. It remains to be seen if you're too rusty and need a lot of work. But, from what I heard, you're ready. And let me tell you this once again for the last time—I kept tabs on you at Indiana State I know what you did, setting up that boxing program and staying in shape. It sends me a message that you want to get back in the ring."

Kevin, nodding anxiously, responded, "Yeah, I'm so ready. I'll do anything to get back into the ring. I've been praying for this moment. Thanks—thanks so much."

Kevin's giddy nervousness, still apparent, caused Montalvo to add: "It's not going to be pretty. I will push you hard, but you can do it if you want. It's in your corner, Mr. Kevin Bolton."

Joe Montalvo knew that he had Kevin in his grasp. He wanted him to not only feel welcomed but to also have faith in himself. This gesture spoke volumes. It said of Montalvo that he valued both his trainers and boxers. He knew talent when he saw it. More importantly, it gave the once-troubled young man a chance. Life is about choices, and Montalvo held the key for Kevin. He could run with it, take a chance, and at least try. If he failed, his legacy was sealed. He had given it all he could.

For Kevin, the offer was a no-brainer. Montalvo had faith that he could get the now more mature and focused young man in the ring with results that might shatter the boxing world. It remained to be seen, but both Montalvo and Kevin were about to embark on an unforeseen journey. The rough road ahead would test the resolve of the most dedicated and hungry of the lot. The destination depended upon the efforts of the young pugilist who now was given the choice.

Yes, life is about choices, and Kevin Bolton knew it. He had come full circle and thought of the dream while languishing in a lonely jail cell. The daily entry of good words to live by was his mantra that kept him going, thanks to the message that his late mom gave him to fulfill his destiny. That day's word—*responsibility*—took on a greater goal. He was overwhelmed by it all. The young man had so much on his plate at the moment but knew this opportunity couldn't be overlooked. He had to make the right choice. He did exactly that by walking into Southside that cool November morning. He would take responsibility knowing full well that he was to embark on a unique albeit challenging journey.

Lloyd Hopkins, a fixture at the gym, had stopped mopping the floor where a spill occurred next to the water cooler. He was close enough to hear the conversation between Montalvo and Kevin that had lasted about seven minutes after Kevin's arrival. Sometimes, it takes a listener, someone like Hopkins, to step forward and offer the best advice.

Hopkins, a widowed septuagenarian, was a fixture at Southside. He was a witness to the changes in Gary over his lifetime. The son of a poor sharecropper, Hopkins's parents moved to Gary, having left the segregated South in rural Alabama. His father worked long hours at the steel plant. Hopkins, an athlete who excelled in football, also gravitated to boxing with the rise of another Southern transplant, Joe Louis. "I got hooked on boxing as Louis's career took off."

Unable to go to college due to limited family funds, Hopkins started working at the gym part-time on weekends to help supplement his large family of four brothers and three sisters. He got a chance to work full-time at the gym soon after graduating from high school and never left. He saw the best and worst as the city experienced the White flight once the factories closed. Hopkins also had his share of tragedy, having lost a nephew to a drive-by shooting and his wife of thirty-nine years to breast cancer. His two daughters, married and successful, had long left Gary. One lived in suburban Chicago and the other in Los Angeles. Now that he was alone, the gym became his sanctuary, his island of peace in a very troubled ocean. He was at home here. He was respected, and when he spoke, which was seldom, it was to make a point. People listened.

Sometimes it takes a person with a solid history of witnessing the good and bad in life and seeing things from afar. Lloyd Hopkins was such a man. His presence made all the difference to ease the tension that cool November morning in a rundown Gary boxing gym. People listened to the old sage. The philosophical, mainstay maintenance man was ready—ready for his walk onto center stage. Like it or not, fate dealt him a role, and he knew he had to play an important role that demanded immediate attention. Hopkins walked up to Montalvo and Kevin. All eyes in the gym were on old Mr. Hopkins.

He came over, smiling, sizing up the young man in front of him. He reached out and shook hands with Kevin. Giving him a bottle of water, the gesture seemed to work. The little things in life, often overlooked, play an important part our psyche. Handing Kevin the plastic Poland Spring water bottle, he looked him squarely in the eyes and said, "I remember you when you were here. Helluva fighter. Time to get back. Yes, indeed, time to get back. Listen to Mr. Montalvo. He doesn't do this every day. Yes, time to get back, son." Turning, Lloyd had said his piece and returned to finish mopping the slight water spill.

Kevin gazed at the elderly gent, who limped slightly as he walked away, knowing that Lloyd Hopkins's mere gesture had made his return accepted. The elderly Hopkins, having been at Southside for thirty-seven years, saw boxers come and go. He knew who was real and who had the talent. He knew who was a phony and who wouldn't last. A good judge of character, his simple greeting to the young and shaky Bolton spoke volumes. The gym was indeed Lloyd Hopkins's life—his little fiefdom. His endorsement of Kevin sealed the young boxer's fate. It eased the tension that Kevin, up to now, had pent up.

Kevin was ready. Turning to Montalvo, Kevin, now confident and excited, asked, "When do you want me to start?"

"Get here tomorrow at 8 a.m. sharp. Tyrone Dawson will be here. I'm going to give him a call later to tell him that you showed up and you're out. You know the layout of this place. Nothing much has changed except for the new owner, Ramirez. I told him about you. He knows your record." Kevin laughed, thinking of his prison time. As if on cue, Montalvo also laughed, "No, not that record. I'm talking about your performance before you went away. Tomorrow, be prepared. We have some scheduled bouts coming up in a few months. I can get a couple of scouts from Chicago here to size you up once you get into the mix. We'll talk about insurance and contracts if they like what they see. And they will like what they see, I'm sure. Don't mess."

"Oh no, no I won't. The thought that Tyrone Dawson is going to train with me, too. Wow."

"Stay away from the broads and booze for the duration." Montalvo gave Kevin a stern glance, knowing his sordid past when it came to relationships.

"Yeah, I don't have nobody in my life—just got out."

Giving Kevin a quizzical look, he said somewhat reluctantly, "I know it's been a long time. If you go places, those women will flock to you. It's expected. Some of them are genuine, while others aren't. You're young; got looks and body. If you're hungry for the title, you'll wait. You waited while you were in the joint. This is your life. I'm offering you a chance of a lifetime. I know you're anxious to meet and date. I'd feel the same if I were in your shoes. But from now on, you're married to this gym. Your whole life will revolve around this place. So, when it comes to going out, think twice. You got plenty of time for friends, girlfriends, and family. As I said, right now, this is your business, your life. Yes?" Montalvo, unsmiling and looking directly at Kevin, waited for his reply.

"Mr. Montalvo," Kevin felt he had to use the formality to make his point. "I'm well aware of the faith and potential investment in me. Believe me. I won't screw up. I promise."

Montalvo, impressed by the comment, thought, *Good, I'm getting to him. It's going to be a struggle, but the kid may just have it.* Montalvo, a solid and no-nonsense trainer, had the presence of mind to lecture the future boxer without sounding condescending. He knew he was getting through to Kevin. Looking at Kevin, he wanted to make sure he had driven home his points. Yet he was pleased at the attitude, response, and apparent interest that Kevin had in resurrecting his incipient career to take off. It was now time to wrap up the lecture he was giving him and get ready for the change. "That's what I want to hear. I'll have a list of dos and don'ts for you plus the diet that you have to follow." Montalvo knew he had reached Kevin. He delivered his message and got the young prospect on board.

Kevin, overwhelmed by the chance to make it big, felt that the dream he had in jail with his mom's endorsement would seal the deal. He had no choice. He wouldn't let her down. He had the right mix going for him this time around. "I won't screw up. I owe it to myself and Mom and Montalvo." Kevin looked back at Montalvo, the one person who, as in the biblical story, let him return. He was the prodigal son, returning after having been away. Now, it was his time to prove to himself and others that he had what it takes. Life is indeed about choices, and Kevin, given the opportunity to make amends, knew what he had to do. "Whatever happens, I'll give it 100 percent. Won't be a jerk this time. I have to prove that I can make it." Yes, making his mark. It was his time.

Kevin, deeply touched by the reception he received from Montalvo and Hopkins, took a deep breath. His head was spinning, and events lingered in his head. He had to get some things off his chest.

"Okay." Kevin, trying to contain his excitement at this chance to make something of his life, added, "I won't let you down." At a loss for words, his limited vocabulary apparent, the frustrated Kevin didn't know how to fully express his feelings. Aware that others were now staring at him, he felt a bit overwhelmed. Feeling a bit ashamed, his glances at Montalvo sent the right message.

A smiling Montalvo knew he had to step in and make sure his young protégé felt at home. Taking the role of not only his trainer but also his teacher and mentor, he nodded at Kevin, adding, "No, I don't want you to let yourself down. It's all in your corner, literally!"

The nervous young man finally spoke up adding: "No worries. I won't mess. I'm so grateful; so grateful." Kevin thought of the dream in jail and his mother's message. His word today—*responsibility*—made sense. He knew this encounter would be a seminal event in his life. He would make every effort to succeed.

Montalvo liked the maturity he saw in Kevin. *He's starting to grow up. It's good to see him in such great shape. I'll mold him into a fighting machine. I'll make sure if he makes it big that he won't end up as some pompous airbag intent on showing off. I'll make sure he doesn't go that route.*

Montalvo, ever the pragmatist, needed to reinforce his concern for the young, handsome boxer. "Like I said, once your name gets back out there and people see you perform in the ring, it will happen. Those nice and not-so-nice ladies will be looking. And guys, too. Right now, this place is your temple, your shrine, and your girlfriend all rolled into one—*comprende*?"

Kevin shook his head to signal that he wasn't about to throw away such an offer. He smiled, taken aback at the litany of things and the nice Spanish spin. "*Si, comprende*," he added.

Montalvo went up to Kevin. He shook Kevin's hand again, adding, "In the meantime, let Lloyd assign you a locker. Yes, go now."

Hopkins, who had cleaned up the spill, motioned to Kevin to follow him. Hopkins knew that Montalvo wanted to assign a locker for Kevin. Hopkins wanted to give him Locker #4—"My lucky number." Hopkins was born on April 4, the fourth day of the fourth month. He always used this number the few times he played the lottery, winning $150. So, it was his number, and he deliberately kept that locker number 4 vacant for three weeks once Montalvo told him of Kevin's pending release. Hopkins had kept the locker vacant, waiting for the next Dawson-like boxer to emerge. The old, custodial sage knew he found it in the returning Kevin Bolton.

Kevin headed to the locker area. He knew he was the center of attention. His head was not totally able to absorb what just transpired. The other young boxers—envious, curious, and mostly silent—knew they had just witnessed an exchange that was seldom duplicated in the boxing world—an upcoming star welcomed back without any strings. That cool November morning was the start of what was to become a major transition in the life of the young boxer. It would shake things up at Southside and beyond. Each of the young boxers in awe could see himself as the next big contender. Kevin's presence would serve as a beacon of light—a goal to be reached by the countless drills of repetitious routines of calisthenics, jumping rope, sparring, and jogging. Day after day was a chance to hone on one's skills. Like good students, the aspiring boxers saw in Kevin a model to emulate. They knew, given the attention and warmth extended to Kevin Bolton, that they, too, could be in the same situation. They could only wish such good fortune would extend to them.

Kevin turned to them and nodded. He had been there. He had gone through the rigors of endless and oftentimes boring routines. He was ready to begin again—so ready. He turned to the young boxers. He saw a bit of himself in them. The wasted two years at the prison may have actually done some good. He had grown up. He had taken himself seriously and didn't blame others for his own misfortunes. The dream that night in jail changed everything. He was, indeed, ready and willing to accept hours of grueling workouts to get to his goal.

Turning to the young boxers, there was no need for words. They and Kevin knew that he was about to begin a unique journey that could catapult him to international fame. He entered into the locker area, with Hopkins holding the door for him. Already, it was apparent that something extraordinary was in the offing. Joe Montalvo wouldn't be disappointed. Young Kevin Bolton didn't even know how far his career would take him. Yes, he was indeed ready. Kevin was about to shake up the boxing world.

CHAPTER ELEVEN

OVER THE NEXT SIX MONTHS, Kevin Bolton became the talk of the boxing word—a rising star with skills not often seen in a rookie. The kid from Gary. Soon, writers and the boxing world wanted to get as much information as they could on the young upstart.

"Montalvo knew that he was destined to go places," Lloyd Hopkins remarked to Tyrone Dawson after Dawson's initial meeting with Kevin. "He wouldn't have taken him in otherwise." Turning to the former boxing star, Dawson, Hopkins added, "I know you, Tyrone. You'll see yourself in that nice, young boxer. He may be White, but life has been a struggle for him, too. And I know you'll be molding him into a champ." Turning to a smiling Tyrone Dawson, Lloyd Hopkins tipped his Chicago Cubs baseball cap, giving Dawson a high five. "Make him the next champ to come out of here." With that comment, Hopkins walked away knowing he had Dawson in Bolton's corner.

Tyrone Dawson still reigned as the pride of Southside—the peripatetic, local ex-champ who nearly made it to the top. Yet, Dawson, true to his word, stayed in Gary helping wannabe boxers. "He didn't forget where he came from," Hopkins would add anytime his name came up. Despite his tough exterior, Dawson had a special soft side for young kids of all backgrounds who were trying to make it. He and his wife had experienced a few miscarriages until his wife gave birth to a daughter named Julie.

When Kevin appeared on the scene, Dawson knew that Kevin Bolton had the potential to go all the way to the top and win a world champion belt. Dawson saw Kevin as fast on his feet—faster than Dawson himself. More importantly, he saw that fast uppercut that landed so many of his sparring partners on the canvas.

Dawson, the seasoned and well-traveled ex-champ, knew that Kevin Bolton was the complete package. "Yes, he can go the top. And I'm going to make sure that I'm part of the act." Dawson saw in Kevin a bit of himself. That belt that eluded the erstwhile boxer. He decided he would channel his energy, his expertise, in getting Kevin to the top. It was with no trepidation or hesitancy that he took on the role of the chief trainer for Kevin.

And the two polar-opposite pugilists—one White, one Black; one with a felony conviction, the other without a criminal record; one single, one married—soon became a closely bonded pair intent on the world title. The title denied to Dawson.

Sparring with Dawson meant that Kevin would be on par with a talented, seasoned, and no-nonsense boxer. Six rounds of sparring never deterred Kevin. Dawson was tested. Kevin was the real deal. Drawn into the ring once more, Dawson saw his role as a mentor in the same category as Montalvo, albeit much more active. Dawson was able to show the still-green, young boxer the special moves in the ring that would count so much—the foot rhythm, the steely gaze at your opponent, the faster uppercut, and weaving in and out to avert both a southpaw and orthodox style. Working the ring, Kevin, back in the mix, proved to be a quick learner. Before long, he had Dawson on the canvas by the third sparring match.

People took notice—not only boxing fans but the sports world, as well. No longer the reclusive, insincere, and introverted young man from three years ago and with his incarceration and parole behind him, Kevin Bolton came into his own. With the patient and loyal trainers, Joe Montalvo and Tyrone Dawson, Kevin became the pride of Southside Boxing Gym. Not only was he the center of attention at the gym, but he soon displayed a rapid development that started the boxing world chatting. He became a fighting machine. Soon, his name was the talk of the boxing world.

"Here comes the next challenger in the heavyweight division," remarked the legendary sports promotor Don King. No doubt King always had his radar on upcoming talent to promote and make money. Don King and others knew that the young kid from Gary was going places fast. Soon, calls came into Southside from not only nearby Chicago but also distant New York and London.

Sports writers, boxing fans, and those greedy promoters, indeed, wanted to get in on the action. Local residents, curious after a television interview, started arriving at the gym to watch this phenomenon in action. They wanted to see the boy wonder in action sparring with the seasoned retired champ, Tyrone Dawson. And they were not disappointed. They were in for an event that few boxers could match.

"Watching that young Kevin Bolton spar is theater," James Ralston, a reporter for the *Chicago Tribune* newspaper wrote after witnessing a grueling sparring with the former champ Dawson. "He moves like a cheetah—calculating, smooth, and then goes in for the kill. His reach is better than any boxer I've seen, and his upper jab connects with a speed not seen in a long time."

The press quickly picked up the cheetah comment, and within a few weeks, another article referred to Kevin as "The Cheetah."

The name stuck, and soon, people started calling the newest boxing upstart The Cheetah. Other writers, both locally and in the greater boxing world, took notice, and Kevin was barraged with many requests for interviews. Montalvo was cautious, keeping Kevin close to the vest, scanning and researching any new interviews. Montalvo wanted Kevin to stay focused as negotiations were underway to introduce Kevin to the boxing world with a gala bout scheduled in just two months. Montalvo knew that Kevin, with his looks, powerful jabs and moves, plus a unique bio, would soon capture the attention of all sorts, both good and bad. He wanted to protect Kevin as long as possible. "I know the barracudas will be out there—promoters who care only about the market value of the kid, gold diggers, both women and men who would want to gravitate and be seen with Kevin."

Feeling that he helped create a power boxer who was soon to be a world challenger, Montalvo had to divide his attention between Kevin's progress in the ring and watching out for him in the wider world. Beset by those trying to make a quick buck and get on board the Kevin Bolton bandwagon, Montalvo got Kevin "The Cheetah" to calm down a bit with reporters. He also sat down with several people who expressed their concern—Claude and Yolanda Evans, the gym owner Ramirez, and a few regulars at the gym.

"The reporters are off-limits to the gym as long as I have a say, and believe me, they'll not come here and disrupt important training for the big bout." Montalvo, along with Yolanda and Claude, decided to keep Kevin isolated from the public in the basement apartment. After a few more discussions, they addressed their concerns and gave Kevin an evaluation that was both candid and sincere. Kevin was ready for any eventuality. He listened. He knew that his inner circle of trainers, fellow boxers, and friends like the

Evanses were there for him. Yet, there was Kevin himself. He had to be the one who had to handle fame and eventual fortune sensibly. Could he could it? Time would tell.

With these assessments, Montalvo knew he and Dawson had created a lethal machine. The intensive daily workouts would have taxed anyone. Kevin, however, was hungry and ready for the kill. His style, polished and smooth, gave the spectator a look into the art of boxing. His unique moves and swift uppercuts indeed earned him the nickname Cheetah. And his personality shone. Montalvo and Dawson liked Kevin and didn't want him to get hurt emotionally. He was approachable and perhaps a bit too naive for fame.

Tyrone Dawson, once the darling of Gary, knew what was going to happen once Kevin got big on the outside. He had been there only to have his fame ended with a catastrophic defeat. Dawson, perhaps a bit nostalgic and envious, could be hard on the upstart. Dawson, sincere and without a flaw, wanted Kevin to go to the top and succeed where he had hadn't—getting a world title belt. With Kevin not having a family, Montalvo, Dawson, Hopkins, Claude and Yolanda Evans, the boxers, and other workers at Southside became an extended family intent on protecting Kevin Bolton.

Yes, Montalvo made sure that Kevin kept to his strict regimen of diet, exercise, and attitude. The big issues, such as dealing with potential fame, became a serious concern for Montalvo. But Kevin rose to the occasion and made inroads not only by being a skilled and quick learner in the ring but also by being loyal to Montalvo, Southside, and the supportive Gary community. As he exited the gym, some of his fans asked for autographs. The once-reclusive and shy, blond, blue-eyed "White hope" became a celebrity. Like it or not, he was getting the attention that Montalvo warned him about. Yet, Kevin kept his cool, staying in the basement apartment of Claude Evans. And Kevin kept to his schedule.

Kevin Bolton rose up to the expectations of those who would eventually invest in him. Up at 4:30 a.m. in all kinds of weather, he could be seen on the dark, mean, and often dangerous streets, jogging his three- to four-mile run with a plastic water bottle in hand, which he would gulp down in the first few minutes of his routine and then discard in a trash bin adjacent to the dark and isolated park.

His run would then consist of shadowboxing as he moved steadily along the periphery of parks; past old and burnt-out schools; dilapidated, boarded-up, and long-abandoned homes; and a few surviving storefronts, churches, and an assortment of burnt-out cars. Eerily quiet and forbidding, the streets, ever a danger, didn't bother young Kevin. He was focused on his run, focused on the prize, and willing to endure the glares of the few most unsavory people out at that hour.

Homeless people, huddled with their newspapers serving as makeshift blankets against the cold winter chill, often nodded to the young boxer. Kevin felt for them. "I'd probably be there if Claude and Joe didn't believe in me." Motivated by his steadfast regimen, even these poor, homeless people appreciated the upstart boxer. One ragged, toothless White guy, usually a bottle of cheap hootch in hand, would smile. His friend, an older Black guy with a beret-like cap, sometimes roused from his sleep at the sound of the jogging boxer, would likewise give an occasional thumbs-up and smile.

Following his morning run, his next regimen consisted of one hundred jumping jacks, one hundred push-ups, two hundred sit-ups, and once back at the basement apartment, jumping rope two hundred times.

While Lloyd Hopkins and Tyrone Dawson cautioned the cocky,

assertive boxer-in-training to be careful, Kevin had no fears. He would witness a few drug deals going on and would continue his run. He knew better than to get involved or stop. "I've been through enough bullshit. Don't need any more—it made me do time." Ignoring the bad, he concentrated on his run and his desire to get ahead.

The few early-morning commuters often would honk their horns as a sign of approval.

Donning a faded gray hoodie and matching sweats, he was reminiscent of the character Rocky Balboa on his daily run. Only, this was the real thing.

Once inside Claude Evans's basement apartment, he would cap things off after his jumping rope by heading to a small refrigerator and stove installed for him. He would have a hearty breakfast, often consisting of three eggs, whole wheat toast, plain tea, and orange juice. He purchased these items, lest he disturb the young family upstairs.

Then, it was time for the gym. Arriving at Southside Gym, he would spar with at least two boxers for three rounds. His sparring with Dawson was always reserved as an afternoon exercise before hitting the shower. Aware of his strength, Kevin often would back off from throwing his now-famous upper jab too hard at his sparring partner. Instead, he would concentrate more on the all-important leg movements. Once out of the ring, he would do additional jumping rope for a full five minutes nonstop followed by additional jumping jacks, a few dips on the pull-up bar, and two hundred sit-ups.

The strict, brutal regimen was repeated twice a day and made Kevin into a powerful boxer. He would end with one-hundred push-ups and some shoulder shrugs using fifty-pound weights.

Witnessing him in action revealed a performance matched by few. By the third and fourth months, he was ready to step into the ring and make his professional debut. "He's become a monster," remarked the young, admiring boxer-in-waiting Gerard Holley. The young boxer emulated Kevin, hoping to be in his place one day. Holley and Kevin bonded well. They sparred a few times. In Holley, Kevin saw promise, which was seconded by both Montalvo and Dawson.

Kevin had won three amateur bouts in Gary and Chicago by the fifth month. Each one of them was a knockout. In two of the three bouts, he floored his opponent by the second round. The last fight with a young Cincinnati boxer named Jeremy White lasted four rounds. White, like all the others, ended up on the canvas. Kevin's amateur record stood at 3–0, all of them by knockouts. He was now going pro.

His upcoming debut fight was scheduled at Madison Square Garden. It was called The Showcase of the Nation and was in just two months. Knowing the pressures on him, he set out to prove to the world he had not only arrived but also would triumph. His mom's dream, always a driving force, gave him the additional incentive to push on. He kept his Mom's Book with him and entered uplifting words to further psyche himself up. The latest entry was *humility*.

Surprising himself, he knew something was about to take place that would catapult him to fame and fortune. He remembered what Montalvo told him: "Don't get a big head. Don't forget where you came from." These were important words to live by, and they further helped him persevere. That sound advice, plus the constant reminders of his mom's dream and his Mom's Book entry of words to live by, kept him focused.

Soon, Montalvo had to limit spectators coming and going, as they were distracting. Many of the young girls, seeing Kevin's picture in the newspaper and his interview with the local ABC affiliate, wanted to see the handsome upstart. Montalvo, with the tacit approval of Ramirez, agreed to limit the throng to fifteen. He also wouldn't let in spectators unless they indicated an interest in joining the gym. Soon, the crowd trickled, and Kevin was relieved that he could channel his interest into boxing routine.

His sparring was a work of art. As with any talent, there are degrees of excellence. His form—posture, feet movement, and jabs—were a work of art. Even the hardened inmates at the jail were aware that Kevin possessed extraordinary talent few could duplicate. As one inmate remarked, "He can beat anybody—anybody!" For Kevin, his primal desire to be the best started to attract others. Events started to unfold, and changes were inevitable as the boxing world took notice of the young Gary fighter.

Soon, calls came into the gym asking for an interview with the young Kevin. But Montalvo, with the blessing of the owner, kept Kevin close to the vest, often checking on him at his basement apartment at Claude Evans's home. He hesitated but finally agreed to an interview, knowing that the publicity would be good not only for Kevin but also for the gym. The curiosity was also too much. Yet the calls kept coming in. "That damn interview on TV and the piece in the paper got people curious," Montalvo told the owner of Southside. "I'm getting calls from promoters in Chicago and even New York."

Finally, Montalvo agreed to an interview for *The Ring*, the premiere boxing magazine. Montalvo knew what this meant. It would be the introduction of the most talked-about talent since Ali to the boxing world. Reluctant at first, Ramirez wanted the interview, knowing that it would give Southside and the dire city of Gary an added boost.

Montalvo agreed after sitting down with Kevin and Tyrone Dawson to prep him for some possible "catch" questions. The interview would include only Kevin and Montalvo. Dawson excused himself, saying he would be busy training Holley and Aquino for an upcoming amateur bout and bided his time with them and Kevin. Montalvo knew that Dawson, now a has-been, felt the limelight had gone onto Kevin. Perhaps he was a bit nostalgic for the old days, or perhaps a bit of jealousy prevailed. Joe Montalvo understood Dawson. He felt for him, knowing how fleeting the boxing world could be when it came to defeated champs. Montalvo felt that Kevin should be given the attention. Dawson agreed.

Montalvo sat Kevin down and told him what to expect. "You're going to be a celebrity after your first pro fight, which will be coming up soon. This interview will put you on the map and get you on your way. Don't get a big head, and don't forget where you came from—understand?" Kevin Bolton was ready for the interview.

Montalvo had avoided a lot of publicity, but when the editor of the premier boxing magazine, *The Ring*, asked for a sit-down interview, Joe Montalvo jumped at the chance. Ramirez wanted it. "Let's show them even in Gary, with all the problems, we still produce champs." Ramirez also wanted the publicity for his gym and was eager for the interview despite Montalvo's initial concerns. For Montalvo knew that the upcoming interview would give notice that his young protege had arrived. Montalvo knew that this was the seminal moment in the young prospect's life. He also knew that Len Burroughs, a tough boxer analyst, would conduct the interview.

Burroughs asked what was so special about Kevin Bolton. A savvy, twenty-two-year career journalist, Burroughs knew what to expect but wanted a few good quotes to highlight the publication in *The Ring*. Montalvo let loose, knowing that the interview would be Kevin Bolton's big break into the boxing world.

Montalvo certainly didn't hold back, saying, "I've been training boxers for a full twenty years. I have yet to see a tougher, more focused and dedicated boxer than Kevin Bolton. He's destined to go places, and I'm determined to get him to the top."

Burroughs then turned to Kevin, asking what kept him motivated.

Without hesitation, he responded, "Fulfill my dream to be the best boxer I can be."

Burroughs pressed a bit more, digging into Kevin's sordid past, asking, "Did your recent incarceration give you time to reflect on where you want to end up?"

Undeterred, Kevin was quick to respond. Smiling at the softball question, Kevin took a deep breath and, glancing at Montalvo, opened up by saying, "In my lonely cell, I had a dream soon after being locked up that my mom told me to make something of my life. To leave the past alone and look forward."

Burroughs probed further: "To be a visionary—someone who doesn't look back and instead looks to the future?"

Kevin glanced at Montalvo, who nodded, a clear indication that it was okay to explain the strange happening that night at Indiana State.

"Yes—"

Kevin, a bit nervous to add to the discussion, was interrupted by Montalvo, "Our young prospect keeps a book or memo which he calls his Mom's Book." Montalvo decided to let the facts roll out concerning Kevin's Mom's Book.

"Mom's Book?" Burroughs asked. Frowning and then smiling,

he needed to get more insight.

Montalvo looked at Kevin, who appeared a bit agitated by the disclosure. He added, "Kevin Bolton can speak for himself. But I know he keeps this bonded loose-leaf paper as memorial for his mom. Each week or day, he adds a new word to live by—right, Kev?" Montalvo was anxious to let Burroughs know that, despite his hard, scrappy life, Kevin was a dedicated and committed person. This approach by Montalvo did indeed loosen up Kevin, who, up to then, was looking at Montalvo nervously.

"I sometimes have a weekly word to live by. Sometimes, I change it twice a week."

Burroughs, a fifty-eight-year-old, seasoned, veteran writer had interviewed many boxers. He found in Kevin a shy, albeit determined and cautious young man. Curious to know why the book was important, he asked Kevin, "Can you share some of these words to live by that you incorporated into your life?"

"Yeah, they're important to me. Words to live by, like *responsibility, caring, loyalty,* and *perseverance.*"

At this, Burroughs, smiling and nodding, added, "Those are words that demand action from all of us. We can all benefit from them."

This comment brought a smile to Montalvo. He felt that Kevin had given a nice spin to his bio, which would certainly be in the *Ring* article.

Kevin, fully in his mold, now looked at Burroughs and smiled. "Thanks, Mr. Burroughs. They are words to live by. I decide on the word based on where I see myself going—hopefully a title fight." This comment drew a few laughs from Burroughs. Kevin looked at a smiling Montalvo, who knew that his young upstart prospect nailed the interview. Kevin had come off as sincere, humble, logical, and ever determined to show his talent.

Montalvo knew that the added publicity and the hopefully good coverage in *The Ring* would set the boxing world talking. It would also, no doubt, give prospective lenders something to invest in—young Kevin Bolton. Montalvo knew that Ramirez would be glad to hear it all went well for the upstart boxer and his gym.

Leaving for his office in downtown Chicago, Len Burroughs let it be known that he would edit the interview and show the result to Montalvo and Kevin before sending off for publication at the main Los Angeles office. "I hope to have the final draft out in a few weeks. The issue in *The Ring* will take a few months. Expect the interview will get a lot of attention, young man. Good luck; I see that you're on your way to the top." Burroughs, not usually accustomed to such accolades wanted to assure Kevin that the interview would be positive and help him get recognized internationally. Shaking hands with both Kevin and Montalvo, he left to a waiting car service sent from his downtown office on State Street in Chicago.

Once Burroughs had left for his nearby Chicago office, Montalvo sat Kevin down and explained the importance of such an interview. From the expression and nonchalant attitude coming from Montalvo, it was apparent that the interview was a success. "You handled yourself well, Kevin. Talking about your past and your rise to the top wasn't easy for you, I know. Before you say anything, let me tell you that writer liked what he saw in you."

Kevin, smiling, asked sheepishly, "You think it went over well?"

"No doubt about it." Montalvo smiled broadly and added, "His writeup should do wonders for you."

Indeed, *The Ring*, first published in 1922, remained the mainstay for boxers, promoters, fans, and the overall boxing world. A feature interview such as the one just completed by Burroughs was destined to draw the attention of important movers and shakers in the myriad boxing world, which had its share of scandal and corruption. Montalvo, ever the optimist, knew his vigilance in maintaining a strict regimen for Kevin would be challenged by a curious and hungry press.

Montalvo was relentless in his pursuit of Kevin. He knew talent and wasn't about to give up this young, rising star. In Kevin, he found a very committed person. Kevin's enthusiasm shone through day after day. With each day, his training improved. From the moment Kevin entered Southside Gym, Montalvo checked on Kevin to make sure that he was ready. That involved getting Tyrone Dawson to spar with him or another heavyweight who had boxed as an amateur in several venues over the span of eleven years. That person was an unemployed Mike Murtha.

He was a formerly fast, thirty-four-year-old who had fallen on hard times when a marriage went south and had had two run-ins with Gary police that involved speeding and eluding the police. Despite this, Montalvo knew and hired the tough, Irish street kid to spar with Kevin when Dawson wasn't available.

After a few sparring sessions, Murtha realized he was up against a powerhouse. Montalvo backed up a bit and told Kevin to slow his punches and work his feet more. Montalvo knew that Kevin had the reach and power to knock out Murtha. So the sparring was a perfunctory exercise to hone Kevin's punch, stressing his fast jab and foot action. Within a few months, he excelled. Montalvo was also aware that the young boxer was quickly becoming a star. Montalvo knew what he had to do.

He started shielding him whenever he suspected someone was trying to muscle in to make a fast buck. Calls came into the gym: so-called promoters promised a lucrative contract, and others just wanted to see Kevin in action. He warned Kevin not to speak to anyone lest he or she be a reporter that would mar his up-to-then stellar rise in the boxing world. His new name, "The Cheetah," had stuck. One of the boxers' girlfriends sent a caricature of Kevin in loin boxing shorts, replete with the words, *The Cheetah*. It got some laughs, but Montalvo shied away from any nicknames, telling Kevin, "I don't give a damn what they or you want to call yourself—when you're here and training, you're concentrating on the fight. Period." The message was clear—stay focused.

Montalvo made sure that Kevin stuck to a rigid routine that included diet, exercise, and rest. To test Kevin's every fiber, Montalvo made sure that Kevin had risen by 4:30 a.m. for a three- to four-mile run. He would page Kevin, having given him a pager in an era predating cell phones. It was 1975; things were changing in America, and technology would eventually usher in the Internet age. But devices such as iPhones would be decades away. The pager went off every morning at 4:30 a.m., Kevin would respond, and Montalvo knew that his main meal ticket was up and about another day. The familiar beep also avoided waking the Evanses upstairs by not using their phone.

Kevin's determination to succeed was only matched by Montalvo and the former boxing champ, Tyrone Dawson. "T" or "Champ," as Dawson was called by most, kept Kevin on the right track. Tough and with an in-your-face-attitude, he kept Kevin focused, often showing up at the front door of Claude Evans's home waiting for Kevin.

The fact that Kevin had a stable environment with the Evans family made his journey easier. They were his extended family, as his sisters and their families had left and remained dysfunctional and oftentimes needy individuals. Either his sisters weren't aware that their brother was on his way to becoming a professional boxer, or they didn't care. It made no difference. Kevin had abandoned them as they had done to him, and he made no attempt to correspond with either sister. When asked whether he would bond in an interview for a local article in the *Gary Morning Journal*, Kevin took a moment before responding: "They're family. Hopefully, they're okay. I wish them the best. If they wanted to contact me, they had a funny way of showing it. They never wrote. But, like I said, they're my family along with my friends and boxing family."

Kevin's comments caused the writer to stop and absorb what was said. The young, aspiring boxer still had a place in his heart for his family. It was probably the result of his dream he had of his mom and his focus on being positive. The Mom's Book entry of the daily word to live by made him reassess his ties with the distant sisters. Kevin's focus was to be positive in all aspects—not dwelling on a past that he couldn't change. He trained harder and harder, and the results were astounding.

Dawson and Montalvo could see the energy, drive, and commitment from Kevin.

During the four hard, enduring months of training, Claude and Yolanda were given some cash by Kevin. The young boxer had a steady cash flow for supplements and protein drinks, plus he was able to pay a rent allowance to Claude and Yolanda. "That's the least I could do for them. If they didn't reach out, I'd be in a bad situation."

Kevin felt blessed that others came forward for him. He especially was impressed with the ex-champ Dawson, who devoted so much time to mold him into a fighting machine. They were so different in many ways. Yet their mutual love of the sport of boxing bonded them. They became friends, as well. Dawson never thought he would gravitate to the upstart White guy who seemed to just walk in and take over.

Skeptical at first, he quickly realized that Kevin indeed was the real thing. He decided to devote his time and energy in getting him to the top as his trainer. Kevin grew to respect and like Tyrone Dawson. He knew he had a short, albeit stellar career as a contender. Aware that emotions were high when Kevin became the center of attention, Dawson ceded his ego and got on board. Dawson felt he could mold Kevin into a dynamo who had more speed, more strength, and more finesse in the ring than he had. Kevin and Dawson soon would swap stories about the boxers that he would have to face.

Dawson invited Kevin to his home, where he met Dawson's wife, Keisha, and their daughter, Monica. They watched Sunday football games while Keisha prepared a home dinner for the aspiring boxer. Dawson gave Kevin sound advice about the pitfalls of fame—the barrage of would-be promoters and the gold diggers at boxing venues ready to seduce.

The resulting outreach to boxing promoters was part of the plan to ensure a good contract for Kevin. In the meantime, he needed a steady flow of cash for essentials. This was part of the agreement Frank Ramirez and Joe Montalvo gave Kevin—a weekly stipend, provided he adhere to the rules. Kevin did just that. He knew a contract was soon to be discussed. He would make some money in upcoming bouts until he got to the big time. His stay at Indiana State indeed molded the "The Cheetah" into a very focused, determined, and stoic individual, set to make his mark. His goal was to make his mark on the boxing world, and no one was going to stop him.

"I'm blessed to have good people in my life. I won't forget them. They were there for me when I was at my lowest." Everything was on track. Unforeseen events would, however, take place. Unforeseen and unexplained events in the dangerous city would impact Kevin once again. They would nearly stop his dream.

CHAPTER TWELVE

Upbeat and ready for his upcoming, big debut at Madison Square Garden, Kevin Bolton was everything a trainer wanted in a boxer—determined, disciplined with his diet and workouts, coupled with a positive attitude. That attitude motivated those lucky enough to be around him.

His daily routine started with the now-familiar pager he set next to the sofa bed in the Evans's basement apartment. It beeped, indicating it was time to rise and get started on his run. These same beepers were used by many not-so-noble people—drug dealers in Gary and other cities. They used them to communicate and pick up or distribute controlled substances that further brought hardship not only to Gary but also many other communities in the nation. While used for practical purposes, such as paging a wandering relative at a mall or warning resident doctors of a life-threatening situation via Code Blue, the pager was a precursor of later technological advances in cyber world. It would, like most inventions, be used for good and bad. For Kevin, it was his means to an end—his meal ticket. Like an alarm clock, it awakened him to get out and begin his routine. The mean streets of Gary soon saw the shadowy figure of the determined young pugilist running in the predawn hours in the darkened and forbidding streets of the city.

It was the '70s, an era that saw further erosion in cities like Gary due to industrial layoffs and a permissive attitude toward drugs, resulting in cheap vials of freebase cocaine on the street corners of LA, Chicago, New York, and small communities in between. Epidemic and controlling, it caused a great deal of angst for families. Starting in 1974, it would within a year spread to cities large and small, and eventually in the 1980s, it would contribute to a disturbing uptick in crime with the introduction of crack.

In Gary, while Kevin was training, freebase cocaine or "white tornado" was hitting the streets. The murder rate soared, and mothers avoided sending their kids out to playgrounds and parks that were now shooting galleries and places to buy and sell coke. It was the start of the downward cycle of drugs affecting large and medium cities, and later small-town America. The War on Drugs, used by politicians to get votes, didn't often address the societal woes of unemployment, racism, poverty, and abuse. Instead, stricter sentences were called for, and the scared electorate agreed. Kevin's arrest a few years earlier for an illegal, albeit nonviolent, purchase of marijuana sent a signal of incarceration over any rehabilitation. By 1975, the country wanted to curb the downward spiral and passed legislation that resulted in punitive and long-term sentences.

Cocaine was mixed with nonpolar solvent, such as ether or benzene separated into two layers. The solvent then evaporated and heated into layers of coke "rock." Put into straw-like pipes, they could be smoked, resulting in a habit that was lethal and hard to break. The sale of extraction kits and smoking accessories soon became a lucrative underground market for dealers with users hooked on the powerful mixture. Self-administered via smoking, the drug soon wreaked havoc on vulnerable towns like Gary. It affected all classes, from the wealthy kids to street sellers who wanted to make a quick buck. Cities and small towns soon had to address the plague.

Local police and federal agencies found themselves grappling with laws that would be stringent and harsh. Laws were passed, but for the hooked addict, it meant nothing. The cities suffered with soaring crime rates and a diminished quality of life. Pagers were used to initiate sales from street corners to high school corridors to small city parks. The cheap vials soon got many hooked, and the ascending crime rate was indicative of a society that hadn't come to terms with the crack epidemic. Celebrities such as Richard Pryor would become victim to the lure of the quick high with catastrophic results.

Cities like Gary saw an increase in crime, testing the resources of the once proud Steel City. One motorist told of being escorted out of a particular drug-infested area after driving to the wrong exit on the highway. In an interview that got attention, he shared that he was told by a sympathetic police officer "not to stop for red lights or stop signs." Such was the impact of the drug culture on cities that local law enforcement grappled with on a daily basis. The pager—or beeper—was scorned by many, and eventually schools started to check students' tote bags, confiscating them in the hope of reducing drug dealing within the schools.

It was different for Kevin. The beeper had a different purpose. The daily *beep* was a godsend; it was his alarm clock, sending him on his way. He was positive and knew his debut was forthcoming. He set out on his daily run as usual at 4:30 a.m. Getting out of bed, normally a challenge, was easier. Joe Montalvo and Tyrone Dawson had finally come through. They worked so hard to make sure he was a full package. Kevin got to like, respect, and feel good around Dawson. He was real, not a phony or washed-up, angry, and envious boxer. Instead, Tyrone Dawson gave his all to Kevin. "He's the real deal; he's going places" was his response to a fellow retired boxer who inquired about the ascendant Kevin.

It was spring 1975. Kevin was getting noticed by the right people. He had a contract now. He was interviewed not only in the greater Chicago market but also on national TV. The gym had never witnessed such enthusiasm. Owner Frank Ramirez was ecstatic that both Montalvo and Dawson had a would-be champ-in-waiting. It would raise the morale in the tested city and give a sense of pride to a native of the city who stayed and didn't join the flight from Gary. Southside Gym became a topic of discussion in the very troubled city. "Kevin Bolton is a breath of fresh air for us and the city," Montalvo told the press once Kevin's contract was signed. By the time the lucrative contract was offered, Kevin had fought and won several amateur bouts and made his debut in Chicago a few weeks earlier, knocking out his opponent in the second round.

Putting on his gray jogging pants and matching hoodie, he smiled when he looked in the small mirror above the wash basin in Claude Evans's basement apartment. "I'm finally on my way to at least make a name of myself. Wish my mom were here to see it. Madison Square Garden—wow!" He was in good spirits despite the slippery, wet pavement from a brief downpour earlier that cool April morning. The quiet spring morning was interrupted only by a few chirping sparrows in nearby trees as he picked up his pace on the still-dark streets on the city's south end. Eerily quiet, Kevin was warned not to wear a headset to listen to music as he jogged.

"The city has problems now; don't become a statistic," warned Joe Montalvo when Kevin began his daily routine a few months earlier.

"Not to worry, man. I got my back covered," Kevin reassured him.

"Don't be a hero; stick to your program. This mess is getting outta control here with the drugs and jobs leaving." Montalvo looked squarely at Kevin, knowing what the dangers of jogging, walking, or being alone in darkened streets could bring. He added, "You may be young and tough and think you're invincible, but don't press your luck—as I said, stick to your workouts and focus on what's going to happen."

Kevin, a product of the city and a felon, was not naive. However, like many young people, he felt he could withstand any dangers that may creep upon him. Up to then, his jogging, stretching, and push-ups outside were uneventful, witnessed only by a few passers-by and bench-warming homeless people along the edge of the park. His daily jog, now familiar to some early risers also, was a welcome sight. Yet, the danger always lurked.

An optimist at heart, with his daily Mom's Book entry, he was euphoric and anticipating a long career in boxing and making it big. Somewhat of a visionary, he thought of his life down the road and liked the fact that he would probably be financially successful and eventually marry and raise a family in a great suburban neighborhood.

He was lonely—he hadn't been on a date, having kept a low profile and concentrating on his upcoming bouts. Yet, like most people, he longed for someone. The warning from Montalvo resonated with him, "You got plenty of time for the broads; keep it in your pants! Focus on your training right now." For now, the emphasis was on getting in the ring and displaying to the world what power he possessed. Yes, he would wait, as uneasy and routinely boring as his life was at the moment.

He was out on his morning jog, like clockwork. Dedicated and ever mindful of the upcoming bouts, he knew he had to be at his best. Kevin looked around at the changing landscape in the stark early morning. The leaves on the trees suggested that the cycle of life continued with the burgeoning undergrowth of weeds that were unattended in the park and alongside the broken cement sidewalk. The trees budding forth leaves gave a more aesthetic look to the dreary surroundings of abandoned buildings and several burnt-out cars parked permanently adjacent to the park.

These unsightly vehicles, plus the unattended parks and playgrounds, made the poor citizens ever aware of what might occur. The garbage, left unattended, sent a malodorous scent that permeated the otherwise clear, crisp early spring morning. For Kevin, these mornings were his real wake-up call. Despite the dreary scenes around him, the early morning light slowly creeping between the clouds made the optimistic boxer feel good. He saw some good in his city—a city he would not give up on. "Like Gary, I'll bounce back. I'll be good, all good."

The leaves on the elm and maple trees were starting to sprout forth after a tough winter, giving some life to a city in need. Despite the city's problems, the prospect of a new beginning that spring morning put Kevin in a good mood. A few blocks from the stench of the garbage, the air smelled fresh after the early downpour. "Amazing how just a few blocks changes everything." He was now near the projects, which were struggling to survive the crack epidemic. They still showed signs of life with benches that weren't ruined and a nearby playground that was still maintained.

It was just a regular day, he assumed. He soon passed the

now-familiar figures of needy, derelict winos and a few homeless stretched out on park benches. The landscape changed once again. He waved to them, and he felt for them. Their condition motivated him further to try to do some good things for the city that industry and government seemed to abandon. He took a deep breath; absorbing the crisp air. It seemed to do the trick. "The air is crisp. It's better here—don't smell the garbage. I feel good today. I should do this routine without the bad smells of the city. The rain cleaned up the stench."

He felt powerful that day. Defying the warnings given to him by Montalvo, he took out his headset and decided he needed to relax. He placed a Barry White tape in his cassette case and listened to the melodic tunes. White's sultry voice made him relax. He especially liked "You're My Everything." He thought of making love to a beautiful woman, and it put some sparkle in his life. Kevin looked around. With no one in sight, he knew music indeed soothed him, and the daily grind wasn't so bad after all. As he ran, he thought of the rapport he established with Tyrone Dawson. "A great champ and a great trainer and friend. I'm fortunate."

He and Dawson had much in common. Both were from dysfunctional families that struggled. Dawson's mother worked as a domestic for a wealthy Toledo family, often working weekends, as well. Kevin appreciated Dawson. Kevin knew he didn't have to channel his energy to some upstart White kid who had nothing.

But they bonded well. They liked the same music—especially the likes of Def Jam Records with Grandmaster Flash and the new, innovative mixing of sounds using scratching to get the unique sound. Music brought the two polar opposites together. They liked disco music, also—Van McCoy's "The Hustle," which was a big hit.

Dawson had finally gravitated toward Bolton. He realized that

Kevin had the combination that made a complete package—speed, hard jabs, good movement with his feet, and use of his body in a rhythmic dance to evade the jabs thrown at him. He was also hungry—anxious to make his mark on the world. Dawson came to the conclusion that Kevin was indeed everything he wanted to be.

Deep down, Tyrone Dawson, a brief champion belt–holder, knew that his protégé—this White kid—had heart and was, in fact, a better fighter than he. Dawson's frustration in the ring now transcended to a rigorous program to get Kevin to the top. He wanted Kevin to go all the way. He wanted him to avoid the mistakes he made in the ring. He had been a contender with the greats in the ring of the 1970s—Ali, Norton, Foreman, Frazier, and Cooney. Dawson liked what he and Montalvo had created—a fast-jabbing dynamo—in Kevin Bolton. Criticized by some for helping "that White boy," Dawson knew that Kevin's success would reap some rewards for him and his wife and kid. He swallowed his pride as a former contender and latched onto a rising star. "The kid has what it takes, period," Dawson said to one of his former opponents in the ring. "You'll soon be hearing about him."

Thanks to Montalvo and Dawson, Kevin's progress started to show. It was clearly evident that the hard work, long hours, constant sparring and jumping rope, and jogging were paying off. Lloyd Hopkins, the sage of Southside, stopped sweeping one morning and, turning to Joe Montalvo, said, "I thought I'd never see live to see this—a Gary boy who has the chance to go all the way. Yep, he's got it, and he can do it. He's got the stuff—all put together, yes sir, the total package." This assessment by Hopkins meant much to Montalvo.

He knew Kevin was ready for the big stage in boxing. Montalvo, keenly aware of the possibility of Kevin's power in the ring, wanted to wait a few months to polish his fighter before introducing him to the boxing world. Montalvo was careful, making sure that young Kevin stuck to his rigorous schedule of exercise, rest, and diet. Montalvo knew that Kevin, however great in the ring, still had personal issues that haunted him. He liked the fact that he kept in his possession his Mom's Book with a daily word to live by. *Trust* was the word for this week.

Kevin, ever a doubting Thomas, had trouble gravitating to others. That was one reason why he didn't write while incarcerated—he felt he was a failure and that no one would be there for him. Given his life up until then, rejection, hurt, pain, and suspicion all combined to keep him wary. It took the likes of Montalvo, Dawson, and the blessing from Ramirez to get him on track. Once there, he was a nonstop dynamo, aggressive and ambitious. Ready for any opponent, he was indeed hungry to be in the game.

Still, Kevin had known hardships and hurts, and didn't want to disappoint himself. Like the struggling city of Gary, he knew he had to listen, learn, and change. The city was a reminder of a once-proud place, now coping with loss of jobs overseas. Kevin didn't like what he saw on his daily jogs. Gary was his home, his only home, and he didn't like the sights of homeless people, addicts, burnt-out buildings used by squatters to shoot up, and the constant fear of crime. He used the headset only once a week to relax. It was also to distract him from the noise and sirens of passing fire and police vehicles. He knew the danger of using it, yet he was circumspect, careful not to listen in more crime-ridden areas. "If Montalvo and even T know I'm breaking their rule, they'd be pissed. I know the city is bad, but I'm pumped and feel good."

Like his native hometown, he witnessed in his young life good and bad episodes. Now a free man, he had a second chance. Yes,

Gary was going through hard times. He saw the misery every day. The steel mills, once the heart of the city's booming economy that attracted many poor Black people to flee the segregated South and hungry Europeans looking for a better life, had closed. With no jobs, many packed up and left. At least, those who could afford to. They started to leave. The poor—mostly Black with some Hispanic and poor White people like Kevin—remained. The tax base started to dry up, and with it, so did social services. Gary became symptomatic of Rust Belt cities struggling to survive in a changing economy that had forgotten its working-class base. Stores closed, and neighborhoods started to become dangerous with vacant homes used by homeless and squatters. Soon, drugs and crime followed. People avoided the city, and the schools, churches, and businesses all started to feel the effects of the economic downturn. The term "Rust Belt" aptly applied to Gary and other cities that once provided so much to America.

Kevin witnessed the deteriorating quality of life in the city. He was angered by the White flight. Gary was indeed his home. His only home. People avoided the city with the rise in crime and loss of jobs in the steel mills. He felt for his city. These daily runs motivated him to persevere. The sights of the once-thriving area he knew as a kid bothered him. The homeless people on the benches seemed to grow during the four months of intense training. "Not all of us are winos, hoes, or druggies," he heard one middle-aged man say to him after a brief hello on his daily run.

It made Kevin stop and take a hard look at life. Despite what he had been through, these individuals, once working and proud, had nowhere to go. He wished he could do something positive. He felt especially for the families with kids. In some way, his dogged determination was replicated by Gary's resident population that remained and wanted to bounce back. He wouldn't leave and would carry on. He had his extended family of Yolanda and Claude Evans, Joe Montalvo, Tyrone Dawson, Lloyd Hopkins, and the boxers and the steady onlookers at the gym. He was no quitter. He had a dream. Not just a dream for himself but a dream for the city.

"If I can bounce back, maybe the city can, too."

That dream of his mom while in jail never left him. Almost like an apparition from beyond like the Virgin at Fátima, he knew it was something. The haunting words of his mom never left him: "Don't give up. Follow your dream, son." It was as if a vision from heaven had touched him. Never much for religion, that dream did the trick for him.

"Maybe it was Mom's way—she always looked out for me." It was a game changer for him. He took the dream seriously and used it as a metaphor for life. It would change him. The daily and weekly words would be his motivation to excel. That day, he wrote the word *endurance* in his Mom's Book.

His workouts became ever challenging, and yet he rose up to the occasion. A pleased Montalvo and Dawson knew that Kevin had special inner qualities. "He's hungry, I can see that," remarked Ramirez, who would step out of his spartan office and check on his boxers. Ramirez, like Montalvo and Dawson, was pleased that they had a showcase boxer who would propel them, as well, into the boxing world. It also would help the much-needed gym get recognition in the tough city. And Kevin—he wouldn't disappoint. His steadfast workout now consisted of jumping rope more times, more shadowboxing while jogging, and keeping his focus on the jabs.

Sharp, solid, and very fast, Kevin's quick responses surprised even Joe Montalvo. And it showed. Dawson also noticed the rapid changes. "He's focusing more on head movement and the important foot work," Dawson remarked after a long day at the gym. Both

Montalvo and Dawson realized that they created a nonstop dynamo, who would soon be the topic of correspondents, pundits, and boxing fans.

"The Cheetah is living up to his name," old Lloyd Hopkins said to Montalvo. "Mark my words, that boy is going to give all those big boxers from Ali, Frazier, Norton, and Holmes a run for the money. He may not beat all of them or even none of them, but he's going places. Yes sir, that White boy is going places." Hopkins was correct. He had indeed seen it all. The Cheetah now was indeed getting attention in the boxing world.

Dawson marveled at Kevin's control of the heavy bag. "I wish that I could have unloaded such power in the ring." Indeed, Kevin had greatly increased his punching power, hitting the bag hard with a barrage of punches.

"He's sharp, solid, very fast with his jabs, and completely in control," remarked Dawson after a very intense workout. Dawson noticed the transformation—the heavy bag was unloaded upon with speed and a rapid volley of punches. Kevin increased his punching power, hitting the bag as hard as he could. Sweat pouring down his brow, he resorted to wearing a yellow bandana to catch the sweat from getting in his eyes. Soon, another yellow bandana was given to him by the young, admiring boxer, Holley, with the word *Cheetah* on it. It provided a much-needed laugh to the serious regimen.

Kevin, focused, hungry, and ready, didn't disappoint. Routine after routine kept getting more grueling and intense. Both Montalvo and Dawson felt that the young dynamo was destined for greatness. They had to search for sparring partners who could just last a few rounds with Kevin. Dawson and Montalvo, satisfied with the rapid progress made by the young boxer, knew he was ready for the big time. "It's his time," Joe Montalvo remarked to Ramirez in the presence of the loyal Lloyd Hopkins.

Nodding at Montalvo, Hopkins added, "I haven't seen such power in the years I've been here. The boy's ready for big time; yes, sir, he's more than ready." This frank assessment brought smiles to both the proud owner and Joe Montalvo.

Kevin's resolve to succeed was relentless. His workouts showed remarkable progress. Each day, he got more intense and more involved in his overall routine. Montalvo admitted, "I've trained a lot of boxers; never have I seen such power come from a glove like that." Continuous and repetitive exercises built strength, amazing anyone who saw Kevin in action. The young boxers, hopeful on their way to the Golden Gloves, marveled at their idol. Holley and Aquino, after their workouts, would stay and watch the champ-in-making perform. It helped them focus and develop their own strategy with the help of their trainers.

Kevin Bolton had indeed touched many with his boxing skills. He would check his Mom's Book each day before and after a workout to see if he lived up to the word of the day. It was a motivational and somewhat spiritual guide for him. It kept him going as his routine kept getting more challenging. To develop more strength, before his daily run, he would unload a barrage of calisthenic exercises that consisted of an incredible three hundred push-ups, two hundred pull-ups, three hundred sit-ups, and one hundred leg raises, all highlighted by a three-mile run along the periphery of the adjoining Glen Park. He would perform these exercises in series of several repetitions. He pushed himself to the limit, even when Montalvo and Dawson told him to break for a few minutes. "Nah, got to finish the push-ups or pull-ups or jump rope." It was all Kevin. He was center stage and in total control.

He knew that his time in the ring was his meal ticket, and he was hungry for the upcoming title fight. It affected his personality, making him a positive and likable person. He indeed did change from the dysfunctional, angry, and bellicose young man of just a few years back. And he was ready, having gone through so much in his young life.

Kevin, anticipating his big coming out at the premiere showcase at Madison Square Garden just a month away, was in a buoyant mood. He didn't let anything deter him. He never complained about the early hours running in all kinds of weather. He never complained about the restrictions placed upon him from socializing at clubs, bars, and restaurants. He didn't complain about the offers he had to turn down when pretty, young, and not-so-pretty and not-so-young women sent him messages at the gym.

Dawson and Kevin would go to a local diner once a week and informally discuss strategies. Often, Kevin would attract the eyes of young women. Dawson, himself in good shape and decent looking, would find it amusing. Having been the center of attention in many of his travels when boxing, he was a good mentor in this regard. "Be careful with who you meet. Focus first on your boxing. The good stuff will follow," Dawson added one afternoon after Kevin spotted a young lady smiling at him over lunch at the diner.

Kevin knew he had a job to do and wouldn't let anything stay in the way. It was apparent to anyone in the gym who witnessed Kevin's progress in the last several months. "You created a monster," remarked the affable old custodian, Lloyd Hopkins, after seeing a brutal and quick sparring episode at Southside between Dawson and Kevin.

Dawson, ever the realist, added, "Kev would have knocked me out in the first round." Dawson's candid assessment was evident. It was clear to everyone that Kevin Bolton was the rising star in the boxing world. The question remained: Just how far could he go?

The new year of 1975 held a lot of promise for Kevin. The upcoming bout at the Garden originally slated as an undercard event was quickly moved up to the main event as a result of his meteoric rise in the boxing world. *The Ring* interview plus a national TV introduction on *60 Minutes* added to his ascending popularity and curiosity in the boxing world.

Charming and with an infectious smile, the handsome young man with the golden locks came off on the *60 Minutes* interview as a shy, polite, yet steady and determined person. The interviewer also referred to him as "The Cheetah." When asked how the name came about, smiling, he gave credit to a homeless man who saw him every day running and jogging. He shouted out to him: "There goes The Cheetah." Every day, the man would shout: "Here comes The Cheetah." The name stuck. Like it or not, Kevin would be The Cheetah. People started taking notice of the fast-climbing boxer and wanted to capitalize on his fame.

After the national exposure that the *60 Minutes* interview generated, daily calls came in from magazines and publishing houses asking for more information. Montalvo made sure that the public was kept at bay. "Don't get a big head, kiddo," Montalvo told Kevin after he received a few alluring letters sent to the gym from wannabes. He and Dawson had a job to do. It was to protect Kevin from these wannabe exploiters. Kevin hadn't been tested on the national scene. The upcoming bout at the Garden would seal the deal, making him a household name. Montalvo didn't want Kevin to be seduced by the adulation from fans, press, and greedy promoters who wanted a piece of him. As for Kevin, he had already won four easy bouts—all by knockouts—and was hungry to strut his stuff at the Garden. He would often bring up the fight from the previous fall between Ali and Foreman. It had a profound effect on the newly released prisoner.

"Ali did it, and I can do it, too—come back and win."

Dawson and Kevin bonded well and learned to respect each other. They were different yet the same. They were different in race but alike in temperament. They were different yet bonded by their love of the sport. They were competitors. They knew they were in an elite group that had witnessed triumphs and tragedies. Dawson, initially a bit jealous of the upstart White kid, warmed up to him once Kevin's uniqueness and power were evident. Dawson learned to respect him.

Kevin, in turn, looked up to Dawson. Kevin knew that Dawson hadn't fulfilled his mission in getting a world belt but had many important and notable fights. They needed each other and worked well together. Kevin appreciated the time, effort, and lessons he learned from Dawson. Once Dawson got to know Kevin, they respected and trusted one another. Kevin listened to Dawson, who he felt should have gotten more recognition for his boxing prowess.

Dawson, in turn, liked the intensity that Kevin put into his routine. He had been there, and despite the fact that he would no longer be the center of attention, he latched onto Kevin and wanted him to go the distance. Dawson knew how instant fame could change a person. He became a mentor socially, telling Kevin about the dangers he'd face once his name and his talent drew attention. "Beware of the barracudas out there—both men and women." Kevin didn't need any explanation. He had heard it from Montalvo and Hopkins, too.

Kevin and Dawson also became good friends. And Kevin needed someone other than Montalvo to be with and have a dialogue. Kevin and Dawson were closer in age. They understood each other.

Dawson had seen it all and wanted Kevin to go the distance without the lure and temptations of making a rash decision once fame and fortune came his way. Dawson was also a faithful person to his wife and to his dedication to the sport of boxing. He instilled good values in Kevin.

For the first time in his life, Kevin had someone who cared about him and took the time to mold him into the champ he wished he could have been. Dawson came on the scene at the right time. We need people in our lives to help in all situations who are unafraid and willing to share their own good and bad events. For Kevin, that person was Tyrone Dawson.

The ex-champ now lived outside Gary in a nice house and drove a BMW. With the money he earned, he was able to provide some amenities in his life to his wife and kid—a ranch-style home in the affluent suburb of Munster, thirteen miles from Gary. Having himself gone through hard times growing up, Dawson wanted Kevin to succeed. He knew that Kevin had a rough family life with few friends or positive role models. He was there for Kevin. They in turn not only trusted one another but also grew to like each other.

After a few weeks of hard training, Dawson had both Kevin and Joe Montalvo over for Sunday dinner. His wife, gracious and impeccably dressed after Sunday service, wore a red dress with white pearls. "The pearls were a gift from Tyrone on our fifth anniversary," she added after Kevin complimented her on her attire.

"Damn, it's been a long season without rain—I could use some solid female company right now." Kevin, knowing how important it was for him to dismiss any relationships right now, still felt the need. Keisha embodied what he saw in a woman—strong, attentive, caring, attractive, and loving. He was envious of Dawson yet happy for him.

Keisha Dawson sang in the choir at her local Baptist church and stayed active in community affairs. She also loved to entertain and was a great cook. She prepared a pork roast complete with mixed vegetables of peas and corn, plus sweet potatoes, salad, and Boston cream pie for dessert. Keisha, sensing Kevin's shyness, knew she had to make the young man feel at home. "So tell me, Mr. Bolton, is my husband killing you yet? Is he making you think twice about him as your trainer?" Smiling and looking at Kevin, Keisha wanted Kevin to feel at home and relaxed.

Looking at a smiling Dawson, he added, "Yeah, he is. Please, call me Kevin or Kev." This started a bit of bantering back and forth between Dawson and Kevin.

"You don't know what's coming next. Just wait till I get you back in the ring tomorrow." More laughs followed.

Keisha, a third-grade teacher and part-time worker at Walmart, had a magnetic personality that made her a favorite with family and friends. She took charge in potluck dinners at her church when an elderly congregant, Maxine Logan, had a hip replacement as a result of a fall. Her potluck dinners were a favorite and raised money for her church activities, such as the daycare center, and organization of a youth program that included basketball and baseball in a nearby rented facility in Munster. She also could get others to help and delegated duties that made for a smooth event both at her church and at school. Keisha was liked by her colleagues. The school's principal, Maureen Murphy, asked her to consider an administrative job at the school, with an increase in salary. She had to turn her offer down, stating that she was a full-time mom and didn't want to be far from her family.

Dawson never wavered. Supportive and always attentive, their marriage to an outsider seemed a perfect union. He had saved much of his earnings, and they led a very middle-class, suburban lifestyle. Keisha, of course, always worried about Dawson driving his classy BMW into Gary. She often told him to use her smaller Chevy. "I'll get less notice and won't be the object of people set out to rob." The boxer in Tyrone Dawson told her not to worry. Yet she did, as often as when he was on the road at various boxing venues. "Gary isn't safe anymore; you need to drive my Chevy." Dawson reassured his wife that he took caution on the way to Southside Gym.

Her concern was real, viewing the news summary on the local TV stations, which showed a sharp rise in crime in Gary. Dawson, a tough, determined fighter, was afraid of no one and wouldn't compromise when it came to his prized BMW. "Nobody's gonna bother me," he boasted to his wife.

When Dawson traveled or was training in another state or country, he called every day.

He stayed loyal at the height of his boxing career despite being away for bouts. The handsome Dawson often noticed a few females in hotel lobbies after his fights or outside an arena. He thwarted the temptations by going only to dinner with his trainer and ringman despite the advances from women and hangers-on. That loyalty was part of his upbringing. He remained a trustworthy person in every aspect, from marriage to friends. "You have to have trust and faith in yourself—without it, you're nothing." Tyrone lived by this code, and it made him a favorite in the boxing world.

Not arrogant or demanding, trainers liked the easygoing, laid-back boxer who treated everyone with respect. Ever loyal to Kevin, too, he had already warned Kevin, as did Montalvo, that once he was in the limelight, others would want a part of him. "Promoters will tempt you and try to lure you away from Montalvo and me."

Shaking his head, Kevin replied, "I won't let it happen—even if I go the distance." Kevin appreciated the advice from Dawson. Feeling comfortable in the comfort of Tyrone and Keisha's home in Munster made Kevin hope one day to replicate by having a family—the family that had eluded him.

Keisha was indeed a great asset for Dawson. Originally from Tulsa, she met Dawson when he was fighting in a fundraiser bout in Enid, Oklahoma. She was in her last year as an education major at Oklahoma State University. When introduced to the boxer, Dawson was smitten by her reserved and gracious demeanor. They seemed to have a lot in common. They had started calling and writing, and within a year, they were married in Tulsa. Their marriage was solid; Kevin could see how much they loved each other. They were a couple that he both envied and was grateful to call friends.

For Kevin Bolton—the poor White kid who most thought would never amount to anything and never ventured anywhere—this was a wake-up call. Montalvo had picked him up in his car for the fifteen-minute drive to Munster. Montalvo could see the sparkle in Kevin's eyes as they left Gary for the more suburban setting. Kevin admired the location, thinking that perhaps one day he could live in a nice, new home with a manicured lawn, picket fence, and stable environment. But Kevin liked the city of Gary and knew he was attached to it. For a moment, it was nice to daydream and wonder if this life and suburban environment would be appealing.

Kevin was in awe at the ranch-style home in Munster that Dawson and Keisha lived in. Keisha had Ethan Allen furniture that was classy, expensive, and indicative of their lifestyle. He especially liked the den area that had pictures, magazine articles, and trophies from Dawson's meteoric rise as a winner of the Golden Gloves to a professional boxer. "Someday, I'll have this, too—a great house with a special room to showcase my career. Don't know where—maybe even in Gary if we can get the city to change."

Dawson had a positive impact on Kevin's lonely life, and Kevin liked the order and calmness surrounding him in Munster. The den, with the triumphs of Dawson's career, motivated him further. Indeed, Kevin had already started an album in Southside containing magazine articles, pictures, and newspaper clips on his recent fights in Chicago and nearby Crown Point. Dawson told Kevin he could have even more, given his talents and the fact that he would have the opportunity to go further toward a world heavyweight champion belt than he ever had.

Kevin admired Dawson. He had a family, financial success from his career as a boxer, gave pep talks to the boxers at Southside, and had his picture on the Wall of Fame. Kevin appreciated the time, effort, and challenges that Tyrone Dawson, the champ, had given him. "He could have trained someone who had already gone pro; I'm glad that he stayed loyal to Montalvo, me, and the gym."

Their differences were diminished when it came to mutual interests—boxing, music, and movies. Their taste in music—rap, jazz, and disco—coincided. Both Dawson and Kevin liked these genres. They also found common ground in action movies from Bruce Lee to Jim Kelly. When it came to food, their love of burgers and fries—despite the ban placed on Kevin for the duration—made for a good chat. They discussed boxing, football, women, and sex. As friends, they learned to depend upon one another.

Disappointed by his fall from grace when he was at the top of his career, Dawson felt he had a second chance at life by staying in the game. One releasee was helping the young Kevin Bolton. Having observed him sparring, he knew he had what it took to go on and make a nice living as a boxer.

Once he came on board and became assistant trainer with Montalvo, he plunged into his role as a person who could transcend from a retired, jaded, and somewhat depressed ex-boxer to a viable and competent asset in Kevin's journey. He, too, would remind Kevin that Ali, despite the problems of having the belt taken from him, resurrected his moribund career to again become a world champ. "Think of yourself as a young man who bounced back," Dawson remarked to Kevin after a brief discussion about the challenges of reentering the world of boxing. It was a good mix to have a seasoned professional mold the young, cocky, and now confident young man.

Dawson knew that boxing could be dirty. It was a sport with a lot of hangers-on, phony promoters, and a fan base that quickly dried up once you started losing. Dawson had been there. He had been at the top and soon fell out once his losses in the ring added up. His interest, now directed at the young Gary boxer, ensured that Kevin would go the distance. With Montalvo and him, Kevin could face any formidable challenger and be a contender for the title. He and Montalvo sounded the message to Kevin Bolton—don't let your guard down, both in and out of the ring. Dawson's presence and expertise motivated Kevin, and the pair got along well.

Feeling good, Kevin knew he would be the center of attention soon. He was ready. Little did he know that unforeseen events would soon challenge his goals.

CHAPTER THIRTEEN

A few days after dining at the Dawsons, Kevin was back on his routine morning jog when he heard his beeper go off. It was Montalvo. He thought nothing of it, as Montalvo usually beeped him during his run. "It's a little early, but I guess he wants to make sure I'm doing it." Montalvo paged Kevin two more times within five minutes. Kevin was in the middle of his three-mile run. "He knows I'm jogging; maybe he or T won't make it to the gym today, but I still have a sparring routine with a few guys. He's never paged me this much." Placing the pager in his deep jogging pocket, he continued his run. Inside, something didn't feel right. He couldn't put his finger on it. There was something happening. He continued on his run.

Kevin had heard the screeching sounds of two patrol cars speeding by. It was not unusual, given the early morning and the lure of drug sales at night. He had experienced this before a few times. He wouldn't let it deter him from his morning run. "Probably out to bring down another drug deal." Kevin's mind was on the upcoming fight; he momentarily dismissed a fourth page from Montalvo. "Damn, Joe, let me finish my run. If you can't make it today, T and I will still get it going." After the last beep, Kevin knew that something was amiss and needed immediate attention. Deep inside, Kevin had a bad feeling about the incessant beeps.

"Something's not right." As he picked up his pace toward the end of his run, he noticed an ambulance speeding by. He stopped jogging. He didn't know why; a racing ambulance never made him stop. In the early hours before 6 a.m., when crime was rife, emergency vehicle sirens were not an uncommon sound. For some reason, today's noisy siren made him stop. As if it were an omen, he stood dead in his tracks. He looked in the direction of the ambulance as it raced in the direction of the nearest hospital, which he knew was a few blocks away. "Got a weird feeling something isn't right. Joe keeps beeping me."

He again looked at his pager, which had two more requests to call. At that point, Kevin knew this wasn't good, as Montalvo never interrupted his routine in such a manner. He had had four beeps within the last six minutes. "All this going on this morning can't be good. Hell no, it can't be good." Unprecedented and unexpected, these pages sent a clear message to the aspiring boxer—connect with Joe Montalvo. There was something that needed attention now. Without any knowledge of possible events that had taken place, Kevin decided to curtail his important daily routine.

Kevin walked briskly back to his basement apartment at Claude Evans's home, nearly bumping into a passerby when distracted by yet another beep on the pager.

By the time Kevin finished his morning run, which was usually a bit after 6 a.m., Yolanda and Claude were usually up getting ready for work and waiting for the Khalid's babysitter, Marge Brown, to arrive. Yolanda, an early riser, usually opened the office where she worked, preparing coffee for the staff. Before heading for work, she usually had breakfast for Claude and Kevin. It worked out well. And Marge Young lived a street away.

A very punctual, reliable, and caring elder, she doted on little Khalid. A widowed grandmother in her late sixties, the gray-haired, diminutive lady had experience raising four children and was there when needed. On occasion, she joined the Evanses and Kevin for breakfast.

As Kevin neared the Evans' home, he noticed something different. The lights in his basement apartment were on. It was unusual. Yolanda and Claude had never gone downstairs before he returned and had time to shower and come up for breakfast. He picked up his pace. "Something isn't right at all." Saying a silent prayer, he knew he had to get to his basement apartment.

Kevin entered the apartment. "Something ain't right here. No, something is wrong."

Claude, hearing Kevin's approach, opened the door. Claude said nothing. Yolanda was holding Khalid. She didn't look Kevin in the eye. Somehow, it didn't seem normal. Kevin noticed that Claude and Yolanda were looking solemn and looking at each other. Kevin instinctively knew there was bad news. But what was happening?

"Good morning." Kevin, feeling uncomfortable, didn't know what else to add. He expected Claude and Yolanda to greet him. They just stared at each other. Claude was clearly uncomfortable.

"Kevin." Claude stared at Yolanda for a few seconds that seemed longer and continued, "Joe Montalvo called us ten minutes ago. He wants you to get to the gym right now."

Kevin got out his pager, as it was beeping once again. "This is the sixth time he's beeped me. What's going on? Is something wrong?" Kevin's instinctive curiosity took over.

“I don’t know.” Yolanda let out an audible sigh, suggesting otherwise. Claude continued, “It’s best that you go the gym. Joe called here about ten minutes ago and told us that he had sent several pages to you on your beeper. When he called here, just before you got here, he said that something happened. I didn’t press him, as I really don’t know him. I’m going to drive you to the gym. It’s 6:20, and Joe said he’d be there early.”

Handing Kevin a bottled water after his run, Yolanda, with a forced smile, proceeded upstairs, carrying Khalid. Marge Young was due at 6:45. As Yolanda started up the stairs, she looked back at Kevin. Pursing her lips, she continued up the narrow wooden stairs, shaking her head a bit. Kevin knew a very serious situation existed.

Kevin looked at his uncomfortable friend. He could see that Claude was struggling to say something. It was all so bizarre. Kevin took a deep breath. He knew he had to get some information now. “This doesn’t sound good. Do you know what’s happened? Is it something about my upcoming fight?” Kevin looked at Claude, hoping he would ease the suspense.

“He didn’t say.” Claude, clearly nervous and feeling uncomfortable, added, “All he said was, ‘tell Kevin to come the gym right away. Don’t bother showering. Just get here.’”

From the look on Claude Evans’s face, Kevin, recalling the sight of police vehicles and an ambulance, and with an uncomfortable gut feeling, suddenly thought aloud, “Oh, Christ, did something happen to Tyrone? I heard lots of sirens, saw an ambulance, and just got a crazy feeling inside.”

He looked at Claude, who finally looked him squarely in the eyes and said: “I’m going to drive you to the gym. You need to be there. Joe wants you there now. Let’s go.” Grabbing his car keys, he told Kevin, “Come on, Kev. Joe is waiting.”

Normally, Kevin would walk the twelve minutes to Southside Gym, a distance of nearly a mile. This morning, as he got into Claude's Chevy Impala, he turned to Claude and said, "I know some damn thing has happened."

Claude, turning the car onto the street that would take them directly to the gym, glanced at Kevin, adding, "Whatever it is, you got a fight coming down soon. You've done so much and are so ready. Remember that; you've been working your butt off getting ready." Kevin, speechless, knew deep down that Claude probably was aware of what happened.

I better not press him further; he and his wife have been so good.

Within seven minutes, Claude pulled up in front of the gym. Two Gary police cars were in front of the gym. Kevin gave Claude Evans a look that only can be described as having fear in his eyes, knowing full well that a devastating event had occurred. Kevin got out and asked, "You coming in?"

"No, I got to get back and drive Yolanda to work as I usually do. But, promise me this—call me. You have my number at the bus station. The direct number for the dispatcher—right?"

Kevin didn't fully register his remarks, his mind preoccupied by a chain of fast events he couldn't and didn't want to understand. "I know this isn't good; I see the cop cars." Kevin looked heavenward as if in silent prayer. Looking at Claude, he added, "This sucks." Turning to Claude, he registered the request to call at Claude's dispatcher office. "Yeah, I do have your number. Thanks, Claude." There was nothing else to say. Closing the car door, he proceeded into the gym.

Since the gym had just opened at 6 a.m., two boxers ready to spar plus Lloyd Hopkins and Frank Ramirez were present. Kevin looked at Ramirez's office. Two officers were in the office. Kevin knew this wasn't good.

Ramirez was standing up from his desk, talking to the police officers. He looked in the direction of Kevin. Joe Montalvo, knowing Kevin was arriving, had left the office. He spotted Kevin and immediately headed toward him.

Before Kevin could blurt out an inane remark, Montalvo, touching Kevin's shoulder, said, "Come into Frank's office. We have to tell you something."

Kevin took a deep breath and blurted out, "I know something bad has happened to Tyrone. I heard a lot of sirens, saw ambulance—"

"Let's go into Frank's office." Joe didn't want to create a scene. At this early hour, there were just a few people.

Lloyd Hopkins walked over to Kevin and handed him a bottle of Poland Spring water, adding, "Take this, son." The sad eyes of the elderly gent quickly confirmed in Kevin's mind that the commotion he heard on his morning jog was about Tyrone Dawson not being present. Kevin felt a pang in his stomach. The ex-champ and his dependable trainer and friend, Tyrone Dawson—what had happened? Hopkins, shaking his head after giving Kevin the bottled water, only added to the drama.

Montalvo and Kevin walked into Ramirez's office. Frank Ramirez normally came in about 7 a.m. It was unusual to see him at this early hour. Today was different. Police were present. They were quiet when Kevin and Montalvo entered the office. Nodding at Kevin and Montalvo, Ramirez, a taciturn and businesslike individual, said nothing and merely pointed to the small leather chair to the left of his desk. He asked Kevin if he wanted to sit.

Saying nothing, Kevin remained standing, clearly uncomfortable and looking in the direction of Joe Montalvo. He knew he was about to get some devastating news.

The silence was deafening. Kevin's anxiety and exasperation got the best of him, and he blurted out, "What the hell is going on? Is T dead?"

Looking at the two officers, his worst fears were realized when Officer Kelly Tolliver said, "There was a drive-by shooting at 5:05 a.m."

"Was it Tyrone Dawson?" Kevin looked at the two officers.

Officer Tolliver added, "Yes, I'm afraid it was."

"Oh no. Oh damn. What happened? Why him? Oh Christ!" Kevin plopped into the seat and put his head in his hands, his voice rising as he repeated, "What happened? How the hell did this happen? I mean, I heard sirens and an ambulance and . . ." At this, Kevin got up from the chair, running his fingers through his hair.

Ramirez, not knowing what to say, offered sheepishly, "Kevin, maybe you should stay sitting down,"

"No." Kevin was clearly agitated and looked at the officers. "Is he dead?"

The other officer, the more seasoned, tall Officer Mike Connelly, looked at his partner and nodded, saying, "I'm so sorry, but we couldn't save him."

Officer Connelly, trying to explain what happened, was interrupted by Kevin, who by this time had grabbed Montalvo's arm for support. "What the hell happened? He's my trainer. He's my friend. It's ain't right. He's got a kid. He's got a nice wife. It's just stupid—it ain't right. No. Damn." Kevin started to sob in the arms of Montalvo.

Lloyd Hopkins, who had been informed of the events before Kevin arrived, could see what transpired. Observing from outside the large glass window, he knew that Kevin needed help. He instinctively walked into Ramirez's office without knocking. He knew he had to act. Giving a nod to the officers, Montalvo, and Ramirez, he walked up to Kevin. The young, vulnerable, and shaken fighter, looking forlorn and dazed, gave Hopkins the opportunity to act. He gently touched his arm and said, "Son, we all know this is bad. I've had things like this happen in my family. But, you owe it to yourself and to especially to Tyrone to go on. Yes, you owe it to yourself and him. This is what he would have wanted." Hopkins, looking directly at Kevin, gave him a strong hug, saying, "I know it hurts. Bad."

Lloyd's gesture seemed to calm Kevin momentarily. He looked at the elderly gent, shook his head, and said, "No." Sometimes it takes a simple gesture—a pat on the shoulder, a nonverbal nod of approval, a smile, hug, or even a frown—to help a person hurt by circumstances come to reality. Old Mr. Hopkins stepped up to the plate and helped calm the tense atmosphere. With reality sinking in, Kevin turned to the officers again and asked, "What happened?'

Officer Connelly, a veteran of twelve years whose father and grandfather were also cops, knew he had to act. Unfortunately, he had responded to too many drive-by shootings in the high-crime areas of Gary. He had consoled many mothers after the shootings in gang and drug areas. Hardened by the responsibilities, he also exhibited a softer side when it came to notifications of devastating crimes.

Tolliver, a young native of Gary, looked at Officer Connelly as he tried to explain what happened. She was a determined recent college graduate who wanted to make a difference in her community. She and Officer Connelly knew that the high-profile murder of the former boxing champ would generate much media coverage. But not now. They knew from past experiences that the families and friends wanted to get details on the sudden, violent death of a loved one. They were the ones who needed help.

Tolliver looked directly at Kevin and said, "We got a call and responded with two other police vans. When we arrived, Mr. Dawson was already beyond our help. The first responding paramedics tried everything—trust me."

Officer Tolliver, an attractive Black woman, spoke softly yet firmly to Kevin. She added, "I was an admirer of Tyrone Dawson. I followed his career. We were pleased to see that he was helping you."

Kevin shouted, "Not now he isn't."

Tolliver added, "Like the gentleman who just came in the office, you should realize that the best thing for you to do is to go on with your fight. I read the articles on you. I've seen the publicity on the TV, and I know you got what it takes." Tolliver gave a nod to both Ramirez and Montalvo. For the first time, Tolliver's approach seemed to touch Kevin. A woman's touch was much needed.

Kevin looked at Tolliver, his watery eyes giving an expression that she cared. He gave her a slight smile, saying, "Thanks very much." Kevin, distraught and bitter over the murder of his friend and mentor, had to add, "I kept telling T not to drive that BMW. He should have used his wife's car, the Chevy. Maybe this wouldn't have happened. I bet the bastard who killed him didn't know who he was and what good he's done for me and this town." Finally, Kevin, coming to terms with the stark reality of the sudden death of his trainer, knew he couldn't add anything else. He looked at the officers and asked, "Did you catch who did this to Tyrone?"

Shaking his head, Connelly added, "We'll do what we can to bring the shooter to justice. There are detectives conducting forensic evidence on the scene now, doing whatever it takes to gather information."

"Did they take his wallet and money?" Kevin felt he needed details, however sketchy.

Connelly continued: "Luxury cars are always a target. But, to be honest, this probably would have happened to him even if he used his wife's car. Crime is rampant now with the drugs and gangs. I know it does little to make you feel better, but even if he hada licensed gun on him, Mr. Dawson was clearly marked. They probably knew the route he took from his home in Munster to here. It's only about eleven miles and a fifteen- or sixteen-minute commute. No doubt he was stalked."

Kevin, listening and shaking his head in disbelief, said, barely audible, "Like I said, I told him. I told him to take his wife's car. The BMW is a target."

Sympathetic, Officer Tolliver answered, "Perhaps so, but we get drive-by shootings with all types of vehicles. But you do have a point—the more expensive cars are prime targets."

Montalvo, listening to the chain of events, asked, "Do you know if there were any witnesses?"

Officer Tolliver quickly interjected, "No, sir. When we arrived, we had responded to shots fired. After we assessed Mr. Dawson's condition, we realized he was beyond aid. A few homeless people were looking on. They heard the shots, and because it was still dark, only said it was a white Toyota. Our detectives will certainly interview them to see if they can shed additional information. It's a sad affair. We're so sorry for your loss." Tolliver's assessment eased the tension somewhat. Officer Tolliver indicated that she knew the gym and its good programs. Officer Tolliver was aware that Dawson was a former professional boxer with a championship belt.

She sighed and said, "Of course I remember some of his fights on TV." Joe Montalvo had accepted a cup of coffee from Ramirez, who was standing up next to Kevin. Ramirez, unaccustomed to the violence having come from a suburban environment, looked at Montalvo as he handed the coffee cup and two packs of sugar. He nodded at Montalvo, as if a signal to gather further information.

“Do you know who called in the shooting?” Montalvo wanted to get as much information as he could, knowing he would have to break the news to the gym rats and regulars that came daily.

“No, but the detectives who will come here after they speak to Mr. Dawson’s wife will probably have more information. They will no doubt interview you and the staff. It seems as if Mr. Dawson had no enemies. I don’t think this was a crime of retribution. It looks like another horrible drive-by that is becoming all too common,” Tolliver said as she looked at Kevin, whose expression begged for as much information as possible.

Kevin stood there saying nothing. He wanted to know who would do this to his friend and trainer. His whole world seemed to be crumbling as a result of this murder. His upcoming fight, normally a stellar event, was the farthest thing from his mind.

Kevin, eager to gather information, waited for the officers to reply to Montalvo’s query.

“We’ll have to wait until forensics and others investigate. Yes, robbery appears to be the main motive, as the driver’s window was shot out, his wallet taken, and it appears that Mr. Dawson put up a struggle.” This comment caused Kevin to let a loud sigh.

Officer Connelly added, “His shirt was ripped, indicating that he probably tried to grab or punch his assailant. Investigators will be gathering more evidence. Let me tell you, your friend did put up a struggle.”

Kevin looked at Officer Connelly, asking, “He did? I’m not surprised. He was not afraid of nobody. One helluva fighter gone by some street punk robbing him. Damn. It sucks!”

Officer Tolliver, aware of the drama that unfolded and the pending media coverage from such a high-profile crime, looked at Kevin, adding, “When we were instructed to come here to tell you about this, the newspaper had already called the department. They had a scoop. They, no doubt, will be here." Montalvo and Ramirez had already put a gag on the fighters in the gym to say nothing about the murder, lest erroneous information seep out. Ramirez and Montalvo wanted to ensure Keisha Dawson's privacy for whatever time interval would allow.

"Did anyone go to his house and tell his wife?" Kevin asked. He liked and appreciated Keisha Dawson and wanted to make sure she was at least informed.

"In these cases, we send two or three detectives to the house. We established his identity and address, and we already sent two to his home in Munster. Mrs. Dawson was informed about an hour ago. We had his information in the glove compartment with his registration. Like I said, his wife knows. I know our police will try to do everything to solve this murder."

"Does she have to ID him, too?" Kevin really felt for Keisha.

"Yes, she or any family member. I know it's difficult, but we have to have a positive ID."

Ramirez spoke up at this point, "Is there anything we can do? I want to level with the staff as Dawson was so well respected. I just hope they find who did this heinous crime. Tyrone Dawson was a pillar in this gym and his community. I hope they find the perpetrators. I surely hope so."

"A lot of these drive-bys don't get solved," Kevin added, knowing the dismal crime statistics that made Gary a city to avoid. Officer Connelly said nothing, knowing how distraught the young boxer was and the pain he, no doubt, was experiencing.

Glances were exchanged until Joe Montalvo decided to speak. He needed more information. He asked, "So his wife already knows?" Tolliver assured Montalvo and Ramirez, who had returned to his desk and was nervously shuffling a few papers.

Ramirez knew as the owner in charge of the gym that he had to act. He said, "We'll have to call her soon. Perhaps we should go the house this afternoon?"

"Yeah," Montalvo agreed, knowing the situation would be somber. He said that a group from the gym should show support for the grieving wife and child. Ramirez indicated that Montalvo, Kevin Bolton, and he himself should drive out to the ex-champ's home.

"I'll have a few calls to make," Ramirez said. "Already I got a call from the local newspaper." He added, "If any press or TV come here looking for an interview, we'll have to brush them off like I said to you when we first heard about this. I don't want the boxers coming in and finding out the news with TV and other reporters sniffing around here. Some of them will probably get the local news before coming in. I'll meet with the other trainers and clients and break this dismal news to them." Shaking his head and holding back what appeared to be a sob, Ramirez added, "Let's not give any interviews until we get back from Tyrone's house. I know this is awful and dreadful. It's going to be a rough time for all of us, but I need to take the time to explain what I can to the staff and boxers."

Ramirez decided, as the owner, to take control of the dire circumstances. He didn't want any adverse or hesitant comments to be made to the local TV or newspaper. He wanted to look out for the gym. He called for Lloyd Hopkins, who had started to fill the dispensers in the bathroom. This was part of his daily chore, along with getting the clean towels delivered overnight from a local laundry. Ramirez called for Lloyd to come into the office.

When the reliable, elderly Hopkins came in, Ramirez told him of the decision to go to offer some comfort to Keisha and her daughter. Hopkins, informed of the possibility of news coverage, assured

Ramirez that no statement would be forthcoming yet. "And make sure right now that none of the boxers or clients make a statement." He would also remind incoming workout clientele of the news of the murder of Dawson. Hopkins agreed that no interviews would be given until Ramirez and others had facts about the incident.

Hopkins, normally low key yet firm, let it be known that he felt this was the correct thing to do. "We need to honor Tyrone in our own way without making a spectacle," he added to a nodding Frank Ramirez. "I'm sure some of the guys coming and going here will have seen or heard about this, and it won't be a surprise for most." Ramirez liked the old gent's logic; he had seen so much in his years as a Gary resident and Southside custodian. Lloyd Hopkins added, "You can count on me to make sure the place is run okay while you're visiting the family."

Ramirez, forcing a smile, nodded to Hopkins. The others—Montalvo, Kevin, and the two officers in the small, crowded office—glanced at Ramirez, knowing that this scenario made sense. The police suggested to Ramirez that he could issue a statement upon return from the condolence visit to Keisha Dawson. Ramirez wanted to honor the slain popular trainer and ex-boxer. "We should draft a statement for when the expected press coverage ensues," he added. In the meantime, the grieving members of Southside, like most families in crisis, would bond together and display a strong solidarity in memory of their famed champion, Tyrone Dawson.

"He was a real champ, a good and decent family man, and he didn't deserve this," Montalvo said, shaking his head and causing a wail from Kevin.

For Kevin, this was the worst day of his life since his mom's death. Ironically, he had his trusty Mom's Book. He always had it in his duffel bag. Today, he had written *faith* as that day's word to live by. He wrote it before he knew the events of the morning. The world *faith* seemed to be appropriate and timely at the moment. It seemed strange that he selected a word that would sustain him in the next weeks. Kevin's path to glory as a champion boxer had hit a roadblock that day. "I feel the same way I did when Mom passed." Yet, deep down, he knew he owed it to Dawson's memory to do the right thing, stay the course, and use his tragic death as a catalyst to succeed.

The human experience is a journey of ups and downs, of good times and bad, of remembering those who impact our lives. Kevin would not be the fighter he had become had it not been for the jaded ex-champ Tyrone Dawson. More determined than ever, Kevin set out to dedicate his debut at the upcoming Garden fight to Dawson. Like most people experiencing loss, he needed people around him to get through the tough weeks ahead. The Southside Gym lived up to its mission of "molding minds and body" by embracing its star boxer as he set out to prove his worth. Southside would be his extended family and a source of strength for Kevin.

CHAPTER FOURTEEN

Tyrone Dawson's funeral was eight days later and attracted an assortment of people from all segments of the social strata. Hammond, Indiana, had not seen such a turnout in years. The funeral was held at his home church—First Baptist of Hammond. The largest church in Indiana, the cavernous setting had a seating capacity of 7,500. It was a draw for many in the Gary area who liked the idea of a megachurch and the myriad activities associated with it. An all-inclusive venue that provided childcare, a food pantry, and activities for all age groups, it was appropriate to have the final services for Tyrone there. Not only was it his home church, it was also large enough to accommodate the expected 3,500 invited guests.

"Tyrone would have been proud that the boxing world, along with family, friends, and fans are here for him," Joe Montalvo told a local ABC affiliate that had interviewed him in the large parking lot adjacent to the church with a quiet and dejected Kevin beside him. Montalvo knew his mission was to get the young and clearly-hurting boxer through this difficult time. Montalvo and the Evans family checked on Kevin in the first three days following the tragic event that ended the former champ's life. A game changer, it made the young boxer more determined than ever to honor his late mentor and friend and excel in the ring. The motivation, clearly evident in the gym within a few days after Dawson's murder, caught the attention of the staff and other trainers.

"The kid's on fire; he's angry, hungry, and nothing is going to stop him," remarked Lloyd Hopkins.

Angry, crestfallen, and in need of an outlet, the gym proved to be the perfect mix for him. He spent more time there, intent on getting the maximum amount of training. Determination coupled with the loss of his trainer gave the up-and-coming boxer a mission to get to the top as quickly as possible. "It's for T—he deserved the best, and I'm going to give it my all."

For the trainers, staff, and other boxers at the gym, the support and love given to Kevin since the murder of Tyrone Dawson resulted in a dynamo in the ring. Relentless, he performed everything from sparring to punching the heavy bag to jogging and jumping rope with reckless abandon.

One young boxer, looking at Kevin's routine, remarked, "Man, nobody can stop this dude." That summation resonated with anyone who witnessed Kevin Bolton in the days following Tyrone Dawson's death.

That would be the saddest day in his life since the passing of his mom. He knew he had a task to perform. It wasn't easy, yet he wanted to give his all as a tribute to the person who helped make him the contender that the boxing world eagerly awaited. He took out his Mom's Book and looked again at the entry for the day.

Kevin had entered the word *faith* in his Mom's Book; it remained the word of the week for him. "I needed to have faith—faith in myself and God, too, I guess—and the strength to move on." Kevin said he had a few very rough, sleepless nights and blamed himself for Dawson's regular early training sessions at Southside that led to the robbery and murder. After a good talk with Claude and Yolanda Evans, he seemed to calm down.

"You owe it to Dawson to continue," Claude told him over morning coffee a few days after the murder.

Yolanda, ever the sound and practical person who had had a rough upbringing and having known a few of her high school graduates who were murdered, added, "It's what Tyrone would want—dedicate the fight at the Garden to him. Believe me, the boxing world and the general public won't forget, and you'll feel better."

Caring and compassion were just what was needed. Surrounded by good people like the Evans family, plus his trainer and others at Southside, Kevin got through this very emotional and anxious time. The comment by Yolanda, "You owe this to Tyrone," worked wonders. This comment brought a sense of calm and a smile to Kevin's face. Yolanda, Claude, and people around Kevin persevered, giving him the encouragement to excel, continue, and dedicate his upcoming big fight to his late trainer and friend.

Kevin had resumed his workout after the talk with the Evans family and Montalvo within three days. With reckless abandon, running faster and farther than on previous jogs, he soon was physically back in his mode. Yes, it had taken a good three days, but now he knew he had to hone up to his late mentor, trainer, and friend, Tyrone Dawson. Inside, he was torn up and wanted to shake the events of that dreadful morning but knew he could do nothing. He felt the same way when his mom died, yet this was different. "With Mom, I knew she was in her last stages and that the end was coming and it was bad, but—this really sucks, what happened with T."

His jog became an elixir, as if to brush away altogether all the misfortune that had befallen him. Not very religious, when asked by Keisha to say a few words at the funeral service, he at first hesitated. Then he decided he owed so much to Dawson that he had to say something. But what to say?

"Just say what's on your mind, son," the trustworthy, avuncular caretaker, Lloyd Hopkins, told Kevin. "You'll do just fine; just say what needs to be said." Once again, old Lloyd emerged as the sage of the gym and a catalyst to accept what transpired. A reality check was much needed. It did the trick. Kevin would speak and now looked forward to sharing some moments with the assembled mourners.

"I want the world to know how one individual can make a change in others' lives."

The day of the funeral soon arrived. The somber mood was matched by the cool, raw wind that swept across Lake Michigan. The cool breeze seemed to invigorate the line of people waiting to enter the sanctuary. With the parking filling up, the church's pastor, Wayne Atkins, knew this funeral would attract national and local news, given the coverage following the drive-by murder of the former champ.

Tyrone Dawson was young, a former champ, and a known humanitarian who took time out to help the youth of Gary and Hammond. This funeral would not only be a sendoff but also an inspiration to those who felt left out and in need. Atkins wanted the choir and the ushers to be on their best behavior and give Dawson the proper and glorious service he deserved.

Pastor Atkins wasn't wrong. People exiting their vehicles represented a laundry list of states near and far—Illinois, Dawson's native Ohio, Pennsylvania, New York, Maryland, Georgia, and of course, Indiana. Along with local police officials, the governor had assigned a special unit of the Indiana State Police to be on hand. Pastor Atkins knew that the officials of the state boxing commission would be on hand, and many current and retired boxers would be flying into nearby Chicago O'Hare Airport from distant places such as Los Angeles, New York, and Philadelphia. Additionally, the mayors of Gary, Hammond, Munster, and Tyrone's native Toledo would be in attendance.

The good ladies of the church welcoming committee had prepared a dinner for invited guests following the expected emotional service. Since Keisha was an active church member, her friends and family contributed to making the reception special and a tribute to a great husband, father, and friend. The reception was standard fare for any church member following a funeral. It was done for all families of deceased parishioners. That day was going to be especially challenging for the ladies, as the church would be hosting some 3,500 invited guests, including family, friends, boxing executives, former national and international boxing champs, media, and some local and national celebrities in the movie industry.

Tyrone Dawson was known internationally. The ladies, ever vigilant and hardworking, knew they had to go the extra mile. And the extra efforts made by the nice ladies of the parish would soon be turned into a sumptuous spread of food, drinks, and desserts. Each table was adorned with a bouquet of flowers. There were several pictures of Tyrone from childhood to the pinnacle of his boxing career and his training with Kevin Bolton.

The ladies would be busy the morning of the service. They wouldn't be attending the service, instead concentrating on the reception that would follow. An excess of 3,500 guests were expected, making the herculean efforts all the more demanding. Chicken, lasagna, salmon, macaroni and cheese, assorted baked vegetables—such as potatoes, broccoli, carrots, and okra—as well as a vegetarian tray of vegetables would be displayed on four large tables that individuals would line up at to select their choice. Beverages such as coffee, tea, assorted sodas, and bottled water also would be on hand. For dessert, chocolate cake, sweet potato and apple pies, plus an assortment of cookies would be available. After working long hours in the kitchen, the church's pastor and assistants were grateful to have such an industrious crew of women and a few men helping out.

Tyrone's mom was staying at her late son's residence with Keisha and her daughter. At the funeral, she would be joined by her two surviving sons, Earl and Lesley, and their wives, plus Tyrone's sole sister, Adrienne, and her husband, Michael, and two teenage kids. Tyrone's surviving siblings were staying at a nearby hotel. Pastor Atkins had a reserved section of three rows for Tyrone's parents, siblings, and extended family sitting alongside his widow. In the other reserved area, two rows were reserved for friends from Southside, elected local officials, and members of the extended boxing family who had flown in to nearby O'Hare Airport in Chicago for the funeral.

The uplifting story of Dawson's dedication to the sport by being there for Kevin would be a focus of the pastor's eulogy. In addition, his love for his wife and kid, church commitments, and community service would also be highlighted. The pastor needed to let the guests know that Dawson dedicated much of his time to coaching sporting events in the church's recreation area—from hitting the boxing bag to getting the youngsters to perform basic calisthenics and jogging. Dawson also served as an usher on Sundays while his wife prepared a post-service breakfast consisting of rolls, assorted pastries, coffee, and tea.

First Baptist Church had to make room for the many reporters, boxing officials, former challengers, family, and friends who had piled into the church to see the open casket showing Dawson in a gray suit, blue tie, and white shirt with his heavyweight belt.

The aroma of fresh flowers permeated the air as one approached the remains of the slain fighter. Several large floral arrangements adorned the sides of the casket as well as two large baskets on the upper level, where the preacher's dais stood. These large floral tributes were from the boxing world—the World Boxing Association and the World Boxing Council. Additional floral arrangements were from some family and friends. Two large sprays of mixed flowers were from Southside Gym, and one personal one from Kevin that read *Always a Champ*. A poignant, small, heart-shaped floral piece that read *Daddy* was placed inside the coffin for all to witness.

Crowds were lined up outside for up to thirty-five minutes before navigating their way into the spacious church interior to view. The ushers of the church, with distinct white sashes across their chests, helped control the pedestrian traffic as they entered the sanctuary. A meeting of church officials had planned this meticulously, knowing the turnout would be great. This was done the previous night, as the notoriety of the crime plus the popularity of Tyrone Dawson were clearly evident, having drawn the expected large crowds and necessitating police crowd control. Each lamenter was given a prayer card with a picture of the boxer that included his birthday and date of death plus a copy of Psalm 23 on the back. It would be a keepsake for the many who knew Dawson only from the sport and the occasional interviews he had given since his recent retirement.

It was decided, with family approval, to allow the viewing to be extended beyond the scheduled 8 o'clock closing the night before.

The crowd was still there at 8 p.m., and the officials kept the church open until 9:30 p.m. Since the service the following day would be by invitation only, it was only fitting that fans could be given a final farewell. Keisha was pleased by the turnout and the fact that the church stayed opened an extra hour and a half to accommodate the overflow crowd lined around the church.

"Despite the seating capacity, there's just not enough room to allow everyone to attend the funeral service. Also, the police and security officials were concerned, as the suspects were still at large," Pastor Atkins had announced. Keisha Dawson wanted the general public to pay their respects, and the opening of the church for the viewing proved to be a good move as it accommodated many who otherwise wouldn't be able to attend the actual service.

"The people are what made him," she remarked. "He came from humble beginnings and gave back so much to the community. I want them to have the chance to see him once last time." Keisha, her assessment right on target, was impressed by the large group of all ages and races coming to pay their respects to the boxer who settled there and wanted to mold other boxers like Kevin Bolton.

Interviewed by the local press, several mourners indicated that they knew Dawson only from his boxing career or to show solidarity to his widow. Many of the women had their young children with them. One woman, Grace Politi, said, "I want my young son of seven to witness this tribute to a man who gave so much of himself." Her sentiments were echoed by many others who had lined up to pay their respects.

Another, a sixteen-year-old Crown Point girl, wanted to be there because "I want to send a message; this gun violence is out of control. Many nonfamous are killed; I just want to show my respects and tell everyone that this horrible madness should stop." She indicated that a friend of hers had been killed just a few weeks earlier by a stray bullet on a Gary street. Her statement, aired on local news and Chicago affiliate, resonated with many of the people in line.

All too aware of the continued violence and abandonment of once-vibrant cities due to outsourcing of industry, the Rust Belt really bore the brunt of the malaise that hit the United States during the 1970s. With little help from the federal government and scandals such as Watergate, the federal government had left cities like Gary to fend for themselves. Continuous migration from the inner, medium-sized cities like Gary made the situation all the more worse. Many of the people paying respects to Tyrone Dawson knew he epitomized someone who tried to make a difference but became a victim. The on-target comments from the people in line were raw, sincere, and made sense.

Comments such as these, given from the heart, made the local news and helped institute a campaign to get guns off the street. The pastor of First Baptist joined with other churches and synagogues in the greater Hammond and Gary area for a gun buyback campaign.

"No questions asked. Just bring in a gun and get $100 for taking these lethal and illegal weapons off the street," said the mayor of Gary in dedicating this movement to Dawson. By the time of the funeral, some 240 guns had been handed in to the various churches participating in the buyback program. Local officials, sports heroes in the boxing and basketball worlds, as well as several large corporations also contributed to this program. It seemed to have a positive effect on the out-of-control gun violence plaguing the inner cities. The tragic loss of a revered sportsman and humanitarian like Dawson galvanized a movement that was soon replicated in cities from Detroit to Chicago to Houston.

Kevin decided to address this issue when he eulogized his friend. "It's something that I've witnessed firsthand growing up in Gary. This has got to stop."

The Hammond Police Department got an assist from the Gary police force, which still hadn't apprehended a suspect. Thus, several detectives working on the case carefully looked for any clues from the mourners paying their respect. "Sometimes the assailant could be in a crowd," the police commissioner of Gary, Alton Wheeler, remarked.

He had seen it before. The fact that a few of the homeless people on the street that early morning had seen a white Toyota with Indiana plates speed away was one avenue of approach. The forensics department was making some headway, but at the time of the funeral, the death of Tyrone Dawson was unsolved. The Hammond and Gary police departments, working in tandem, asked the governor for additional security during the funeral. As a result, there was a contingent of Indiana State Police to allow for crowd control and monitor overall traffic. They, too, would be vigilant and perhaps see the Toyota used in the killing. But that day, the focus was on a victim of senseless gun violence, and it was time to pay tribute to someone who made a big difference in the life of Kevin Bolton.

CHAPTER FIFTEEN

KEVIN BOLTON'S NAME APPEARED ON THE PROGRAM with the other invited speakers—Pastor Atkins, the Indiana Boxing Commissioner; neighbor and friend Tracy Cummings; and Dawson's brother, Lesley. Each invited guest received a program with a cover picture of Tyrone Dawson. It also included a brief biography of his life, beginning with his childhood in Toledo, Ohio, and listed the schools he attended. It also covered his meteoric rise to world champ and the belts he won. In addition, the program listed his surviving family members—wife, daughter, parents, siblings—and friends at Southside. As with each program, it listed the speakers, songs to be sung, and a thank-you on the back page from Keisha Dawson to all who helped during the time of bereavement. Called a "Journey Home," it would be a keepsake for the attendees.

The service started with a welcome from the pastor, followed by "Amazing Grace." The adult choir, consisting of twenty-two members dressed in red robes, raised the emotional level with their rendition of the old spiritual. This was followed by several speakers, who spoke of Dawson in personal ways: his fondness for disco music, his love of dance, his favorite food—burgers with onions and fries—his love of boxing, and his dedication to his family.

Tracy Cummings, a single mom, added a few anecdotes as a neighbor for whom Dawson, often without any notice, would take her garbage bags to the curb, mow her lawn, and make sure she was attended to. "He knew I like the small pizzas at 7-Eleven and would surprise me sometimes with a pizza for my son and me." Cummings gave a human, albeit brief, touch to the person she called a friend and neighbor. She was able to get the crowd to smile, often describing how Dawson would ask if she wanted to meet some of his single or divorced male friends.

She was followed by a few members of First Baptist, who glowingly spoke of Dawson being on hand for setting up tables, putting up decorations, or going shopping for goodies following Sunday 11 a.m. service. Despite the somber occasion, the congregation nodded in agreement as speakers spoke glowingly about the man cut down needlessly in his prime.

The adult choir then followed by singing a favorite hymn of Tyrone's, "How Great Thou Art." The hymn was midway through the service. The adult choir's rendition of "How Great Thou Art" moved many to tears. Also, many swayed with the rhythm as the choir sang the final stanzas. The invited guests clearly witnessed a tribute to someone special.

Following the song, Kevin Bolton was asked by Pastor Atkins to come up and say a few words. Kevin didn't feel comfortable at first when asked to speak. But, after Keisha and Pastor Atkins assured him that it would be an honor for him to participate, he agreed. He was a novice in this area—he had never attended a Baptist funeral, had never spoken in front of a large crowd, and was still quite a private and shy individual. Yet, when Keisha asked him, he couldn't say no.

Slowly and with some trepidation, Kevin ascended the eight steps to the pulpit to deliver a sincere and from-the-heart tribute to his late friend. Looking down at the coffin, he gave a nod to Dawson's widow. He began to speak. Slowly at first, then with more confidence and a feeling of gratitude, his words resonated throughout the church. Yes, this would be the most difficult moment of his life since the death of his mother. Yet, he knew he owed it to his friend, his trainer and mentor, to tell the assembled mourners what he felt in his heart.

Without any notes save for a passage from the Old Testament—First Corinthians—that he would read, Kevin knew he had to say what was on his mind. Reaching into the breast pocket of his beige herringbone jacket, he said to the assembled, "Sorry, Pastor, I don't know much about the Bible or scripture, but allow me to share this passage from First Corinthians that I want to read. The message jumped out at me, and I think it help us understand our dear friend, Tyrone." Kevin began:

"Love is patient, love is kind. It does not envy, it doesn't not boast, it is not proud. It is not rude, it is not self-seeking, it is not easily angered, it keeps no account of wrongs. Love takes no pleasure in evil, but rejoices in the truth. It bears all things, believes all things, hopes all things, endures all things . . . And now three remain: faith, hope, and love; but the greatest of these is love."

A nervous Kevin looked out and knew he had the crowd in his grasp. He wanted the passage to sink in. After reading the Biblical passage, he said, "I believe we see a lot of Tyrone in that passage on love." It had to be said. He wouldn't let his friend down; he would tell all present that the person killed had, along with Montalvo, saved his life. Kevin had a goal, he had a life, he had a reason to excel, and it was all due to the trainers in his life. He knew the passage was a good introduction for what needed to be said. Looking again at Tyrone Dawson's widow and daughter and then glancing at the pew where Joe Montalvo, Frank Ramirez, Lloyd Hopkins, and the young boxers Aquino and Holley were sitting, he began:

"Unlike Tyrone, my life was a mess. Some say it still is." This brief comment brought forth a much-needed laugh from the congregation. He went on, feeling more confident. "Here I was this crazy, White, angry, and lonely kid from Gary. I had just been released from Indiana State Prison. I knew I wanted to get back to boxing. It was the only thing I thought I could do. But, I didn't know what to do. Thanks to my friend Claude and his wife Yolanda, they encouraged me to go back to the gym and let the chips fall as they may. So that's what I did. If you think it was easy to walk into Southside thinking no one would want me back, you would be right." This comment brought about a few laughs as Kevin made his point, "I never wrote to any of the people who had helped me. Sorry, Mr. Montalvo." He nodded to Montalvo, who smiled.

Kevin continued, "Yes, I was a lost soul; had no place to go when people came into my life. I had no home. My two sisters weren't around, and it's probably good that they weren't. What did I have to offer?" More laughs as Kevin, now taking a deep breath, added, "People like Claude and Yolanda Evans, who took me in and never asked me for anything helped save me. Also, people like Joe Montalvo, a great trainer who I had let down by getting in trouble, was at the gym when I walked in. When Joe Montalvo saw me, he welcomed me, telling everyone that I would be in the ring again. I had already before my incarceration won the state and national amateur bouts.

"I let it go. When I got out of Indiana State Prison, I was welcomed back at Southside like the prodigal son." Turning to the pastor, Kevin added, "I know the reverend knows that story." The comment brought about additional laughter.

Kevin at this point knew he had the audience in his hand and was ready to drive his main attention to his late friend. "And then there was T. Tyrone, the accomplished professional who took me aside that very day and told me that he was willing to help me get back into the ring. A great champ taking the time to share his ability on a loser like me. That was Tyrone. But he did so much more. That was just the start.

"How do I thank someone who really got my life back on track? How do I thank someone who believed in me when many others didn't? How do I thank someone who got up early in all kinds of weather in the dark, driving from Crown Point to meet me at Southside? How do I thank someone who got me to believe in myself?" At this point, Kevin had everyone in his grasp. A few of the people shouted "Amen," while others waved their hands upwards in approval. Kevin added, "And how do I thank someone who never gave up on me?" At this point, the congregation, nodding, some on their feet, with more audible amens resonating, were captivated by what had been said thus far.

Kevin looked out, his eyes welling up, and took a deep breath. He cleared his throat and went on, saying, "I just hope I can be half the man he was—righteous, fair, and someone who made me feel that I, too, could go the distance. Someone who believed in me. Today is a sad day for all of us, but I know his spirit is with us." His voice rising, Kevin hit home by adding, "I know that he would want me and others to focus on our future. It's real hard, Champ, but I will do it for you, Tyrone." Several more people responded with amens as Kevin continued, "You deserved so much more. I always looked forward to coming to the gym. I looked forward to working out with you, learning moves from you, and feeling good. I hated getting up early, don't misunderstand me." This comment brought some levity to an otherwise very somber moment.

Kevin concluded by adding, "Despite whatever the weather, the darkness, and the dangers on the streets of Gary, I loved being part of a program that Tyrone and Joe Montalvo put together for me. No, I didn't really mind the early hours, knowing that I would get sound and practical advice and training from the best. I looked forward to going to Southside. And yes, I will continue to pursue my dream with even more determination." Breaking down a bit, biting his lip, Kevin beautifully summed it up by saying, "Life is about choices. Tyrone Dawson helped me make the right one and put me on a path to success. Without him, I would not be here today. I probably would be another locked-up individual at Indiana State Prison, forgotten by all.

"Now, when I go to Southside, I will take with me his energy, his love of the sport of boxing, his friendship, and yes, his love. And I was asked by our owner Frank Ramirez to inform all of you that as a tribute to the champ, Southside Gym will now be known as the Tyrone Dawson Memorial Gym." This comment brought about a standing ovation. It was spontaneous, and the applause lasted a full thirty seconds. Looking down, Kevin took a deep breath and knew it was the climax to his uplifting tribute.

Kevin, glancing at Tyrone's widow, smiled at her, as did the row of boxers, including Montalvo and Ramirez. There weren't many dry eyes in the church. Kevin beautifully summed up his eulogy to his friend, mentor, and trainer by adding, "I will continue to train. I will continue to pursue my career as I know Tyrone would want me to do. Yet, somehow, each day I arrive Southside—excuse me, the Tyrone Dawson Memorial Gym—I will never, never be quite the same without Tyrone Dawson." With that, Kevin ended his eulogy for his friend. Many in the congregation continued to dab their eyes with their handkerchiefs. Pastor Atkins gave Kevin a hug, and Kevin then proceeded to sit next to Joe Montalvo, who gave him a strong pat on his shoulder.

Without knowing it, Kevin gave a visceral, real, from-the-heart talk. It was the highlight of the service, whether intended or not. For Kevin, it was a cathartic moment—he realized he owed others for his meteoric rise. The candid and poignant speech moved many, and Kevin won over their hearts. They knew he was the real deal. As he sat down, he received another pat from one of the officials of the boxing commission, who whispered, "Great tribute, young man." Kevin paused, took a deep breath, and, overcome with emotion, cried softly. It was then that the choir ended the service with the old spiritual "Going Home."

There followed a service with an interment ceremony at the cemetery. The cemetery was just around the corner from the church. Many of the people in attendance had left their cars in the lot and walked the three minutes to the small cemetery. Following a few prayers, Pastor Atkins invited everyone in attendance for a reception in the church basement. Kevin and the family and guests gathered at the large cafeteria downstairs, where the Dawson family greeted everyone.

The church basement was a large area that could accommodate the people in attendance at the funeral. In addition, several reporters and security, including several police officers, were also invited.

When Kevin arrived with the contingent from Southside, many of the people who were in attendance came forward. Shaking of hands, pats on the back, and nods of approval were some of the gestures that indicated a job well done.

An elderly woman dressed in a black dress and matching black hat approached him, saying, "Your words were wonderful. It was very emotional. I'm Gladys Gibson, a member of the church and a friend of Mrs. Dawson. Thank you, young man. I know how much Tyrone meant to you." Kevin was overcome with feelings of gratitude and gave the elderly matron a hug. As she headed to a table where some of her friends were waiting, she turned, adding, "With your positive attitude, you'll be a success in the ring or whatever endeavor you chose." Kevin smiled at the woman as she left for her seat.

Others said, "Nicely done; you really touched us with your tribute." Kevin knew that he had done justice for his friend, and for the first time, the anxiety and nervousness left him as he proceeded to the smorgasbord table lined with the many foods prepared by the church committee.

As he approached the two long tables loaded with food, he was approached by a familiar face. It was the reporter—the same female reporter who interviewed him at Southside. Dressed in a dark-blue skirt and white blouse, she caught Kevin's attention. It was Marie Russo. Coming up to Kevin, she smiled, adding, "Mr. Bolton, you remember me?"

"Of course I do." Kevin liked the fact that she addressed him formally.

"I'm here to write an article on the service for Mr. Dawson. I want to express my sincerest condolences to you."

"Thanks," Kevin replied to the pretty, smiling, Italian-American brunette, and added, "I have to focus and make sure I get on with what he wanted—a win at Madison Square Garden." Filling his plate with chicken, biscuits, sweet potatoes, and okra, he invited the reporter to sit with him and the other boxers from Southside.

"Thanks, but I should sit with my colleagues from the paper. I just want you to know that your tribute was magnificent; it brought tears to my eyes. I plan on writing a piece in the next edition of the *Crusader*." Kevin had his hands full of food and smiled, asking her to contact him with the article once finished.

"I appreciate it." Kevin was smitten with the likes of Marie. "Damn, she's nice. Once I get some wins under my belt, I may ask her out." The momentary lapse alleviated the melancholy he felt for the loss of Dawson. It was a good distraction, however brief.

Marie Russo handed the handsome young boxer her card, adding, "You can call me if you want to add any anecdotes or any information on Mr. Dawson." Kevin liked the young reporter. Attractive, real, and soft spoken, he wished he could ask her out for dinner. He was also aware that she had a job to do, and so did he. Yet, he had feelings for her and longed for affection at this time, especially. It was difficult for him to repress his feelings, given the anxiety and pain of the last week with the death of his trainer and friend. He wished he could sit with her and just talk as the nice ladies of the church group started coming around with beverages. He knew he had to join his friends and trainer at the table.

As Marie left him to join her fellow journalist, Craig Lindstrom, she added, "I wish you the best, and yes, I'll be in touch." Kevin felt like asking her to dinner or just to spend some time together. He stared at her for a few seconds as Marie proceeded to her table with her fellow journalist.

Kevin, taking a plate of the homemade food, sat with Joe Montalvo, Frank Ramirez, Lloyd Hopkins, and the young boxers

Aquino and Holley. Aquino, a large grin on his face, said to Kevin, "I see you have a nice friend."

This comment brought a laugh from the elder Hopkins. "Maybe so, but first you got the Garden. Concentrate on the fight. You've done so much, and Tyrone would expect nothing else. Nothing else. By the way, you did a great job in what you said about Tyrone. A great job."

Ramirez and Montalvo nodded in agreement. Montalvo added, "I'm proud of you as a man, a person who has heart. Channel that energy and determination in the ring. We all have suffered through this. I know it was so hard for you to do what you did. But you rose to the occasion. It was appropriate for you and you only to represent the gym, and you were great. You put a human side to the Tyrone that we all knew. And I know that Tyrone would have been so proud of you. I'm so proud of you, too." Montalvo put his head down, shook his head, and added, "You and all of us are hurting, Kevin. But we got to get through this, and, hard as it is, we will."

This comment brought nods from Hopkins and a thumbs-up from Holley. Frank Ramirez, putting down his fork after biting on a piece of chicken, added, "That's what Tyrone would expect from you. Your tribute to Dawson was the best I've heard. And I've been to too many funerals. You made him real to those who didn't know him. You put a human side to him. The Tyrone we knew and loved. I briefly spoke to Mrs. Bertha Dawson, his mom, and she was very overcome with your tribute. I'm so proud of you, Kevin, so proud." Ramirez, bit into a roll and looked at Kevin with a smile.

Kevin, still mourning his mentor and friend, stared at his food and said in a barely audible voice, "Thanks very much. I needed that." With that, the group from the gym started eating and exchanging memories of their murdered friend. For Kevin, it was a seminal moment. He remembered what he wrote in his Mom's Book for the day of funeral—*courage*. It seemed appropriate for the occasion. He knew he needed courage to give his friend a tribute worthy of his stature. Courage to go on despite the hurt. The fact that he spoke from the heart and touched so many was evident by the accolades he received from those present. Despite the somber and melancholy aura surrounding the funeral, Kevin Bolton once again showed he had the right stuff to excel.

For a moment, while gulping down a Pepsi, he thought of his mother and knew he could conquer this dark episode. Kevin was grateful for his friends—they were his family. He had a goal to succeed and knew he could put it together. His late mom and now Dawson would be the catalyst to motivate him to succeed. Kevin knew that he had a job to do. He wouldn't falter; he would persevere, win or lose in the ring. There could be no turning back. It was his destiny to be a world champion boxer, and despite the circumstances of the last week, he felt strengthened in his resolve to move ahead. He glanced at Marie Russo sitting with her fellow reporter. He liked what she said to him, and deep down, he wanted to know her better. But, for the moment, that would have to wait. He indeed had a job to do, and nothing would stand in his way. He would now use his talents and expertise learned from his late mentor, Tyrone Dawson, to succeed in the ring. He was ready—so ready!

CHAPTER SIXTEEN

IN THE WEEKS FOLLOWING THE MURDER OF TYRONE DAWSON, Kevin resumed his daily routine with even more intensity. "I'm more focused than ever. I owe it to Tyrone." As the days grew close to his long-awaited, big boxing debut at Madison Square Garden, Kevin, more determined than ever to channel his energy into his morning workout, ran an extra mile. He then would end up at the newly named Tyrone Dawson Memorial Gym.

His Mom's Book entry for the week was *believe*. He knew he had what it takes but had to have faith and believe that he was the real deal. Never one to inflate his ego, his goal was to hit the ground running and show the rest of the world that he had arrived. Already with a 5–0 record as a professional fighter, he had triumphed over mostly club fighters in the Midwest and East. Prior to Dawson's murder, Kevin had won all five fights, which went largely unnoticed until upcoming heavyweights challenged him, and promoters who were in for the money.

All of the club fighters came from local gyms like Southside that were scattered throughout the country and provided an opportunity for promoters to check out the aspiring champs. Up till then, Kevin made less than $50,000 fighting. It was lucrative for a down-and-out aspirant club boxer. But Kevin was the real deal. He was destined to go the distance. He had what it took to be a contender on the world stage according to Southside, which had expressed an interest in the upstart Bolton. Kevin was now ready. Shortly before his murder, Dawson had invited several top promoters to the gym; after Kevin's first two fights, they realized they had a potential world champ in the making. Everything changed quickly.

Kevin, recognized for his talent, got good press coverage. Also, promoters knew they could make money with the young and talented, fast Cheetah. The bout at the Garden was the end result after the five quick victories over six months. With the scheduled fifteen-round bout at the Garden, Kevin's match would become the main mvent. It was also a triumph despite the tragic loss of Tyrone Dawson. The upcoming Garden fight would be his coming out as a boxer that others in the boxing world would have to take notice.

He owed it to Dawson to excel and be the best. And he owed it to himself. Deep inside, he felt anger and rage and would have liked to rip apart those responsible for the murder of his trainer, mentor, and friend. But, he knew better. His checkered past would serve as a catalyst to go the distance. So *believe* was an appropriate word this week.

Walking through his old neighborhood, now looking like the aftermath of a World War II bombing site, he stopped in front of his old church. Surrounding the vacant lot next to it were discarded beer bottles, cans, and garbage in the growing weed lot. "I remember how nice this used to look—the church, the parochial school, and the homes along the street. Wish we could get back to what was."

Kevin hadn't been inside the church since his mom's funeral. For some reason, he was drawn inside, slowly meandering his way down the nave. In need of painting, the church, like the city, needed help. A declining congregation in the old Polish neighborhood contributed to the church's decline. The nave, once adorned with beautiful stained-glass windows, was a mere shadow of itself, with paint peeling on either side of the once-glorious nave that had seen baptisms, weddings, funerals, and festivals. Now, like the once-proud city, it was destined for the wreckers' ball.

Kevin passed the empty pews and stopped at a side altar. This was the church where he was baptized and made his first communion. The side altar where he stopped was dedicated to St. Joseph. Looking down on him from above his perch, the former colorfully painted saint with a sad smile still held a lily in his hand. It, too, needed a cosmetic overhaul, with chipping paint on the hands and feet of the statue.

Kevin stared at the statue and reached into his pocket. He took out a $1 bill and lit a votive candle to St. Joseph. It was Saturday afternoon, and soon about twenty people started to come in for the 4:30 Mass, which was to begin in twenty-five minutes. So desolate and eerie, he felt the presence of his mom once again. Sitting down in a left-side pew, he gazed at the high ceiling, remembering a joyful day years earlier when, dressed in all-white suit, he received the sacrament of Holy Communion. The thought of that day brought a smile to his face. He continued to sit.

Kevin decided to stay for Mass. It was scheduled to begin in twenty-five minutes. "It was peaceful, and I felt calm." He sat looking at the old church's stained-glass windows and thinking of his mom and Polish grandparents who frequented the church. In a meditative trance, his thoughts were interrupted by an elderly priest.

The priest had just walked down the main aisle. He stopped where Kevin was sitting, recognizing him from the media coverage. The old priest, Father James Petronis—probably in his late seventies with thin white hair—smiled and came up to him. "You're the boxer, aren't you? I saw you on TV—The Cheetah, right?" This reference to his now-famous nickname caused Kevin to smile.

"I am, Father." Kevin didn't know what to add. But the priest did. He sat down next to him and began to speak.

Father Petronis told him he was not alone in grief. "I know the recent murder of your friend has been a major upheaval and a tragic and senseless act." The old priest told him of the changes that had occurred and the recent spike in murders. "I had to preside over a few teenagers' funerals as well as husbands and sons killed by needless gun violence. We even have been broken into and have to shut our doors before dark. This was not the way it used to be. There are good people here from all walks of life, and we have set our goals on the positive. But we also have to try and change. So many have moved away, fearful of the deteriorating quality of life. It's hard to maintain this church; they're talking about closing."

Kevin felt for Father Petronis. Like him, the city was on life support and needed people to make the changes, however dismal and depressing. Kevin listened intently, knowing full well the dangers in Gary. Kevin also realized that the old priest, dedicated and humble, wouldn't give up. He then turned to Kevin.

Father Petronis told him that what he saw in the interview that Marie Russo aired showed much compassion. Father Petronis spoke from the heart, and he told Kevin that he was young and had his whole life ahead of him. He was especially pleased to hear from the interview that he would honor his late friend by dedicating the big fight at the Garden in his memory.

It touched Kevin, whose eyes welled up, and he said, "Thank you." Not knowing what to say next, he looked at Father Petronis and added, "I haven't been to church since my mom's funeral. I think you said the Mass for her." Nodding affirmatively, Kevin continued, "I was walking by, and I felt the need to come when I saw the doors open."

Kevin ended up talking to the priest for an additional ten minutes. The priest had to get ready to say Mass. But he moved Kevin. Kevin asked if he could hear his confession. Surrounded by the beautiful stained-glass windows and the statues of the saints in need of a painting, Kevin was at ease. "I guess maybe my mom is sending another message."

Deciding that some spiritual enrichment was in order, he stayed for the Mass after the priest heard his confession. When it was time, he took Communion—all the while absorbing the quiet and peaceful atmosphere. It helped him calm down and focus more. He indeed felt better and was now anxious to get to New York. "It's so sad that so few people are left in the neighborhood. Only about twenty-five people here in a church that I think could seat six hundred."

The visit to the church helped him—he knew others were feeling his pain and wanted to show it. The priest, like Kevin, wanted to make a difference despite the odds. He motivated Kevin to excel. Kevin left more confident. The visit and the attendance at Mass had an effect on him. Leaving St. Hedwig's Church, he was aware of what the old priest said: "Many of the old attendees had left for the suburbs. The church could barely keep up with expenses."

He knew that the old ethnic parish would probably shut its doors permanently in the near future. Yet, the visit made him feel good. He put some pep in his step and headed for the basement apartment in the Evans's home. The fight was coming up, but first, an important ceremony, however spontaneous, was in order at the gym. It involved the name change in honor of Tyrone Dawson. The gym lived up to its commitment to honor Tyrone Dawson. The gym erected a new sign—blue and white—over the main entrance. It sent a clear message—an honor to a hero cut down too early and a notice that the gym would prevail.

The message was that this boxing venue would cherish the memory of Tyrone Dawson. Future contenders, serious or not, would ask, "Who was Tyrone Dawson?" The looming picture of the slain champ and the plaque under it would be a source of discussion to a young man or woman wanting to hone in on their boxing skills.

Kevin, with mixed feelings, added, "No cheap-ass street punk is going to have the last word. Tyrone's memory will live on." Kevin, renewed and invigorated by his desire to display his worth, was running faster, punching the bag harder, jumping rope with more vigor, and sparring with the greatest intensity. He was the dynamo that both Montalvo and Dawson molded. Relentless and in total control, his routines at the gym amazed even the veteran trainer Montalvo and Lloyd Hopkins.

The elderly caretaker said to Joe Montalvo, "I've been here many years. I ain't never seen a fighter like that Kevin Bolton. He destined for glory; yes sir, destined for glory."

Kevin was pleased with his results. When the sign officially went up renaming the gym, he made sure that Marie Russo was on hand to record the event for the local TV news. Dawson's widow was on hand one week after his funeral to witness the hoisting of the new sign. Added to that was a large black-and-white photo of Dawson at his peak. It was placed on the Wall of Fame. A plaque next to the pictures read: *A champion of the people—Tyrone Dawson.*

Keisha, with her young daughter, Monica, was interviewed by Marie Russo of ABC local news and Clay Wheeler of the *Post-Tribune* newspaper.

Marie, the ABC reporter and writer, gave Keisha latitude, allowing her to express her appreciation to the people of Gary, Munster, Hammond, and neighboring Chicago for their support. Marie Russo's interview would appear on the nightly news. Brown also approached Kevin and asked his take on the brief ceremony. He and Marie were now communicating as the date of his debut at the Garden neared. She had given him some good press on his eulogy at the funeral.

Kevin wanted to make sure that the attention was to Dawson's widow and child. He mentioned to Marie that he hoped that the Gary Police Department would soon apprehend a suspect or suspects in his trainer's murder. Kevin mentioned that the people at the gym liked the coverage, both on TV and the article in the newspaper, and thought it gave a good spin for both the gym and Dawson. The article was well received, and Frank Ramirez, aware that Kevin was in touch with Marie, invited her to the dedication and name changing of the gym. Marie's supervisor at ABC sent the news reporter Clay Wheeler to accompany Marie to write a joint article on the dedication.

Aware that her interest went beyond Kevin's talent, the publisher of the *Post-Tribune*, Joseph Parker, wanted a candid and balanced spread in the paper. "Let's keep it real. Interview a few of the boxers and workers there, as well as Dawson's widow, and stress the need for the police to apprehend a suspect. It's a tribute to the slain trainer and a clarion call to arrest the suspects." Parker knew the enraged community wanted the police to broaden their investigation, resulting in suspects. In the meantime, he assigned Wheeler to aid Marie Russo to ensure a feature article that addressed the concerns of the community while honoring Tyrone Dawson.

At twenty-four, Marie Russo, two years older than Kevin, witnessed a strong, albeit sensitive, man who had been through a lot in his young life. She admired him. They kept in touch, and soon, Kevin and Marie were seen at a few diners and theaters in the Gary area. Aware of her reputation as an upstart reporter, she still had a soft spot for Kevin. He, too, found in Marie a smart, ambitious, and talented writer, who pursued a career in a male-dominated venue. "She doesn't care what others think; she likes me, and I like being with her."

They found a niche, resulting in a calmer Kevin. For the young, ambitious boxer, Marie's interest in Kevin went beyond her role as a reporter. Both were sharp, intense, and ready to make their marks. Marie recused herself from writing or reporting about Kevin, lest it cloud her mind. Her supervisor, realizing that her interest in Kevin was not entirely professional, willingly assigned her to other venues in the sports world in the Gary area. Relieved at this action, Kevin and Marie were seen more often. She and Kevin were an item, and others had indeed taken notice.

Marie, also an ace cook, could create a great pasta sauce. "It's my grandma's recipe, and it never fails." Topped with meatballs and pork, her meals did the trick. Her Neapolitan grandparents and mother taught her to prepare a dinner that anyone would savor. It was good for the young boxer. Kevin could cheat once a week on his diet, and Marie was eager to entertain the young boxer. He looked forward to the special Sundays. What resulted was a mutual and, at first, platonic relationship. But true to her profession, Marie Russo, a climber who envisioned working for ABC in Chicago or writing for the *Chicago Tribune*, kept her profession at the forefront. The action by her superiors avoided the conflict of mixing business with pleasure.

Yet, she knew that Kevin and she would ultimately end up together. At one point after Sunday dinner, she remarked, "You have a life outside boxing. You know it, and so do I. We've grown closer, and I'm not going to stand in the way of your career. I asked that my assignments not include interviewing you, as I think it would compromise both of us."

Listening intently, Kevin nodded and smiled at the candid assessment of their growing relationship. "Yeah, I think you know better than me, but, like you said, we have feelings for each other, and that's great. I know that you've done so much good for the reporting you did on the gym and the help with interviews after Tyrone's murder . . ." Kevin's voice grew softer, thinking of his late friend and feeling a bit guilty about his own desires.

Marie knew that Kevin, in his own rather boyish way, was having difficulty in expressing his feelings for her. Catching wind of what he implied, she summed it up, "It's good that we can talk. You and I have big dreams ahead. Where it goes, we'll let fate determine it. I like you, like being with you, and I hope we can grow." Again, Marie said what Kevin had on his mind.

He picked up his fork, dug into the plate of spaghetti and meatballs, and gave her a big smile. Kevin wanted to say more; he wanted to stay overnight with her and make love, but that would have to wait. He had a strict regimen of diet, exercise, and rest that was not to be interrupted. He knew it. Marie knew it. The attraction, growing by the day, would have to wait.

Two days later, Marie was assigned to report on the gym's name change; it also gave her an opportunity to once again see Kevin and get his take on his upcoming fight at the Garden in just two weeks. She and Kevin were all business, but they fooled no one.

Montalvo knew that Marie was a professional and had Kevin's best interests at heart. Without mentioning Marie by name, he reminded Kevin to focus on the upcoming fight. Montalvo knew that Kevin was lonely and in need of comfort. He didn't want to be overbearing. Montalvo had spoken to Marie, who expressed her feelings openly to Montalvo and the newly assigned trainer to replace the late Tyrone Dawson, Hank Montgomery.

Montalvo kept Kevin busy. Checking daily on his runs, he also wanted him to know that, along with Claude and Yolanda Evans and now Marie Russo, he had an extended network of caring and determined people who wouldn't let barriers stand in his way to the top. Montalvo was relieved that Marie was looking out for Kevin's best interests. "She's good for him. I'm glad that she, and not one of the crazies, got him interested in her."

Marie, alerting Montalvo and Montgomery that she was at the gym to report on the tribute to Dawson, assured the trainers that all was well. An upcoming fight meant a very focused Kevin, and Marie, a writer with enough experience, knew to stay clear.

Marie mentioned to Kevin that she was invited to New York as a local reporter to witness Kevin's big debut fight. She indicated that she was going to New York as a tourist with her friend, Mike Davis, assigned to the fight. Her job was to stay clear of interviewing the young boxer. Davis would report on the fight.

Kevin, mindful that each had a task to perform, didn't waver, saying, "We both have priorities. But, that won't change my feelings for you."

Marie, against some colleagues' advice, let her growing relationship with the aspiring young pugilist foster. "I'll just get different assignments; I know how to handle a situation." This comment made her at once vulnerable but also honest with her coworkers, many of whom supported her. Finally, her boss told her that she could go at her own expense, and Davis could report objectively on the upcoming bout at the Garden. He wanted her to recuse herself on any story or article on Kevin.

Meanwhile, Kevin, anxious and hungry, prepared hard for the fight. His opponent was a popular cult figure—an Eastern European named Anton Burachek, who was a native of the Ukraine and who had held the title of European Heavyweight Champion for the past two years. Tough, well liked, and well spoken, the twenty-seven-year-old Burachek would face Bolton with a 27–2 record. His two loses were controversial and by decision. One took place in Las Vegas; the other in Berlin. The one in Berlin was against a German fighter named Mark Wolfe, known as the Wolf Man. The judges in the Berlin bout were said to be favorable to their favorite son, and a later investigation resulted in the indictment of one of the judges.

Burachek, always the optimist, remarked, "I know I won the fight against Wolfe. They in Germany have to wrestle with their conscience. The Vegas fight was fairer, and the decision was uncontested." Burachek also fought a Philly fighter named Norm Fellows. The split decision was judged fair. Burachek's corner never doubted the aggressive and competitive Fellows, a seasoned fighter, who would probably challenge the winner of the upcoming Bolton–Burachek fight.

Kevin knew what the odds were. He would face a very formidable southpaw in Burachek. He was the champ and, like any champ, didn't want to relinquish his title to some young, cocky upstart boxer like Bolton. Kevin Bolton's mission was to become a champion, and he was ready.

Having reviewed VCR tapes of the young Gary fighter, the boastful, brash, and bellicose Ukrainian said, "I'll take him out by the fourth round."

Kevin also viewed tapes of Burachek and studied his moves, his jabs, and his overall technique. After his easy victories before turning professional, Kevin knew he was now in the big league. Equally confident, Kevin Bolton had told the *60 Minutes* interviewer Mike Wallace that he was "ready to show the world he arrived." The fight was hyped up by the New York media, and Montalvo received calls asking where the Bolton staff were staying and if Bolton was available for interviews and TV coverage. Montalvo, aware of the publicity, kept things close to the vest, saying little. Only, "After he wins, you fellas can have your piece of him. Right now, he's focusing on the fight." Montalvo and Kevin's entourage were aware of the aggressive and often-tough New York media wanting to get information on Kevin, from his personal life to the reaction of the Dawson murder, to his upcoming strategies in the ring.

If fortune were on his side, Kevin would emerge victorious at Madison Square Garden. And if a win was in the cards, it could ante up for an eventual fight at Vegas against others who once or currently held the World Boxing Council belt—Ali, Foreman, or Frazier. The purse would be in the millions, and he knew, win or lose, fighting in Vegas would be the premiere, nationally televised fight. It would resonate with the boxing world, letting him make his mark. He thought of the match between Ali and Foreman a few days after his prison release. Ali was his hero. He identified with him. The resurgent champ, Ali, inspired him to get on with his life and do what he wanted—fight. Ali's triumph against Foreman had its effect. "Despite all odds, he believed in himself. He knew he could win, and so do I."

His Mom's Book, now a bit yellowed and frayed, nevertheless, was his guidepost. He entered the word *humility*. He always remembered what his mom said to him, "Don't be a wiseass, Kevin—it will catch up with you." He smiled when he thought about this comment, knowing its relevancy now.

"I'm headed for the biggest challenge of my life. Wish my mom were here. I won't forget where I came from, no matter how far or rich I get. Yeah, I don't want to have a big head. It's all about attitude, Montalvo tells me. He and Mom were right—so right." The added tragedy of Dawson's untimely death further cemented his desire to display his talents and show the world that he had arrived. Using the wisdom of his mom and his trainer, he would never allow his emotions get in the way. "I owe so much to these people; don't wanna be a jerk with a big head." He remembered being angry and a bully at school and the many calls to his home after fights with fellow students. The two suspensions. Failing most classes by hanging out and causing problems with the truancy school staff.

He felt guilty misdirecting his anger at others. He didn't know as a wounded young man that his rage at his father impacted him so much with others. Realizing, indeed, that much of the anger was misdirected, he acknowledged he was a troubled young kid who witnessed too much abuse leveled against his mom and him by his alcoholic father. He wanted to desperately show the world that he had arrived as a boxer who demanded respect. But he looked into his soul, taking out his Mom's Book, and looking at the word *humility*. It was a powerful word to live by. He knew he was destined to go places, given his skills and the pros in the boxing world who saw his potential. He also owed much to Dawson and Montalvo.

A few days before leaving for New York, Kevin Bolton got a surprise phone call from his older sister, who was now settled in San

Antonio. She had given birth to a son two weeks earlier and had married Frankie Ortiz once his divorce was settled. Skeptical and not wanting to let his past influence him and upset him, Kevin at first thought of not taking the call. Yet something was to be said about his entry in his Mom's Book—the word *humility*. What resulted was an amicable and friendly chat with his older sister. She named her son Kevin Bolton Ortiz, adding, "I'm so proud of you. I saw your interview on *60 Minutes*. Frankie was right in telling me to touch base with you. I hope you'll forgive me for my stupid past. With Dad and our youngest sister always in trouble and Mom's death, I just bugged out."

Kevin, absorbing all this information, responded, "Yeah, it's time we were a family. I'm so happy for you and Frankie. Wow, you named your son after me." What followed was silence for a few seconds. He shook his head and added, "Sounds like Frankie's a good guy, after all. Just hope he treats you well." Kevin was elated at the sound of his sister's voice.

Her tone positive, she added, "He's the best thing that happened to me. He made me grow up, take responsibility, and be the mom I should be. Frankie's got a good job with the city sanitation department and gets a lot of overtime. His family is very nice—good Mexican people that took a liking to me. I'm learning a little Spanish, too."

This bought a laugh from Bolton, who added, "Good for you. We have been wounded, and now it's time to get along."

Laura added, "Amen to that."

Kevin was happy for his older sister. She also told him of his younger sister: "Charlene has also cleaned up and went to rehab in Fort Wayne. She's now with our cousin Marlene in Columbus and got away from the mess she was in. Too many people not in her best interest." This comment brought a nod from Kevin. Laura continued, "I'm in touch; she sends her love. I want to give you her number as well as mine. We're so happy that you're making it, Kev. You deserve it. I'm sorry for the bitch I was."

Speechless for the moment, Kevin smiled, looking at the word *humility*, and added, "It's all good. Mom would want this too. Yes, give me Charlene's number. I don't have Marlene's number. I'm glad she's with our cousin. I remember Marlene being very decent. You said she's now clean from all those pills and pot smoking. Like the rest of us hanging out and not doing a damn thing. Glad she's clean. That's great. Is she working?"

"She's in a tech school learning computers. It sounds like a good thing to me," Laura added almost matter-of-factly. "She's smart; she just never applied herself. Always with the wrong people, you know how it was."

"Yeah, we were a mess, I admit." Kevin's bit of good family news got to him. "So happy that you seem to be doing well and have someone good in Frankie."

"Yeah, once I got pregnant, he was all serious. Wanted to do good, looked for a good job, and got settled. His family likes me, too. Its's working out good, Kev."

Kevin, almost near tears, felt that his mom had somehow intervened. Like most events in our lives, this was a seminal one. Grateful to receive a call from a contrite and changed sister, he felt good. Elated that she apparently was happy and not subject to manipulative men in her life, Kevin was relieved also to hear the good news that his younger sister was living what appeared to be a normal life with their cousin in Columbus. The call, totally unexpected, made his day.

"Well, brother, I hope to see you win at the Garden on TV. I know it's on HBO. Frankie is going to have his whole family watching, from his mom and two brothers and a sister. I'm popular, thanks to you, at my job at Walmart. Because I don't speak Spanish, I'm in the office away from the crowd—preparing outgoing orders. The people in my department found out that I'm the famous Kevin Bolton's sister—Da Cheetah!" This comment brought about a light moment. Laura went on, "The girls I work with and the guys, too, have become big boxing fans. They all ask for you. Of course, the younger girls want your picture or phone number!" Kevin laughed out loud, and this bantering helped ease whatever tension initially felt.

"That's nice, but I have a friend named Marie. We're starting to form a good mix."

Kevin felt a bit awkward. As a young man living in Gary, the girls were there, and he tried his charm and good looks. The comment brought back an incident. He remembered Sally Lamar. The incident still haunted him nearly a decade later.

He remembered the trouble he got into at the fair. They were at a county fair. Sally looked good to Kevin—a shy, pretty blond with an infectious smile that Kevin liked. He asked her to go up on the Ferris wheel with him. She did, and once they got to the top, he started to get frisky at age thirteen, trying to feel her up.

She screamed and created a scene. When the Ferris wheel descended, crying and yelling at him, Sally made her point. A cop was called, and Kevin was told to leave the fairgrounds after Sally composed herself and told the police officer that he just tried to get loose. Sally's parents were told, and Sally's dad, Richard Lamar, a tall, heavyset man, came to his house.

Kevin admitted that he got frisky, apologizing to Lamar. Seeing his dire family situation, Lamar gave Kevin a stern warning. "Actually, I think I was stronger than Sally's dad even at thirteen, but didn't want to upset Mom. Told him I stepped out of line and apologized. He left, but my mom told me to be careful and not ever touch someone without permission. It was a lesson I learned the hard way." Yet, the damage was done. Despite his looks, Kevin was avoided by most people.

"Gossip and exaggerated version of the 'Ferris wheel' didn't help."

It was soon the news all over his class. Kevin was nasty and was to be avoided. He became known as someone to not ever be messed with. When the now-bully displayed his bad attitude or looked them in the eye, they usually backed off. This was the brother that Laura had to live with, in addition to a fatherless household once their dad had absconded and left for good.

The day of their call was very different. She heard a mature, focused individual on the other end of the phone and liked it. With Ortiz's divorce finalized, she felt good about her move to Texas and getting married. Frank Ortiz proved to be a doting and caring individual. His first marriage was to an itinerant Mexican girl whom he met when working in a fast food restaurant. "Mercedes was a great girl, but we grew apart, and she up and left and went back to her family. It was for the best." Ortiz had found in Laura a strong and independent woman, who, when aware of her pregnancy, stopped smoking cold turkey and fell for Ortiz totally. He liked the fact that she wanted a healthy baby, and upon returning to Texas, he got a decent job with the city and started saving for his family.

As Laura related to her brother, "Kev, it somehow worked out. I don't know how. Frankie cares about me. He's the only person that has. And, I'm glad for you, because I know you've been through a lot, too, with Dad, and I understand why you wouldn't write when you were locked up." Listening to her *mea culpa*, he remembered to be humble. Kevin was happy for his sister. The move to San Antonio was indeed a good thing for her. Before she hung up, she wished him well, telling him halfheartedly, "Just don't forget where you came from, bro." This comment brought a laugh on both ends and helped wrap up the call.

Kevin hung up the phone, feeling good knowing that at least his sisters were trying to make it. He thought of his mom and knew he was destined to go somewhere. He would not revert to the bad days and would embrace his family. Before hanging up, he also wrote down his younger sister Charlene's number as well as Laura's.

The call made his day. He also thought of his late trainer, Tyrone Dawson. He would use the memory of Dawson to triumph. Kevin Bolton, the throwaway kid from the inner city of Gary, the White kid who had been dismissed by most as a loser, was determined to strut his stuff and show the world that he had indeed arrived. He owed so much to Montalvo. "Without Joe, I would probably be back in jail or dead." With the support of Ramirez, his trainer Montalvo, and promoters, his Garden debut would be a life changer. Events in our lives have impact, and the upcoming do-or-die moment at Madison Square Garden would be Kevin's "day in the sun" moment. And he was ready.

"Yes, I know life is about choices. I made the right one for a change when I stepped into the gym after Claude and Yolanda encouraged me. Yes, I'm blessed to have special people in my life. Without their support, I would never have made it."

He thought of his mom and Dawson, and he knew he owed it to them to show the world he had arrived. His zest for life—to explore, to find love, to grow into a respected boxer—was awaiting him. He knew his time had come.

At the time of the bout at the Garden in 1975, the World Boxing Council and the World Boxing Association were the premiere belts.

A boxer who held these two belts would be the world champ. It would demand much: going the distance and fighting bout after bout until one reached the pinnacle. The belts! The trophies of the boxing world. Kevin knew he had the strength and stamina to fight any of the world champs. "Even if I lose to one of these great champs, I know I left my mark. This is my destiny, and no one will stop me."

CHAPTER SEVENTEEN

New York! The great city at long last had given Kevin Bolton the venue that talented people lusted for—an appearance at the Garden. A ticket to the Madison Square Garden sent a clear message. Reaching your pinnacle in life, the adoring fans at concerts, political events, or games with the New York Knicks or New York Rangers said it all: you have arrived! Such was the case for Kevin Bolton, the confident young fighter from Gary.

He was ready to delve into the ring and display his unique and quick jabs. The much-awaited bout with the Ukrainian champ became known as The Cheetah Romp. The event would showcase Kevin against the cocky, somewhat arrogant, Eastern European champ. The event was sold out within an hour. The *New York Daily News*, with its bold tabloid headline picked up on the event, generating more interest in the boxing world. It would be "East vs. West," as the headline put a political spin during the height of the Cold War.

No doubt, all eyes would be on the upstart from the Rust Belt. Young Kevin became emblematic of what was good—young,

American, with a challenging route to the Garden via prison, abuse, and rejection. As the writer Ben Alsop of the *News* summed up: "Young Bolton represents hope over adversity and a chance to prove oneself despite obstacles that the average person would succumb to. He has the grit, stamina, and hunger to get to the top. The May bout at the Garden will be his entry into the gritty, often dirty, boxing world. Right now, all eyes will be on the young Gary pugilist. He, like the tough and often-neglected city of Gary, has a chance to prove himself. Like the once great Steel City it was, Kevin Bolton will rise above it all and display his talent."

Alsop's article hit home. It was read in the boxing world. It reinforced the hype and contributed to the sellout at the Garden. And it got the attention of big promoters, eager to witness The Cheetah in action. Kevin's entry into the big time at the Garden also drew New York's celebrities and political figures. Ringside tickets would soon be dispersed to Mayor Abe Beame, Broadway stars, and a host of wealthy real estate moguls and Wall Street fat cats.

Yet, for the young Kevin, none of the hype really mattered. He wanted to enter the ring and display his quick and lethal jab. Told by Montalvo and his ring attendants not to be overwhelmed by the accolades and attention, he focused only on the upcoming fight. Right then, none of the hype mattered to the naive and hungry fighter. Seeing the city as his rented van inched closer to Midtown, Kevin, eager to be recognized as the professional kid wonder, was, in some ways, like every tourist who sees the city for the first time. The city does that to both seasoned travelers and first-time visitors. The Big Apple, the city on the Hudson, awed Kevin. He already had had a good experience when, after retrieving his bags, he was recognized by both service staff and a few passengers at the airport McDonalds.

Arriving at JFK airport, the fighter was accompanied by Montalvo, Montgomery, Ramirez, and two cornermen—Stacy Jenkins and Mike Lombardo. "Are you The Cheetah?" asked a passing young traveler. A shy but awkward nod resulted in the fan adding, "I wish you the best at the Garden. I saw your interview on *60 Minutes*." The young traveler, carrying a large tote bag, indicated that he was a boxing fan and was going to Atlanta to visit family.

Buoyed by this brief encounter, Kevin smiled at the traveler. The young man, Keith Stark, asked if he could have Kevin's autograph. The surprised, upstart boxer signed his name to a loose-leaf binder the young traveler had. It was the first time that someone had asked for his signature. He had won several bouts prior to this but was never asked for an autograph. The fact that media-savvy New Yorkers gravitated toward celebrities and bestowed some special status made the encounter with young Stark all the more satisfying.

Thanking Kevin, the Atlanta-bound young man shook his hand and headed to his departure gate. Turning around, he gave Bolton a high five and wished him the best in his upcoming bout at the Garden. This impromptu, Atlanta-bound man would have a good conversation piece with family and others. The encounter with the young passenger brought a smile to Kevin Bolton. It was a good start and a good omen, he hoped. "A nice entry to the big city."

"I see you're a celebrity already, Cheetah," a smiling Stacy Jenkins remarked. Bolton, featured in *The Ring* and the *New York Times* sports section got much coverage, including the TV interview on *60 Minutes* in which he discussed his hard and often turbulent upbringing in a tough city coupled with an abusive, alcoholic father and sick mother. The personal touch gave Bolton the leg up. His spirits soared after the surprise encounter, giving him the boost he needed.

His arrival in New York not only showed excitement and enthusiasm of a young talent but also cemented his place in the boxing world. The Garden. A different world altogether with the writers and cynical boxing analysts who would scrutinize his every move in the ring. He would indeed now be looked over critically. And his every move in the ring would be analyzed by would-be contenders. It would be a lot on anyone's plate, but the determined young man, ever ready to display his talents, came into the city prepared. Yet, to others, despite the chance encounter with the Georgia-bound fan, Kevin Bolton was just another tourist in the Big Apple. And, like most first-time visitors to the great city, New York captivated him. The city, known to seduce the most cynical out-of-towners, didn't disappoint the visitor from Gary.

Coming into Manhattan, the first-time visitor marveled at the size of the buildings, the expanse of the city, the fast pace, the frenetic, noisy honking of taxis, and the endless multitudes on the streets. The city often overwhelms the first-time visitor—the loud honks from jaded taxi drivers, the aroma emanating from the hot dog and pretzel vendors in Midtown, the crowds on the sidewalk on their way to work, and the tall buildings ever rising to the sky.

New York! The pace of the city excited him. "Wow, I thought Chicago was big—this is crazy." His crew of trainers, staff, and cornermen found an innocence that was at once somewhat refreshing. Jenkins, the cornerman, looked at Mike Lombardo, causing Lombardo to remark, "Just remember, kiddo, what you're here for—you got plenty of time to see the sights after you win. Once you win, I'll show you the sites. You can come and eat some good homemade Italian food in Bensonhurst, where I'm from."

The Brooklyn neighborhood, known for its fine restaurants, boasted as having the best pizzerias and pastry shops in the city.

This would be a treat for Kevin. Lombardo quickly added, "That is, only after you win." This remark brought about a few laughs from the crew in the rented van that headed toward the Hotel Pennsylvania, directly across from the Garden.

Montgomery, Jenkins, and Lombardo had seen the potential in Kevin and left for Gary when Montalvo asked them to come on board for Team Bolton. In the aftermath of the tragedy of Dawson's death, their presence brought a solid, experienced team together. Both Jenkins and Lombardo had trained and worked with fighters over a span of twelve years. Jenkins, a Pittsburgh native, and Lombardo, the tough, former street fighter from Brooklyn, saw the potential in Kevin. Hank Montgomery was from South Bend, near Gary. They were glad to get a call from Montalvo when given the opportunity. They had seen videos of the fights that Kevin won decisively and knew raw and hungry talent when they saw it. They gladly joined The Cheetah Team Bolton. Now, everyone connected with the upcoming bout concentrated on the fight, just two nights hence.

Madison Square Garden. The Showcase of the Nation. Making it to the Garden is a dream come true, whether you're a rock star, playing for the Knicks or Rangers, or rallying for a just cause. And for Kevin Bolton, his entry on the international professional boxing stage took place in the summer of 1975 with his first nationally televised fight. It was a time of mixed emotions for the young boxer so soon after the tragedy surrounding his trainer, friend, and mentor, Tyrone Dawson.

Joe Montalvo, the night before the fight, remarked to the young pugilist in his hotel room after a dinner at the local Greek diner located in the lobby, "This is your moment to shine. We're all still suffering from the loss of Tyrone, but your dedication to the sport will show him and us that you have arrived." Handing Kevin a bottle of water, Joe Montalvo gave a gentle tap to Kevin's right shoulder. He knew that they all had sustained a terrible setback with the demise of Dawson. Yet, the desire to have some good come from such a tragedy resonated with the entire team—even the newcomers, Jenkins and Lombardo, felt it. They knew they could make history.

And for Kevin, this was not just another major bout. It was about him. About Dawson. About his mom. About his inner soul, to prove to himself and the rest of the world that he had indeed arrived and demanded the respect and adulation of the art of boxing.

The boxing world was eager to see the young upstart from Gary. Veteran analysts and writers were on hand to witness what one writer, having seen Kevin in several bouts in the Chicago and Gary area, said. "You're going to see a boxer swift on his feet, with a cunning, hungry, lethal uppercut, that makes The Cheetah a name appropriate and fearsome. Watch out, boxing greats from Norton to Ali—this kid from Gary has it all—drive, speed, dedication to the sport, and a determined tribute to his late trainer."

This was indeed a special night; just two days earlier, the Gary Police Department informed the Bolton team that they had arrested two young alleged murderers. They were teens who bragged about killing someone big. Their bravado ultimately did them in, and they were arrested for the murder of Tyrone Dawson.

For Kevin, it was a Pyrrhic victory, knowing that at least justice would hopefully be served. "These kids are wasting their lives for a quick buck. Doesn't make any sense—no, no sense." His outrage at the murder of his trainer was coupled with an empathetic feeling for the two lost souls now destined to a life behind bars. Despite the intensity and full attention to his showcase fight, he asked Montalvo and his cornermen, Montgomery and Lombardo, to keep him posted on events in Gary. He knew the upcoming fight was everything; he, nevertheless, wanted justice for his slain trainer.

Meanwhile, the arraignment was scheduled the day of the fight. It gave Kevin and his trainer and manager some comfort. It also eased the burden on Kevin, who was eager to enter into the ring and show the world that he had indeed arrived. The dedication to Tyrone Dawson took on more meaning. For Kevin, it also reaffirmed what his mom had always instilled despite his own checkered past—"Do good, and don't be a smartass, Kev." He took a deep breath, knowing that his big debut was about to unfold.

Joe Montalvo looked at Kevin and gave him a plastic water bottle. This small gesture did the trick. Kevin, who up till then had had his head down, smiled at his trainer. "He knows me too well. Thank God I have him in my corner."

Finishing the water bottle, he got up and looked at the entry in his Mom's Book for the night of the fight. He wrote: *confidence*. He knew he could and would emerge triumphant and would display his lethal right jab for the world and potential contenders to respect.

The night of the fight—May 22, 1975, was a warm, muggy, late spring night. A rainstorm did little to alleviate the uncomfortable, hot, sticky New York night. No doubt a harbinger of what would probably be a long, steamy summer. It didn't matter. This was the big night for Kevin Bolton, and he would be the center of attention. He knew it, his trainer and fans knew it, and Marie Russo knew it. Ready to make his entrance into the iconic symbol of American sporting events, Kevin Bolton's dream had come full circle. A sellout crowd of nearly 22,000 was on hand, eagerly awaiting the arrival of The Cheetah.

Kevin, wearing a simple pair of black-and-white trunks, entered the ring humbled, yet determined. The spotlight on him gave the crowd the energy and hype to cheer him on. Looking at the Megatron above the ring, he saw his and his opponent's images on the screen. Reality set in as he slowly inched his way down the main aisle to the ring.

He knew he was in the lion's den. It would be his moment. Aware of the publicity that would greet him in New York City, the Robert Redford look-alike boxer was aware of the possible dangers that awaited him if a reporter shoved a microphone in his face. Already, Montalvo had received calls from NBC asking for an interview and an appearance on *The Tonight Show* with Johnny Carson. Montalvo, focusing on the fight, didn't bring the invitation up. "I'll wait until after the fight; then, the press and the public can have a piece of him."

As expected, the young fighter from Gary soundly defeated the European champ in four rounds. A TKO—a technical knockout—Kevin's continuous jabs proved too much for the champ. This, despite the prediction that Burachek would put Bolton on the canvass by the third round. Getting up, the dazed and frazzled Ukrainian fighter had never faced such a formidable opponent.

The ref, Calvin Foster, decided to stop the fight within ten seconds when once again Kevin sent the champ to the canvas. Foster, waving and crisscrossing his hands over the embattled champ sent the message that this bout was over. Kevin knew he had finished the loquacious and oftentimes arrogant Burachek. Bolton had said he would triumph, and he succeeded beyond anyone's imagination so early in the fight. As a gesture to the late trainer Dawson and his mom, Kevin Bolton looked upward and, smiling, thew a kiss to both. The crowd, aware of the recent tragedy in his life, roared.

Fans yelling "Cheetah, Cheetah" inspired Kevin. With the bright lights and crowd roaring, the scene, surreal and exhilarating, those in attendance knew history was made. Kevin had finally come to the pinnacle of his career—a win at the Garden against a defending champ.

"It's doesn't get any better than this," he remembered what his cornerman Lombardo had said. He was hot, sweaty, and had a slight cut on his lower lip that oozed a small, bloody drip and was attended to by his cornermen. Yet, none of that mattered. What was important was that he had made it.

Life throws obstacles in the way of one's dreams. For some, it means giving up. Others use it as an instrument to excel and excite the world. For Kevin Bolton, his fast rise to the top took a mere sixteen months despite the tragedies and hurdles he and his team faced. Ridiculed in the boxing world by some, the former castaway displayed his art in the ring. To show the come-from-behind ne'er-do-well could make it through dogged perseverance and a commitment to his mom made the humble Gary boxer shine. His message was to the underdogs of the world and the people who were the unheard and unsung everyday heroes.

These were the ones who worked hard in the mills and factories, producing the goods that landed on dining room tables. These were the people who worked hard, watched the football and baseball games on TV, and bonded with friends and family. They appreciated the rise of the young boxer from the Midwest city that many gave up on. The people of Gary, like the rest of America, saw in Kevin Bolton someone who could rise above after the loneliness of incarceration, the alienation from family, and the rejections from cynics in the boxing world. Like it or not, Kevin Bolton was emblematic of the struggles of people. His rise to fame from the abyss to champ, despite pressure and occasional ridicule from fellow boxers, writers, and cynics, was now in the history books. That hot, muggy night at the Garden would go into the history books.

It was his moment to shine. With mixed emotions, he bowed, raising both hands heavenward. The sweat still pouring down his face under the lights of the hot, muggy, late spring night, Kevin Bolton had indeed arrived. He had achieved something special. Very special. His Rocky moment had come true. The castaway kid whose own family and society had abandoned him had found his niche. He was one of the lucky ones whose unique skills brought him to this moment. He knew that the victory came with a price. As of this moment, he would be fodder for greedy promoters, journalists, and other competitors. Boxing was his meal ticket. He knew that. He thanked God that he listened to Claude and went to his old boxing gym that morning just a year ago. "So much has happened; I got to focus and take in this moment." The crowd, still on its feet and cheering, allowed that moment to sink in. "It can't get any better than this." Looking at his corner as the ref raised his hand in triumph, he smiled at Montalvo, Lombardo, Montgomery, and Jenkins. He did it.

In life, challenges come in many forms. For Kevin, these started early with the abuse he witnessed against his mom and himself from an alcoholic father who abandoned his family. Kevin's anger in school and society had made him a bit of a social pariah. Deprived of a responsible social network from both school and home, he became the bully that people avoided, ending up alone and angry. He knew how much the pain of seeing his mom verbally abused by his dad meant.

His brief incarceration, his dream, the programs he started in the prison yard, and the caring administration as shown by Ms. Matos changed him. He was no longer an angry, often violent, young man. Instead, with the help of others, he came into his own. What resulted was a caring individual who bonded well with others and became a mentor. Kevin Bolton, the poor kid from the raw, rough, and drug-infested part of the city, made it at last. His was a come-from-behind story that Hollywood would love to show on the big screen. He proved to everyone who had previously dismissed him as another throw-away youth that society gave up on. Instead of the downward spiral as a lost youth in the custodial care of the state, he proved otherwise.

Emerging from the nightmarish prison system, he rose to the top in the boxing world. That meteoric rise to the top sent the boxing world and Vegas in a whirl. He was the formidable contender who, despite all odds, made it. No longer the amateur club fighter, he was now a top contender for the world title. His unique journey of persistence and focused dedication to the art of boxing paid off. More importantly, Kevin Bolton was an inspiration to other young kids living in similar situations to hold on, persevere, and go for their dreams.

Kevin would never forget his roots, his city of Gary. His body was his meal ticket, and that, along with a now humble and grateful self, would get him far. He was hot, and promoters, Hollywood, and fans were there to pounce and get a part of him. Yet, he remained loyal—loyal to his boxing family in Gary, to Marie Russo, and to his once-estranged sisters with whom he had now bonded. True to form, his victory secured in the annals of boxing history, he was ready for his moment in the sun.

No doubt, offers would be rolling in with promoters wanting a piece of the action. Fleeting though it may be, the fame and fortune that waited the young boxer from Gary were a dream come true. The sweat pouring down his face, he looked in the direction of where Marie Russo was sitting in the first row. Standing, like most of the crowd still chanting "Cheetah, Cheetah," she blew him a kiss, forcing a painful smile on his battered face.

Triumph over a great win. "I'm blessed." Like everything in his young life, his victory was bittersweet. Triumph in the ring was mixed with a somber mood for those who were no longer with him. The sensitive side that he always felt began to show. The crowd, cheering at the newly crowned champ, continued to roar. This should have given Kevin the added adrenaline to continue waving to the crowd. But, as he scanned the crowd, grateful to all, he suddenly felt alone. Weakness took over; he smiled when he thought of his mom and his late mentor. The crowd really didn't matter. Nothing did. Strange that at the height of his quest, his thoughts turned to others who weren't there. He wished that others—Tyrone Dawson and his mom—who got him to this place were present.

Thinking of them brought a smile to his face, but his thoughts were quickly interrupted within a few seconds. The ref came over and raised his sweaty right hand in victory. Sweat pouring down his face and obscuring his vision, the crowd became a surreal haze. His losing opponent, who had come to center ring, reached out with a forced smile and gave him a hug.

His ego tarnished, the Ukrainian now ex-champ, walked back to his corner, a trickle of blood still evident over his left eye. Waving to the crowd, he received a polite but muted applause. He then went back to Kevin, saying in his broken English, "You the champ and will remain one for a good while." The crowd responded with a big round of applause as Kevin's fans continued to shout: "Cheetah, Cheetah."

A realistic, albeit somber, Kevin Bolton had entered the word *humility* as the word to remember and live by in his Mom's Book that morning. He had come so far beyond anyone's imagination. While others brushed him off as a loser destined to the revolving door of prison, Kevin defied all odds and proved to everyone that he had the stamina and ability to excel.

Reaching this point in his young life, Kevin Bolton realized how fortunate life's journey had become. Had he not ventured into the gym the day after his release from prison, who knows where he would have ended up. Thankful to people at the prison and friends like Ms. Matos and Claude and Yolanda Evans, a network of responsible and caring individuals paved the way for his success. The acceptance by Joe Montalvo and the dedication by the former champ Tyrone Dawson redirected his life. The result was a journey that was unique, notable, and moving. That journey to the top, despite the misfortunes that beset him, proved that the human spirit could accomplish what was considered the impossible. Kevin was catapulted to the top by a determined and confident self. He knew that boxing was his meal ticket. The dynamo in the ring that evolved that night at the Garden would be the topic at bars, pool halls, and water coolers throughout America.

Coming from behind with nothing, his story, no doubt, would serve to inspire young pugilists throughout the country. *If Kevin Bolton could do it, maybe I can, too.* That grit, drive, and determination to get ahead has been replicated time and again. Like the wounded city he came from, Kevin Bolton epitomized the American spirit. Yes, others helping him along his path made the once reclusive and rebellious young man mature. Along the way, he proved to everyone, including himself, that perseverance, determination, and a goal were not a pipe dream. His rise to the top of the boxing world, historic and unique in many ways, would inspire others. Indeed, it did just that. Asked how he felt about his hometown, without hesitation he replied, "Gary is tough and will rebound just like I did. It will always be a part of me, regardless of where my career takes me."

Kevin would go on to a stellar career that ultimately opened doors. He traveled many places and married Marie Russo, who gave birth to twin boys, named appropriately Tyrone Dawson Bolton and Joe Montalvo Bolton. Never forgetting his roots, he returned often to the gym where it all started. Gary, however battered and bruised by outsourcing of jobs and crime, would eventually rebound just like Bolton. Tough and unwilling to give up, the city, like the young boxer, served as a catalyst for change. And together, the boxer and the only city he knew rebounded for all to witness.

ACKNOWLEDGMENTS

Writing a novel about a dysfunctional young man who, despite having the odds stacked against him, emerges triumphantly in life was a challenge for me as a writer. Creating the fictional character of Kevin Bolton was the result of many years of observing and experiencing both amateur and professional boxers. My years in New York City as an inner-city assistant principal and teacher also allowed me to interact and learn from others. I decided that writing was a good outlet and wanted to share some events on paper. Thus, the story of Kevin Bolton emerged. *Leaving Gary* is the story of a man whose achievements allow him to reflect on his past. The journey of Kevin Bolton is replicated throughout the book, observing the struggles of real-life challenges both inside and outside the ring—a human life drama for all to witness. I'm thankful for family and friends who encouraged me to continue writing. These include my sisters, Carol Krajewski and Linda Gulli, my nieces and nephews, and other extended family members. Their advice, time, and encouragement allowed me to persevere during the COVID-19 pandemic, when motivation was needed. My New York-connected friends, such as Jerry Adam, Dr. Patrick Burke, Gerard Guglielmo, Laurette Oldewurtel, Lois Feigen, and Dr. Marge Valleau were the most supportive. In addition, my upstate "Breakfast Club" members, who meet regularly at Bubble's Restaurant in Mechanicville provided a much-needed respite, allowing me to get away from my desk. Charlie Mone's expertise as a computer maven was a real asset and a great help in formatting the text. To you all, a most hearty thank you.

John V. Amodeo

ABOUT THE AUTHOR

JOHN V. AMODEO is a retired school administrator and adjunct professor of political science and US history. For many years, he lived in the Hell's Kitchen neighborhood of New York City. He now lives in Mechanicville in Upstate New York. This is his eighth book.